BELLEGARDE

H. BEDFORD-JONES

BELLEGARDE

H. BEDFORD-JONES

COVER BY
PAUL STAHR

ALTUS PRESS • 2014

EDITED AND DESIGNED BY
Matthew Moring

PUBLISHING HISTORY
"Bellegarde" originally appeared in the January 28, February 4, 11, 18, 25 and March 4, 1933 issues of *Argosy* magazine. Copyright 1933 by The Frank A. Munsey Company. Copyright renewed 1960 and assigned to Steeger Properties, LLC. All Rights Reserved.

THANKS TO
Joel Frieman, Everard P. Digges LaTouche and Gerd Pircher

TABLE OF CONTENTS

CHAPTER I

BELLEGARDE IS BORN

A DEAD MAN lay in the road, his neck broken, his horse cropping the hedge beside him.

Except that he had died of a broken neck instead of a sword-thrust, this was not so very astonishing. In this year of grace 1604, France was nominally at peace, but not within herself. The queen was Italian, of the Medici house; many Italians had come into France in her train, and some of the greatest nobles at court were foreigners. These hated the French, the French hated them.

The nobility, still independent of the crown in a country that was but a collection of provinces, fought each other bitterly. Religious strife was even more bitter. And Henry IV cared no whit how many dead men strewed the roads, so long as he kept his crown secure, his life safe, and his many mistresses content; all of which he did beyond reproach.

The dead man lay in mud where his horse had slipped and crashed, for a heavy midsummer rain had fallen that morning. The rider who had just halted, and who now sat his saddle and gazed down at the dead man, had evidently ridden hard and fast, for his horse was exhausted; horse and man alike were splattered with mud, but the man's face was also blurred behind a beard of some days' growth. The rapier at his side, curiously enough, was heavily daubed with mud over the hilt. His garments and cloak were of fine blue velvet touched with gold.

He turned in his saddle and glanced up and down the road.

In the distance, toward Tours, showed a spurt of dust denoting an approaching rider. The cavalier swung out of the saddle with lithe grace, and his eyes showed gray, clear and piercing as a flame of light.

"Not yet cold," he muttered, after touching the dead man, who was clad in traveling garments of stout leather. "Fell from the saddle and broke his neck. Evidently a gentleman. A tall fellow, eh? Like myself. Now, have I outridden those assassins or not?"

He looked back in the direction whence he had come, but the rolling country hid the road there from his sight. He was a tall man, slender, with wide shoulders and arms. After a moment he turned and watched the rider coming from the direction of Tours, which city still lay long leagues distant.

This rider was revealed as a cloaked and plumed cavalier, all in gray, astride a gray horse, who approached at a gallop and then drew rein suddenly. The mud-daubed gentleman bowed and removed his broken-plumed hat.

"You ride hard, *monsieur*," he said gayly. "Good day to you!"

"And who may you be?" came the sharp response.

"The Marquis de Brisac, entirely at your service."

"Brisac! You—why, impossible, impossible!" exclaimed the other. "Have you killed this gentleman?"

Brisac's gray eyes widened slightly, as he looked up at the smooth features above.

"Heaven forbid!" he said, and laughed a little. "As you can see, he fell from his horse and broke his neck. Who is he, then?"

"He is the Sieur de Bellegarde, under passport to Italy from Paris. He stopped last night with us, at the château—" The speaker broke off. "But, *monsieur!* How dare you claim to be a nobleman? The Marquis de Brisac is in Hungary, with other gentlemen serving against the Turk. Your imposture is a hanging matter."

"Faith, that's news!" exclaimed Brisac gayly. "Twice within

"Witchcraft!" they shouted, closing in on Bellegarde.

the past twenty-four hours assassins have tried to kill me. Now
it appears, a woman is about to hang me."

A WOMAN, indeed. She stared down at him with cold
violet eyes, furious at his tone, at his laughter.

But before she could speak, he went on quickly, changing
his manner to one of warm and friendly appeal.

"I pray you, push not irritation to the wall, for it's a devilish
bad opponent. Instead, have the goodness to tell me where lies
the Tour de Gisy, and the gentleman of that name. I'm lost in
these accursed hill roads, so far from the highways."

A startled expression leaped in her face, as she stared at him.

"What! Do you claim to know the Sieur de Gisy, then?"

"Naturally. For the past two years we have been campaigning
together in Hungary under the Duc de Nemours. Two campaigns against the Turks, one against the Cossacks—"

Her violet eyes widened.

"Are you really—but you cannot be Brisac! You don't know
what's happened?"

"Faith, at least I don't know what's in your mind," and Brisac laughed whimsically. "I know that I've had the devil's own time getting here from Italy alive, and if I mistake not, certain gentry in these very parts want to kill me—"

"And you ask for Gisy!"

"Devil take you!" exclaimed Brisac half angrily. "Who are you, and why all this—"

"He is not at the Tour de Gisy," she broke in. "That, and all his lands, have been given to the Italian captain, Giulio Spanuto. Raoul himself is in hiding, a fugitive without a *denier* to his name. His lands, everything, now belong to Spanuto, who is hunting him down."

"Why?" cried out Brisac, astounded. "In the devil's name, what has he done?"

"Conspired to assassinate the king; and you also. Your arrival here has been expected. It was known you were coming from Italy. Raoul knew it, and they knew it as well."

"Are you mad?" Brisac stared up at her, incredulous.

"So I have thought, at times," she replied bitterly. He saw that her violet eyes were very excited, but her face was cool and firm and sweet. "I can direct you to where Raoul is hiding, but I advise you to fly for your life, and get back outside the frontier of France. You are under the ban for treason also—"

"Bah!" cried Brisac angrily. "I don't understand all this; but a pox take me if I run and leave Gisy! Why, I'm bringing money for him, three hundred *livres* in gold—a thousand good crowns! Tell me where he is, then."

Her face changed. She looked down at him gravely, steadily.

"*Monsieur*," she said, "if you are indeed the Marquis de Brisac, you are in peril. Letters from you were produced as evidence; Raoul claims they were forged, but what of that? Lies were told the king. Raoul had to flee from Paris to avoid the Bastille. He is outlawed. Let me advise you—"

"Thanks; I don't welcome advice," said Brisac. "I've some of my own. Turn your back, for there's work to be done that's not for your eyes! Turn your back! Devil take it, I understand now why they attacked me—"

He unbuckled his baldric, and began to tear off his garments. The woman moved her horse about so that her back was turned, but she spoke calmly as she sat looking away.

"What do you mean to do, *monsieur?*"

"Change clothes with this poor devil. All this story of yours sounds like madness, but you're an angel and I believe you."

She made no response. Brisac, indeed, for all the confusion of the moment, was acting with promptness. Her words explained a good deal that had mystified him, and here at his feet was all he needed to evade the men who were no doubt searching every road for him. And the Marquis de Brisac, who had made such a name for himself in Hungary, was no man to stand idle and let destiny overwhelm him.

H E S T R I P P E D the leather garments from the body of the man before him, replaced them with his own, then swiftly got into the bulky leather. His slim body vanished; he took on a deceptive air of girth and appeared a very giant in these clumsy garments.

He donned the other's velvet cap with trailing plume, and buckled his own baldric in place again.

"All's well, gray angel!" he exclaimed gayly, and drew a folded vellum from his pocket "Ha! What's this—a passport from the hand of M. de Rosny, the minister!" He glanced at it swiftly. The document stated that M. de Bellegarde, a distant relative of the Grand Equerry and duke of that name, was *en route* to Italy.

"Why, this is sheer destiny! Brisac now becomes Bellegarde; a very handsome name, which suits me perfectly! Bellegarde is dead; long live Bellegarde! By all means, *monsieur,* accept my hearty thanks. You have provided me with a name, fresh garments, perfect security—poor devil, I salute you! *Requiscat in pace.*"

He bowed low to the twisted body by the hedge. In his bow

was no mockery, but a certain courtly grace, an unwonted gravity. Then the voice of the woman struck down at him.

"*Monsieur!* Here is your chance," she said rapidly. "Escape, I warn you—"

"Escape be damned," said Bellegarde cheerfully. "Where do I find Raoul de Gisy?"

"Go back to the first crossroads, and take the road leading north. In five miles you'll reach the village of Santour. Go to the tavern there, the White Horse; the inn-keeper is a faithful man and is hiding him. His leg is hurt. You understand?"

"Devilish little," said Bellegarde. "First, who are you?"

She had lifted her head, and he saw the color drain out of her face.

"Wipe the foam from your horse quickly! Men are spurring fast—"

Turning, Bellegarde glimpsed dust and a knot of riders coming by the road he had just followed. Three men riding hard. They must have picked up his trail somewhere. His hands moved rapidly, wiping off the foam-flecks from the flanks of his horse.

"Closer than I thought, eh?" he observed. "Poor fools! They think they're in luck to have run me down, no doubt. Only three, after all."

"You think well of yourself!" Her voice was sharply edged.

"I know my faults, which are many. My virtues are so few that I'd be a fool indeed not to be aware of them! Thanks for your warning. I was so absorbed in your loveliness—"

"Devil take your tongue! Can't you be serious at such a moment?" she cried angrily.

"Well, you are lovely, *mademoiselle*. And in anger you are positively divine—"

"Listen!" she broke in. "That first man is one of Spanuto's friends from Paris, a gentleman of the court named Praslin—"

"I don't know him."

"Behind him is one Mendoza, a gentleman from Spain, who is also a guest—"

"And unknown to me."

"The third is Florio, the Italian lieutenant, an old soldier—"

"What a devilish lot of knowledge you have, my angel!" said Bellegarde gayly. "What are all these foreigners doing in the heart of France?"

"Precisely what I'd like to know," she snapped. "If you ever reach Raoul, tell him to come to the Feast of Ravens on Tuesday night. Information and help will await him."

"If that means you, *mademoiselle,* then on the faith of a gentleman he'll not come alone!"

She gave him one angry look, but he swung around, laughing, to meet the three arrivals.

These had drawn rein amid rising dust, and dismounted. They came stamping forward, while Bellegarde leaned negligently against his saddle. His gray eyes swept the three with swift and accurate appraisal.

P R A S L I N H E passed over; a court gallant, a stout wenching fellow, proud and hotly passionate. Florio was intensely dangerous; gaunt, dark, steady-eyed, a veteran. Mendoza, too, had his points. A treacherous, soft-eyed man, smiling and intent.

"Mlle. de Chanlay!" exclaimed Praslin, and like the others, bowed to her. "I did not know you at first. Pray, have you seen a man clad in blue velvet edged with gold—"

His words died. He and his companions caught sight of the huddled corpse.

"Apparently that's your man, *messieurs,*" said Bellegarde negligently. He was aware of the keen, penetrating gaze of the Italian. "*Mademoiselle* and I were riding in this direction, and had just discovered him."

"It is he, it is he!" cried out Mendoza.

He plunged forward, not at the man but at the hurt horse,

and Praslin joined him. But Florio, after a swift roving glance around, advanced to Bellegarde and bowed slightly.

"*Monsieur,* your name if you please?"

"I do not please, fellow. Who may you be?"

"I am the lieutenant of Captain Spanuto, lord of Gisy," said Florio calmly, "on whose lands you are, and who holds the power of high, middle and low justice. I demand your name."

"Sieur de Bellegarde, under passport from the minister." As he spoke, Bellegarde produced the folded vellum. Florio took it, and was plainly able to read French, for after a glance he returned it with a very polite bow.

"Sufficient, *monsieur*—"

At this instant a furious cry broke from Praslin. The Spaniard, Mendoza, came plunging at Florio and gripped his arm.

"Gone! The saddlebags are empty!"

"Evidently," said the Italian coolly, "some one was ahead of us. Is he our man?"

"Of course," assented Praslin, with a low and bitter oath.

Bellegarde watched the three with a half-amused smile. They wanted the Marquis de Brisac, not only to take his life, but also to take the gold he carried; so they knew of it! Well, this helped to make matters clear. And in a flash, Bellegarde read in the eyes of Florio that in another moment or two this man would guess his imposture. There was no escape. This impassive, cool Italian veteran could not be tricked.

But he could be killed.

Florio regarded his two companions, then his gaze went to Bellegarde and he took a step forward. Before he could speak, Bellegarde straightened up and beckoned to him.

"Signor Florio," he said cheerfully, "allow me a word in private, of your courtesy. Perhaps I can give you certain valuable information, if we may step aside. You will pardon us, *mademoiselle?* This is not a matter, you understand, to be discussed before ladies."

WITH A curt nod, Florio joined him. They walked a few paces up the road, all three of the others frowning after them, puzzled yet hesitant.

"From what part of Italy, if I may inquire?" asked Bellegarde genially.

"Milan, *monsieur.*"

"Ah! I was there not long ago. Admirable wine, a charming city—"

"A detestable city, *monsieur;* that is why I left it." Florio stopped short. "Come! What have you to say to me?"

Bellegarde turned to him. "You are, I take it, a soldier?"

"Naturally, being what I am," was the dry retort.

"So am I." Bellegarde tapped him earnestly on the shoulder, gazing into the dark eyes. "I have made two campaigns against the Turks of Belgrade, one against the Cossacks; and that is precisely the reason—"

"*Per Bacco!*" exclaimed the Italian suddenly. "You have gray eyes! I believe—"

"I was about to say," intervened Bellegarde, "that for this reason I could not put my poniard in your back. But—"

Swiftly, sharply, he struck the other twice across the face, buffeting him shrewdly.

Like a flash, the rapier of Florio was out, lunging forward; an oath burst from him, a deep and furious oath of comprehension. His blade swerved, was flicked aside as it met that of Bellegarde. He plunged forward madly.

His hot and furious attack drove Bellegarde back; then the latter disengaged, drew clear, but his foot apparently slipped in the dust. He came down to one knee, bowed forward. Instantly Florio leaped in upon him with a deadly lunge aimed to transfix his back—a lunge swift as light itself.

Bellegarde's left hand shot up. The long poniard caught the lunge, deflected the blade. Like a flame, his rapier glittered in the sunlight, driven upward with all the weight of his perfectly balanced body behind it. The point went in under the

Italian's breast and came out at the back of his neck, killing him instantly.

Jerking free his blade, Bellegarde shook his head sadly.

"A ruse to betray a soldier, not a gentleman; farewell, my Florio! Had you been more of a gentleman and less of a soldier, you'd not have died this day. May you rest in peace!"

He turned toward the others.

These were far from comprehending what had taken place, why this sudden quarrel had arisen. Mendoza was drawn back against his horse, awaiting the upshot; but Praslin, sword in hand, hot fury in his eyes, was advancing. The woman sat her horse and watched with very bright and eager eyes beneath her wide hat-brim.

"Murderer!" cried Praslin hoarsely. "It was a base trick! By the saints, Spanuto will nail you alive to a door for this! Hand over your sword instantly, base fellow—"

Bellegarde broke into a laugh of genuine amusement.

"Surrender, cried the hare to the wolf. Be off, my good *monsieur*, for I have no quarrel—"

The laughter, the mocking jest, stung Praslin to maniacal fury. He uttered a raging cry at Mendoza, who now advanced with his rapier in the left hand, his right hand beneath his cloak. Without awaiting him, Praslin hurled himself directly at Bellegarde.

Although fencing, as it later became, was at this period practically unknown outside of Italy, there were none the less certain rules. And Bellegarde now found himself in that most dangerous of all positions—facing a poor swordsman so insensate with rage as to disregard everything. His long rapier caught Praslin's steel, parried desperately for a moment.

"Look out!" It was the woman's voice, urgent. "The Spaniard—"

Bellegarde glanced around, swiftly threw himself to one side. Mendoza was directly upon him, but now his right hand was in sight, holding a long pistol; this he fired point-blank.

What followed was swift and terrible.

Although discharged in haste, the bullet came close; it jerked off Bellegarde's hat, streaking a fiery finger across his scalp. But he, suddenly enraged, flung himself forward into the burst of smoke, with sword and poniard.

He collided headlong with Praslin. The dagger drove in and out, stabbed a second time, and Praslin went down in the dust, choking as the life ebbed from his throat. Bellegarde's rapier darted at Mendoza. The Spaniard, desperate, white-faced, gave back as he tried to parry the savage thrusts. His rapier, almost wild, none the less pricked Bellegarde's left arm. Back he stumbled, in sudden awful fear of those blazing gray eyes—until one thrust missed its aim, yet tore through his wrist. His rapier clattered down on the instant.

"You—you would murder me?" he panted out, throwing his arms wide.

Bellegarde, meeting those soft, dark eyes, smiled bitterly. He quite understood the subtle strategy, and lowered his blade.

"So you know a gentleman when you meet one?" he said, and leaned forward. Swiftly, his hand smashed across the Spaniard's face, and a second time; no light blows. "When we next meet, reptile, have a care! Go quickly."

Mendoza uttered a cry of anguished fury as he staggered back. Then, gaining his horse, he leaped into the saddle and went careering away at a mad gallop.

"FOOL! OH, fool, to let him go when you might have slain him!"

Bellegarde wiped his sword, sheathed it, and turned to her with his gay smile.

"Breathing fire and blood, my lovely lady? Are you never satisfied?"

"Fool!" She was lovely when really furious, he thought; her pale cheeks all color, her violet eyes aflash. "He is Spanuto's evil genius! Raoul says it is he who probably schemed all the accusations and the false evidence—I tell you, he should be slain!"

"You're late in the telling," said Bellegarde complacently. "If you're so eager to see him die, go after him yourself!"

To his intense astonishment, she struck in her spurs. Her horse leaped out and away; not in pursuit of the Spaniard, but in the direction whence she had come. Bellegarde stared after her blankly for a long moment, then came to himself.

"Devil take her! And me as well," he said angrily. "Why didn't she stay and explain this damned story? I wonder what she'd look like, without that big hat!"

He turned, glanced down at the dead Praslin, then over at the body of Florio.

"So, watching for the Marquis de Brisac, eh! By the saints, that girl must have told me the truth. Poor Gisy an outlaw? It's impossible. Not to mention the Marquis de Brisac! But these fellows had my description; they probably got it at that roadside smithy where I paused. Word about the gold must have gone ahead of me from Italy. Well, this might be Hungary instead of France, from the looks of things. Being on campaign, I'd best act the part."

In Genoa, he had obtained the gold awaiting him and Gisy for the sale of certain loot; but the agent there had given him no warning. Probably had known nothing, after all. Hm! If there were some plot with false evidence, false letters from Brisac, then they would assuredly try to kill Brisac before he could reach Paris and deny any accusations. It was all plausible enough. The king was prone to turn upon his best friends with the most astounding charges that had been whispered into his ear, even without an atom of proof; and with forged letters—

Bellegarde shrugged, took from Praslin a dozen gold-pieces and a diamond ring worth at least two hundred crowns, and went to the body of Florio.

War, public or private, was like private life in this day and age; it had few niceties. To the victor belonged the spoils, in full measure and overflowing, and it was a sorry victory that did not repay campaign costs. From the Italian, Bellegarde got no gold, but he pouched a stamped document proclaiming Antonio to be lieutenant and bailiff under Giulio Spanuto, lord of Corthia and seigneur of Gisy, with right of search and seizure. Then he unbuckled the Italian's baldric, weighing his rapier in delight.

"A pretty bit of steel, this! Nothing like my own Ferrara, but a beauty none the less. Better fitted for a gentleman than a soldier who'd stab in the back. We'll take this along. And as for the horses—"

He changed his equipment to the horse of Florio, a powerful, deep-chested bay of tiny nostrils and delicate head; no doubt some Arab strain out of Spanish hands. This done, he pulled up his leathern sleeve and set his lips to a smarting, bleeding tear in the flesh of his left forearm. He spat out the blood, shrugged, and swung up into the saddle.

"*Adieu,* gentlemen!" he said, and saluted the dead. "Florio, if you hadn't chased me so hard, I'd have run slap into your hands at the Tour de Gisy. That's your bad luck. Well, a merry reunion in hell, *messieurs!*"

He caught the reins of the second horse and rode off at a fast clip. Mlle. de Chanlay, eh? A brave, eager spirit. Whatever the Feast of Ravens might prove to be, the Sieur de Bellegarde would ride thither on the Tuesday night despite of all hell!

CHAPTER II

A FRIEND IN NEED

SUNSET CAME and went. Twilight was at hand when Bellegarde rode into the little village of Santour, a mile off the Orleans highway. He turned in at the courtyard of the White Horse and dismounted.

A hostler came hurriedly to take the two horses.

"I'm in need of a room," said Bellegarde, "so fetch the weapons and saddlebags inside, and wipe down the leather. Where is the inn-keeper?"

"Inside, *monsieur*," said the groom, pointing. "Tending the spits."

Bellegarde stamped into the great room of the inn. The mud had been wiped off the hilt of his rapier by sweat and use, so that it glittered with chased gold and gleaming stones. By the enormous hearth, where was a whole array of turning spits with weights and chains, a huge fat fellow in leathern apron sat tending some roasting fowl. He sprang up as Bellegarde advanced toward the fire, and bowed hastily.

"Welcome, noble lord, welcome!" he exclaimed.

"Say you so?" Bellegarde eyed him with a grin, and plucked out his rapier. "Come! Where is the Sieur de Gisy?"

The fat man's jaw dropped in utter astonishment.

"I never heard the name, *monsieur!* I know of no such man," he returned. His shrewd roving gaze was taking in every detail of Bellegarde's appearance. "True, there is an estate of that name, but many miles from here, back among the hills."

Bellegarde plucked out a gold piece and tossed it over.

"Five more like that, my friend," he said in a low voice. "Hark you! I am the lieutenant of Captain Spanuto—you know the name, eh? Come! Tell me where to find the fellow."

The fat man turned a queer mottled color, and clasped his paunch in fright, but shook his head stoutly.

"I would, your worship—aye, gladly, did I know! True, there was a strange gentleman here some days since, but he departed hurriedly, owing me two crowns. May the devil follow him!"

Bellegarde laughed suddenly and put up his rapier. He took out five more gold pieces and laid them in the huge fat hand of the blinking man, and clapped the huge shoulder gayly.

"Take them. Go tell Gisy that the Sieur de Bellegarde is here, with money for him, a sword, a good horse, and help. From Chanlay. Then get ready the best dinner you can find for us, with your noblest wine and plenty of it; you're paid in advance. And my compliments on your loyalty."

The other peered hard at him, and nodded. "I'll see if any one here knows such a person, your worship," he returned cautiously, and went padding away. Bellegarde chuckled, dropped on the settle, pulled the hat-brim over his eyes, and waited.

Presently he heard a halting step in the obscurity. A man, sword in hand, was limping forward across the room; a huge man with square stubborn features, black mustache and chintuft, thick black hair that fell about his shoulders.

"You, there!" he exclaimed. "Devil take me if I know any Bellegarde! *Par Dieu*, if this is some trap, I'm ready for it. Stand up, *monsieur!*"

BELLEGARDE ROSE obediently, bulking as large as the other in the awkward leather garments. Gisy regarded him, suspiciously.

"You seek me?"

"Aye, *monsieur.* Do you remember that girl in Venice who

died of the plague two days after you spent the night with her? And small blame to the poor soul."

Gisy's jaw fell. "You—how know you of that?" he stammered.

"I know everything," said Bellegarde in a gruff voice. "D'you recall that party with General Rosworm and the Landgrave of Hesse, when you put brandy into Bassompierre's wine?"

The eyes of Gisy flew open. "You are Satan in person!" he cried out violently. "No one knew of that except—except—"

"Brisac."

So saying, Bellegarde flung off his hat, burst into a great laugh, and caught the other in his arms. Then Gisy recognized him despite the ragged beard, and emitted a roar of delight that shook the rafters.

Now their talk rose fast and furious, incoherent, leaping here and there across the year of separation, while the overjoyed inn-keeper arranged a table and brought forth his best to load it down.

Bellegarde motioned toward the huge shape.

"Safe to talk before him, of course?"

"Absolutely!" roared Gisy. "Ho, Michel! This is my best friend, my more than brother, the Sieur de Brisac of whom I've told you—"

"Bellegarde. I have papers to prove it!"

"Aye, you would," and Gisy laughed again. "I've a sprained ankle, but it's coming along in good shape. A few more days— how come you here like this? You fetched my money from Genoa for the sale of that Turkish loot?"

"Aye; all safe. But damned if I understand the state of affairs here!"

"No more do I," said Gisy. "You've become a marquis since we last met; I should congratulate you on succeeding to the title and estates. How did you find me?"

"Through an angel. Do you know an Italian named Florio?"

"That accursed emissary of Satan—"

"Tut, tut! Speak only good of the dead, *mon ami.*"

"Eh?" Gisy stared. "That scoundrel wasn't dead yesterday, for I saw him ride down this very street with six of his troopers!"

"But he met me to-day," and Bellegarde chuckled. "Only two were with him. A fool named Praslin, who had the imprudence to think he could kill me, and a sly soft Spanish devil—"

"Mendoza!"

"Exactly. Praslin is supping in hell just now with good Antonio Florio. I let Mendoza go, somewhat hurt—"

A groan burst from Gisy. "You let him go! Oh, my sacred guardian angel, do you hear that? This blockhead let Mendoza go—that fiend whose wits and intrigue bolster up Spanuto more than a hundred swords could do!"

"Faith, you seem upset about it! Listen to the story, then do you explain matters to me, for a murrain on me if I can understand this whole affair."

Bellegarde sketched his journey hither and the incidents of this culminating day. As he finished, fat Michel bade them to table, where smoking joints, fowl, and an admirable Spanish wine awaited them. Bellegarde, having done his talking, now listened to Gisy while he ate.

THE LORD of Gisy was a stolid, straightforward sort of person, admittedly no sage. On returning to Paris from Hungary, and rejoining the court, he made certain mistakes. One was to run foul of some Italians in a tavern brawl, kill one of them, and lay out another with a broken nose. This other was Captain Spanuto.

Wise men in Paris steered clear of Italians these days. When Marie de Medici married Henry IV, she brought with her many favorites, one of them the sly Concini. Foreigners who enjoyed the king's favor waxed powerful, but those who enjoyed the queen's favor waxed rich. The court was rife with intrigue, jealousy, plots. Spain openly hoped for the king's death, and Spanish agents stirred up dissension on all sides.

Gisy was no courtier. The storm burst upon him without

warning, and he laughed at it. When the proofs were presented to Parliament and to the king, he was on a drinking bout with Bassompierre, who had served in Hungary with him. As he now confessed, it was all so absurd that he paid no attention to it.

Others did. Gisy had plotted to kill the king; and letters from the Marquis de Brisac, still in Hungary, proved complicity. Some obscure fellow made a complete confession. Before poor Gisy could realize that the accusations were real, he was a lost man. His estates were confiscated and handed over to Spanuto, who, like many another, thus became a lord in his own land and in France at the same time. And the Bastille and block awaited Raoul de Gisy.

Barely in time he was warned of impending arrest, and took to flight.

"But why?" questioned Bellegarde. "Why should they fasten such charges on you?"

"I know not, but they did. And on you also. Well, you can disprove them! I cannot. I am outlawed. If I faced trial, false testimony would overwhelm me."

"Why, then?" said Bellegarde again. "This passes comprehension. Vengeance for a tavern brawl? Not likely. There's something more behind it. They'd make use of me, knowing that I was far away, and that you and I are comrades and friends. But the attack was directed on you. For what reason?"

"How the devil can I tell? Well, I came here, naturally."

He went on with his tale. Spanuto, unlike others, was not content to sit in Paris and spend the revenues of his new lands. He took men unto himself, said farewell to the court, and came to take possession of Gisy in person.

"Spanuto fills the part," said Gisy with an oath. "That accursed Spaniard was with him, and fifty troopers—veterans recruited from the wars in Flanders. What could my poor devils of peasants do against such men? Nothing. There was burning and slaying, torturing, a reign of terror. A week ago they took and hanged the last of my men. I barely slipped through."

"No friends?" queried Bellegarde.

"Aye, but in terror of Spanuto. The chiefest is the Comte de Chanlay, whose daughter, Angele, you met to-day."

"She's poorly named, then. Little of the angel about her!"

GISY LAUGHED, and emptied his big flagon at a draught.

"Wait till you know her better! An outlaw has no friends, but Chanlay means me well; he is impoverished and spineless, however. The wars of the League ruined him. He's a shadow of a man; Angele wears the spurs in that family. She told you how to find me, eh?"

Bellegarde nodded. He had not as yet mentioned the message he carried.

"She was cursed suspicious of me, too."

"*Par Dieu!* If you could see yourself, you'd know why!" Gisy roared with laughter, which like all impulses came readily to his jovial heart. "Remember Sybilla, daughter of that Hungarian nobleman? If she'd seen you as you are now—my faith! She'd never have preferred you to Bassompierre, or even to me. And the good God knows I've no wit with women. Well, you'll share my chamber for to-night?"

"I've commanded one of my own. Better come along, look at Florio's rapier, take over your money, and make plans."

Gisy looked at him hard. "You're riding on your way in the morning. I'm an outlaw. You'll be the same, if you don't reach Paris—"

"Paris be damned." Bellegarde stretched out comfortably. "You and I are going to see this cursed business through together."

"It's impossible! You'll lose everything. The Spaniard knows who you are—"

"Not he. Florio guessed, but I killed him before he could

speak. I'm Bellegarde to all here, and Bellegarde I remain until you get out of this affair."

"I'm sunk already."

"Bah! We have money. With money we can raise men. With men, drive that Italian rascal to the devil!"

"But your future—"

"Lies bound up in yours, so shut up." Bellegarde poured more wine. "Tell me something! Are you in love with the fair Angele?"

"Ten thousand devils, no!" cried Gisy. Then he slapped his thigh and burst into roaring laughter. "So that's it! That's why you're so willing to stay and jeopardize everything, eh? Faith, I might have known it. Once you clap eyes on a pretty woman—"

"Stop your nonsense!" roared out Bellegarde, suddenly coming to his feet. So fierce was his burst of anger, so icy were his gray eyes, that Gisy's laughter was checked instantly. "I don't even know what she looks like, you consummate blockhead! Shut up your silly talk. I'm here to stick with you."

"Oh, I know it," and Gisy rose, putting out his hand. "Plague take me, I know it; but upon the faith of a gentleman, I want you to go. I haven't a shred of hope to pull through, and damned if I'll run and leave Spanuto sitting in my place!"

Their hands gripped, and the gray eyes glowed warmly into the despairing black ones.

"Am I only a fair-weather comrade, then?" said Bellegarde gently, firmly, resolutely. "No, my friend. We ride this course together, for well or ill. You're an outlaw, but I'm not one yet, and if you can't ride the roads, Bellegarde can and will! So that's settled. Come up to my room. I've a message from Angele. What day is this? I've lost track of them."

"Sunday. Art a heathen, then?"

Bellegarde shrugged. "Church can wait till life's safer, as any priest would agree. Ho, Michel! Lights and guidance, fat rascal!"

Michel appeared, took down one of the lanterns and lighted them up a narrow staircase to the rooms above. That of Gisy overlooked the street; that of Bellegarde, directly across the little corridor, looked into the courtyard of the inn. From the end of the corridor, a door gave access to an outside staircase that went down the side of the building into the courtyard.

IN HIS room, Bellegarde found all his gear neatly stowed. Closing the door, he got out his saddlebags, while Gisy admiringly balanced the Italian rapier.

"A lovely blade!" he exclaimed in delight. "Far better than mine, which I lost in getting away from them—it went into a rascal and was torn out of my hand as he fell. Thanks, comrade! This is a gift worth while. A shrewd bit of steel; look at this notch near the hilt, to catch an enemy's blade! That Italian was certainly a rogue!"

"Well, here's your gold," said Bellegarde, drawing up a chair to the table. "Part of the sum, at least. The rest is drawn on a Jew in Tours, so it's better than gold and available at will. That Turkish loot netted us both a small fortune."

"Thanks be to the saints! This is the right moment to cash in on it," said Gisy solemnly. "What will we do with so much— yours and mine?"

"Let Michel hide it here, to use as we need it. What is the Feast of Ravens, or where?"

"Eh?" Gisy stared. "The Feast of Ravens? How the devil should I know? Never heard of it before."

"What?" Bellegarde frowned. "Angele said that vital information and help would be awaiting you at the Feast of Ravens on Tuesday night. We're to come there."

Gisy wrinkled up his brows in perplexity for a moment, then his face cleared.

"Oh! I have it now. She was still none too certain about you, eh? So she talked in riddles, knowing that I have a fairly alert brain and would understand, while if the message reached any one else, it would mean nothing to them."

Gisy's broad features beamed as he congratulated himself.

"You are a very paragon of wit and wisdom!" said Bellegarde.

"But suppose you come to the point. I'm a mere dullard who can't understand the riddle."

"It's quite simple," came the response. "The ravens have been feasting for the past week on three of my poor devils whom Spanuto hung. She means to meet us in the wood near there."

"Eh?" said Bellegarde, staring. "At a gallows? What the devil makes you think that?"

"For one thing, the gallows is convenient to the Chanlay lands," returned Gisy complacently. "And for another thing, I myself appointed the gallows as a meeting place, the last time I saw Chanlay, if any help offered. So it's really simple."

"Evidently," was Bellegarde's dry comment. "I almost believe you're right!"

"Look you, comrade," went on the other earnestly. "You don't know the lay of the land hereabouts. The Tour de Gisy is not in the center of my estate, but far at one side, where a stream runs down past the village. The stream goes on and enters the Chanlay lands. The road comes up between the two, and near the bridge is the gallows for all to see. It is well down below the Tour de Gisy. Close by is a thickly wooded covert. An excellent meeting place."

"If it suits your fancy," and Bellegarde shrugged. Then he removed his awkward leather garments and stretched out on the bed. "I need clothes. Have you any to spare?"

"A chest filled with all sorts of stuff, yes. I stored it with Michel, together with a few valuables, when the storm broke. Michel's brother, you see, is the seneschal of the Tour—a queer old chap, quite harmless. Spanuto took a fancy to him because he knows every inch of the place and watches the provisions and wine like a hawk. It's his one business in life."

"So! Is he faithful to you?"

"If he had the chance, probably. I have an idea, comrade! Those leather garments entirely change your appearance. Go on wearing them, and Mendoza would recognize you again; so would any who had your description. With decent clothes and a razored face, that devil himself would meet you eye to eye and never know you!" Gisy sat up excitedly. "Do you understand?"

"Perfectly," said Bellegarde, and stifled a grin. He had cherished the same idea for some time past. "And if you happen to know where I can obtain a few men, having the gold to pay them, I'll ride out to-morrow and try my luck."

"Raise men?" answered Gisy. "Do you mean to go to war?"

"What the devil! You don't expect me to sit here and swill wine all day, do you? Comrade, we're on campaign—and the sooner it opens the better! And the sooner you let me make up some lost sleep the better," and Bellegarde yawned.

CHAPTER III

AN ENCOUNTER

BELLEGARDE DID not set forth upon the following day, for the excellent reason that he slept through most of it.

Raoul de Gisy roused him up in the afternoon, brought shears and razor, and was vastly pleased with the result of his operation. So was Bellegarde. In the mirror he saw a clean, hard face with laughing gray eyes and a firmly chiseled chin, a thin hawk-nose and thin lips; strength and energy in every line of it. A resolute, reckless face, its wild impulse belied by the steady, penetrating eyes.

"Beards were all in style for the past generation," observed Bellegarde whimsically, "which explains why so many old men's wives have young lovers, eh? Where are my clothes?"

Gisy laughed. "I gave them to Michel, to bestow where he would. They have value. Come into my room, and I'll fit you out from my chest."

They were about to cross into the opposite chamber when a sound of voices rising from the courtyard checked Bellegarde, who beckoned the other to the window. Below stood a rickety cart and spavined, shambling horse, whose owner was bargaining heatedly with fat Michel for the leather garments. A peddler, obviously; the cart was crammed with all sorts of gear.

"Good riddance to them!" and Bellegarde laughed, smote the broad back of Gisy, and darted across the corridor. A glance showed him that the scratch in his arm was in clean condition, so he gave his attention to the work at hand.

Opening a huge chest filled with clothes, plumes, weapons and documents in mad confusion, Gisy drew out a suit and cloak of excellent dark crimson velvet, with silver-gilt buttons, slashed and pointed in black.

"I had this in mind for you," he said. "It was made for me three years ago, just before I left for Hungary. I hadn't filled out then. Now it's far too small for me, and should be nearly right for you, comrade. A bit out of style, but as we're not at court, who cares?"

"Not I," said Bellegarde. "And hat to match—ha! A splendid black plume, there! Fit or no fit, I'll take it. What's that glittering in the corner?"

He reached down curiously into the chest, and drew up a double handful of fine-meshed steel links.

"That?" Gisy sniffed contemptuously. "That belonged to my grandfather, who had it from somebody else, back in the time of François I. It's said to be of great value, made by the Saracens, but it's a damned nuisance to get in and out of, I assure you!"

Bellegarde spread it out and discovered it to be a sleeveless shirt, far finer in workmanship than any he had ever seen. He caught up a cumbrous, old-fashioned poniard and drove down with all his strength against the shirt as it lay on the floor. The fine links were driven into the wood by the force of the blow, but when he jerked them out they were unbroken, unhurt.

"Upon my word! This is something worth while, Raoul!" he cried. "Here, take it and wear it by all means—"

"I will not," said the other with finality. "If you want the thing, take it with my blessing, but don't ask me to wear it! If I can't keep a steel point out of my hide without its help, then I'll quit."

Bellegarde knew the futility of trying to break any stubborn resolution of his friend, so he tried on the shirt, found it light, a fair fit, quite forgotten once it was in place.

"Good! This is a companion worth the having," he said. "Now for the blood-red velvet! Any shirts to spare? Thanks; mine is finished."

Ten minutes later he was arrayed. If the crimson velvet did not fit perfectly, at least it served his purpose and he was well content. Gisy surveyed him admiringly.

"Upon my word, you look a prince of the blood at the very least! Here, wait—" and plunging into the chest, he drew out a golden chain. "Take this to match it; a present from the last Valois to my father. Just the touch you need, comrade! Now for your rapier—wait, I'll get it! I've had it polished up, too—"

He hastened from the room and returned with the rapier, its golden, gem-studded hilt now cleansed and polished. A magnificent weapon, in all truth; and yet better than it seemed, for in that glorious hilt was set a blade of true Ferrara make, with an edge like a razor. When Bellegarde had buckled it on, he stood laughing at Gisy's open admiration.

"Laugh and be damned to you!" said Gisy, with a sigh, and glanced down at his massive chest and legs. "But if I had your looks, bless me if I'd not take away the laurels from every gallant at court, even Bassompierre! And he, certainly, stops at nothing. Do you know that the princess herself—"

And he rumbled out a tale which, despite its scandalous audacity, was true in every word. For, indeed, nothing stopped the reckless Betstein, who, under the French equivalent of his German name, carried his gallantries into the very shadow of the throne itself—and what was more, successfully thumbed his nose at any and all consequences.

SO THE afternoon drew to its close, and that evening Bellegarde stooped above the sanded floor of the tavern, scratched lines in the sand with his poniard, and while the scowling Gisy aided him at this unwonted labor, gained a more or less accurate knowledge of the whole countryside. Fat Michel and his stupid, faithful hostler stared in huge delight at their new guest, while Michel's wife gathered her brood about her and glared with fierce peasant's eyes at these two lords who diced with death and laughed over the wager.

They drank deep that night; but an hour after sunrise Bellegarde was up and astir, ordered his horse saddled, and had his morning draught to clear his head. He slipped the steel mesh over his shirt, dressed in the crimson velvet, buckled on his sword, and with the crimson cloak over his shoulders descended to the courtyard.

"Listen well, Michel!" he said to the fat host. "The Sieur de Gisy sleeps, as always after hard drinking. No use waking him. Tell him that if I don't return by mid-afternoon, I'll meet him an hour after sunset."

"Where, *monsieur?*"

"He knows the place. *Au revoir!*"

With a laugh, Bellegarde swung up to the saddle, put in his spurs, and clattered out of the inn-yard. He headed for the east, being minded to visit the small town of Courcelles, the closest place of any size to the Tour de Gisy. His friend had told him of a man there to seek.

An hour passed, and another. He jogged along easily, unhurried, having the full day before him and a pocket filled with gold—although on the preceding night, fat Michel had hidden away most of their riches under a stone in the hearth. It pleased Bellegarde's fancy to take with him only his plunder of the other day, with which to hire men.

Nor were men far to seek. Prosperity had come under the rule of Henri of Navarre, but none the less was France filled with masterless men, veterans from the foreign wars and from the fierce civil fighting; German and Swiss mercenaries, Spaniards returning out of Italy or Flanders, swaggering Gascons in search of fortune. And with these, many and many a broken gentleman of the lesser noblesse, for Paris spewed them out broadcast. That great heart and pulse of France, wide open to debauchery, gambling, duelling, was swift to ruin the gentry who gathered like moths about the flame.

In France, still torn by civil dissension, still a collection of
provinces rather than a united kingdom, all these found good
hunting.

As he rode, Bellegarde recalled with satisfaction that he had
given his name, had shown his passport, only to Florio; the
Spaniard had been busy rifling the dead man's belongings and
had paid no heed. Therefore, Mendoza could not have report-
ed his name. Good!

Noon was approaching when he sighted a crossroads ahead
and recognized certain landmarks told him by Gisy. To his left,
hills, woods, broken country. Off to his right and ahead, farms
and a rich spreading valley. He came to the crossroads and drew
rein; the way to Courcelles lay dead ahead, but he sat gazing
off to his left.

There where the road wound upward, a mile distant, he saw
what appeared to be a grim, round tower perched above an
abrupt descent. It did not stand out against the sky, for hills lay
behind it from this viewpoint. This was the Tour de Gisy, not
a tower but a castle, which had obtained its name from this
particular view.

Bellegarde was about to ride on when a shout halted him.
He turned in the saddle. Coming along the road to his right
was a spurting cloud of dust, and the sun glimmered on steel
under the dust. Half a dozen riders in all, he reckoned swiftly;
well, his brass pistols were fresh primed now! He sat, coolly
watching their approach, his attention gradually fastened on
the man who headed them. The other five, he perceived, were
men-at-arms in steel morion and breastplate.

THEIR LEADER rode like a centaur. He was a very
slender man and graceful, all in black, but beneath his black
cloak was steel and not velvet. He wore a light black velvet cap,
in which was set a heron's feather; his horse was black also, a
magnificent animal. It was his face, as he drew closer, which
held Bellegarde's attention.

This face was oval, of a light olive complexion, with a trim mustache. The nose jutted out in a great curve, and so did the prominent chin; the heavy-lidded, masterful eyes were hot and eager, flashing with fire.

"Halt, lest ye raise the dust upon us," he ordered his men, checking them thirty feet away and riding on alone to where Bellegarde waited. His French was tinged with a soft and liquid accent. Upon closer approach, Bellegarde perceived that the devil sat in this man's eyes, yet his face was very pleasant and extremely handsome—proud, warm.

He saluted Bellegarde with a very courteous gesture.

"Good day, *monsieur!* I am Giulio Spanuto, lord of Corthia and seigneur of Gisy, in whose lands you are. May I pray your name and estate?"

Bellegarde returned the greeting, gave his assumed name, noted that Spanuto's high nose still bore some sign of its breakage under Gisy's hand.

"Faith, I'm in trouble!" he went on cheerfully. "I'm bound for Italy, for which M. de Rosny gave me passport, but I met some friends in Tours and we split a few bottles. I sent my lackeys and luggage on to a small place named Courcelles, somewhere near here. An old nurse of mine is living there, and I promised my worthy mother to see her *en route,* but damme if I can find the place! I've been lost on your roads since yesterday."

Spanuto laughed.

"Courcelles is not four leagues away, *monsieur,* straight on this road before you. But why be in haste? It would give me great pleasure and honor to enjoy a visit from you, and my castle is close by. What say you? We have excellent wine, and good company, though I regret to say that no ladies are of our company. Still, that might be remedied, if it please you."

Bellegarde shook his head. "My lord, your words have a most joyous sound, but at the present moment I am somewhat set on finding my lackeys and luggage, which contains most of my funds. Later, perhaps, I may accept of your hospitality."

"Good!" exclaimed Spanuto vigorously, obviously pleased.

"And I'll give you letters to friends in Florence which will advantage you in Italy, *monsieur*. Shall I lend you one of my men to accompany you to Courcelles? By all means. The roads are none too safe hereabouts. By the way, have you chanced to encounter a very stout, thick-set rascal—"

His eye lit upon Bellegarde's horse, but Bellegarde caught the glance and cursed his own lack of foresight. Spanuto should know this horse, of course! Upon the instant, Bellegarde burst into a great laugh, and smote his thigh.

"Ha! Did I not, my lord—and only last evening!" he exclaimed. "A big fellow in leather garments, unshaven and unshorn?"

"Aye, *monsieur*, the same!" said the Italian quickly, a sudden spasm of fury in his face, his eyes lighting up with a frightful glare. "The rascal murdered a friend of mine and foully slew my honest lieutenant. You have met him?"

"At a village tavern last night," said Bellegarde, and slapped his horse's neck. "I took his horse—my own had foundered—and a dozen gold pieces at dice, and left him drunk under the table."

Flame leaped suddenly in the dark eyes.

"Where was this, *monsieur?*" cried Spanuto eagerly.

Bellegarde recalled a village through which he had passed, before his meeting with Angele and Florio, and named it. This would put Spanuto far off the track of Raoul de Gisy.

"By the saints! My warmest thanks!" broke out Spanuto, and whirled his horse. "We shall expect you at Gisy to-morrow, when you like! *Andiam!*" He whirled a hand toward his men. "Ride! After me! Stuart, accompany this gentleman to Courcelles, then return to the tower."

HE WAS gone in a spurt of dust, four of his men spurring after him. One remained; a lean, dour Scot, a wiry veteran, who came riding up to Bellegarde and saluted him.

"At your service, *monsieur*," he said, a queer burr in his voice. "And glad of it. We've ridden eight leagues already this day."

"Eh? Eight leagues?" said Bellegarde. "But that's a good march in itself!"

"Not for Captain Spanuto," and the Scot shrugged. "Good leader, good men, good horses—that's his motto, and work them like the devil. He's the toughest among us, and the pay is good, so there's ho harm in it."

They rode away side by side down the road, and talking with Stuart, Bellegarde found that the man had been serving one side or another for the past ten years. He was a cynical, hard-bitten Scot who looked on everything around him with a jaundiced eye, and talked of wine, women and loot without illusions. He admitted that Captain Spanuto was no angel, but admired him sturdily, as did all his fellows.

"He can outfight any three among us," said Stuart with relish. "Learned his trade over in Italy, and learned it well. Uses either hand with equal skill; I've seen him, with rapier and poniard, hold three men in play."

"Why did he give up Paris, then," asked Bellegarde, "to hide himself away down in this part of the country, away below Tours?"

"Nay, ask him that yourself, *monsieur*," returned the Scot, giving him a shrewd sidewise look that startled Bellegarde. For some reason, the idle query had probed deep into something the Scot knew or guessed.

For the first time, Bellegarde began to ponder that question himself, in sober earnest. Praslin had been a court gallant; not at all the type to accompany Spanuto here without some good reason.

"Your master said there were no women at Gisy, Stuart. Why? Does he dwell all alone?"

Stuart shrugged. "Women enough in the village, and at Courcelles. Aye, he dwells alone for the present; we've only just got a good grip on the place. But he has his eye on a wench he means to marry. He intended to visit the château to-night and arrange with her father. Look you, *monsieur!* Courcelles is no safe place this day for us, or at least for me. You're safe enough."

"Why not?"

"Some of us were there the first of the week," and the Scot grinned. "We did some damage, pinked one or two shopkeepers, and carried off three of their girls to play with. Most of them are Huguenots there and can't take a joke. They turned out with rusty harness and arquebuses left over from the civil wars and gave us a hot time, I can tell you. Only six of us all told, and they clapped three into prison. The captain and Mendoza went over there yesterday and got the boys out, paid some money, and made amends generally, but Courcelles isn't safe for us by a good deal. So we've been told."

Bellegarde laughed. "So much the better. Who's Mendoza?"

"Oh, he's one of the captain's friends from Paris. Two more gentlemen coming this week, or so the courier said."

"Courier? Faith, you're well civilized to have such service!"

Stuart bit his lip at this and refused further comment, relapsing into dour silence. But Bellegarde rode on thoughtfully.

The man had given him hungry cause for thought. Courier service to this district, given over to huge estates mostly devastated in the religious wars, was an astonishing thing. Two more gentlemen coming from Paris—why? There were no attractions here, Courcelles being the only town of any size, unless the company of Spanuto presented some attraction. And Stuart was suspicious; he had some secret to guard warily, and now there was no hope of surprising anything more from him.

And the Italian was thinking of marriage, no doubt to consolidate his position.

"If you don't want to go to Courcelles," said Bellegarde suddenly, looking at the Scot, "by all means, turn back! I'll not need you."

"Thanks, your worship, but I might as well. Mendoza is there with a dozen of our lads, and I'll join them. The don is buying provisions, and there'll be wagons to guard."

"A Spaniard, this Mendoza? I think I have met him at Paris. A small man, with soft, eager eyes, and very shrewd?"

"The same," and Stuart nodded. "Not a man to love, *pardie!* But a cursed good man to be on the best side of, let me tell you! A marvelous head, that fellow has. He's straightened out more trouble than I could tell in a week. He can handle these sour Huguenots, too. They're hot enough to have our money, even if they don't like our ways."

Evidently Mendoza stood well with Captain Spanuto's following.

THEY COVERED the twelve miles to Courcelles, unhurried, and at noon sighted the towers of the town, lying below them on the river. Bellegarde handed the Scot a silver piece for his trouble, anxious to be rid of the man; then, abruptly, a cloud of dust ahead at the edge of town developed into three wagons and a dozen riders. Stuart uttered an oath.

"There's Mendoza now! Look you, *monsieur*—have the goodness to back up what I say! Damned if I want to turn around and ride back, without so much as a draught of wine or bite to eat!"

Bellegarde nodded calmly. Might as well try out Mendoza at once and see if the Spaniard recognized him or not. But he must lower his voice a tone; a voice lingers in the memory.

Mendoza, his face bandaged and one arm in a sling, rode out ahead of his wagons, and Stuart went ahead to meet him.

"A friend of the captain's, some sort of a nobleman," he replied to the Spaniard's quick query. "I'm to guide him into town and return later."

Only the black eyes of Mendoza were visible as he nodded, and saluted Bellegarde.

"A friend, *monsieur?*" he said. "I am glad to meet you. Shall you be returning to Gisy?"

"It is possible," answered Bellegarde, not giving his name. He saw no recognition in those soft, crafty eyes. "I may return there to-morrow or next day, to accept an invitation from your

master. Kindly tell him as much. I shall have lackeys with me,
if I do come."

Mendoza bowed in the saddle. "There is no lack of room,
señor," he said. Bellegarde gave him a cool nod and rode on, and
saw furtive grins on the faces of the men-at-arms riding beside
the wagons. His assumption that Mendoza was a mere servant,
his own air of a great lord, had tickled them all. Stuart exchanged a word with one of his friends, then caught up, chuckling to himself.

"Mendoza has smoothed things over in the town, my lord,"
he said. "All the same, it's best to have an eye out, for these folk
are an independent lot. Well, thanks to you, I'll get my drink
and a bite to eat, and perhaps a word with a certain girl I know,
before returning."

"Off with you, then!" said Bellegarde, as they entered into
the main street of the town. "I need you no longer. If your master
asks any questions, say that I detained you to guide me about
town, and I'll swear to it. *Au revoir!*"

The Scot bade him hearty farewell, and turned his horse into
a side street. Bellegarde, seeing a little knot of men talking
before a smithy, headed for them, drew rein, and met their
scowling looks with his gay smile.

"Good day, *messieurs*," he said. "I have an errand with a certain
Jean le Borgne, but know not where to find him. I was told that
any one here could direct me."

"What's your business with him?" demanded one of the
group suspiciously.

"That's to his advantage, my friend, not to yours," said Bellegarde.

"He's a hostler at the Arms of Navarre," came the sour reply.
"Straight down the street, and turn right at the clock-tower."

Bellegarde nodded and rode on. One of the group called
softly, and a lad came running out of the smithy. The man
pointed to Bellegarde, spoke rapidly, and then the lad went

darting down the street, passing Bellegarde, threading his way among the folk, and vanishing.

Unhurried, Bellegarde rode on. At this inn, no doubt, he could eat and drink, thus combining two errands in one. The narrow street was well thronged, and he walked his horse slowly along, curiously interested in this town that was given over almost entirely to Huguenots. It did not occur to him that, having entered town with the Scot, he also might be taken for one of Spanuto's friends.

So, after a bit, he came to the Arms of Navarre, turned into the courtyard, and dismounted. A lad with leathern apron and blackened face slipped out and departed hurriedly. As a groom came to take his horse, Bellegarde asked for Jean le Borgne.

"Inside, master. He just went in a moment ago."

Bellegarde nodded, turned, and swung into the big room of the tavern. The sudden transition from sunlight to cool darkness blinded him for an instant, but he was aware of a shuffling step at his back, and glanced around. He had one sharp glimpse of a man there, with poniard uplifted; no other warning.

The figure leaped, and the poniard came down squarely between the shoulders of Bellegarde.

"There's one of them gone to hell!" rang out a raucous voice, as the crimson figure went headlong.

THE FORCE of the blow, which knocked the dagger from the hand of the assassin, sent Bellegarde headlong forward; but the mail shirt saved him from anything worse than a bruise.

He struck against a second figure, sent it sprawling, then was on his feet like a cat, his rapier out. The room was full of shapes circling around, and knowing himself trapped here, Bellegarde made the best of it.

One leap and he gained the fireplace. On either side was a long, high oaken settle, which fully protected him from any flank attack. His back to the fire, he stood ready, astonished by the quick outburst of cries and dismayed voices arising.

"Witchcraft!" shouted one man, brandishing a cudgel. "Le

Borgne poniarded him—and there's the blade on the floor! It wouldn't pierce him!"

Bellegarde perceived a dozen men ringing him round, armed with all sorts of weapons, but wisely hesitating in their attack. Then came explanation.

"He's one of them!" came a shrill voice. "I saw him ride into town with one of those accursed ravishers! Pull him down and finish him!"

"Pull him down yourself, if you like," came the retort "Where's Le Borgne?"

"Aye, where is he?" spoke out Bellegarde, beginning to comprehend the situation. "Have him out here, one of you! I want a word with him."

There was a concerted movement. The name of Spanuto volleyed on the air, with a rain of curses. Then came a shrill cry of alarm, and an instant of startled silence; every head was turned toward the door, where a man had appeared.

"What's going on here?" rang out a loud, authoritative voice. "Pistols out, men! In after me. You rascals, drop your weapons, or we'll empty bullets into your dirty hides! What's this, a gentleman? *Mort de ma vie!* To me, comrades! Clear the room—"

Bellegarde was no less astounded than the others. These broke hastily, as a cavalier advanced with two pistols covering them, and behind him two other men. A third appeared, dragging a shrinking figure.

"They've got Le Borgne!" went up a shrill shout. "Flee! Save yourselves!"

The townfolk in the tavern fled incontinently. The cavalier fired his pistol over their heads, laughed, and swaggered toward Bellegarde. His dusty garments showed hard riding; he was obviously a person of quality.

"Whether sent from heaven or hell, *monsieur,*" said Bellegarde gayly, "accept my thanks!"

The other chuckled. "A lucky meeting! Some one yelled in the street they were killing one of Spanuto's men in here, so we jumped in to the rescue. I've been all over town trying to find your comrades; we heard Mendoza was here buying provisions. Allow me; I am the Chevalier Duguet, of the household of the Prince of Sedan, bearing a letter for Captain Spanuto. I've been two days trying to find this accursed Tour de Gisy; I have to get on to Tours without an instant's delay. Curse the luck!"

Bellegarde sheathed his blade and returned the other's bow.

"I am Antonio Florio, chevalier," he said coolly, "lieutenant to Captain Spanuto. Mendoza has returned to the castle."

"Eh?" Duguet regarded him with sudden suspicion. "I understood Florio was an Italian!"

CHAPTER IV

BELLEGARDE MASQUERADES

"WELL, AM I not Italian?" said Bellegarde, with a disarming laugh. "Florio is an Italian name, at least. Since we're in force here, why not break our fast? Devil take it, I'm hungry and thirsty both."

"So are we, *par Dieu!*" Duguet, still on guard, turned to his three men. Two of them he sent after the landlord, bidding them get food and wine in a hurry, then he swaggered over to a table, beckoned Bellegarde to join him, and summoned the third man, who held his prisoner securely.

"Fetch the rogue hither! He's yours, Florio; do what you like with him."

So this was Jean le Borgne! His one eye proved the name; a dirty, unkempt rogue, with no strength in his body. Only Bellegarde knew that he was one of Gisy's best men, who had been sore wounded and left here in Courcelles to recover of his hurt. The one eye glared furiously back at him, as the prisoner was tied to a chair, and after an instant Bellegarde spoke.

"So, fellow! You tried to put a dagger into Antonio Florio, did you? Well and good! For that I shall take you back with me and give you a proper hanging."

"Hang him, eh? By the Mass," said Duguet, stretching out comfortably, "better to put the lousy rascal on the rack! Well, have it your own way. Spanuto is well?"

"Aye, well enough," answered Bellegarde.

The other two lackeys entered, driving the host before them, laden down with bottles. The frightened inn-keeper received orders. Jean le Borgne never took his one eye from Bellegarde.

"You say you are in haste to reach Tours?" asked the latter, tasting his wine.

"Aye." The chevalier frowned. "A lady there—you comprehend! And now I must ride another few leagues in the wrong direction. A full day lost."

"Merely to deliver a letter? Nonsense! Give me your letter. I'll have it at Gisy ere sunset. It will go to Spanuto, I promise you, by a safe hand. Whose safer, indeed?"

"Not so fast!" Duguet shook his head. "I'd be glad, aye, but I'm not turning over a missive from the prince to any one who says he's so-and-so! While I don't doubt it, all the same I don't know you—"

"Perhaps this will convince you." Bellegarde, laughing, produced the folded vellum he had taken from Florio. "My commission under the captain's own hand."

"Aye, I know his writing." Duguet glanced over the document and his face cleared. "Praise be to the Saints! Give me a receipt for the letter and I'll be delighted by your kindness. You must pardon my hesitation, *monsieur*."

"Duty exacts no pardon," and Bellegarde shouted for the landlord.

Writing materials were produced after some search. The required receipt was written and signed with Florio's name, and Bellegarde pocketed a small sealed letter.

Food and wine were already loading down the table. Duguet looked at the captive.

"What about this hangdog rogue? I'll be off for Tours as quickly as we can get started—"

"Leave him, leave him," said Bellegarde complacently. "I've half a dozen men coming ere long. We'll truss him up and carry him back to amuse the captain."

Le Borgne sat motionless all the while, his one eye glaring at Bellegarde.

EATING AND drinking, Duguet talked of Paris, which he did not know too well, and of Sedan, which he knew thoroughly. Bellegarde said little, but now and again drove in a query that provoked information.

"The captain told me to-day that two more gentlemen arrive soon."

"Aye. Vicomte de Theleme and Count Solbeig, of my master's guards. Once it's over, Solbeig gets a marshal's baton," and Duguet winked knowingly. "I'll remain at Tours. The courier from Madrid should arrive in a week or ten days, and I'll send over the word when it comes."

Bellegarde itched for more, but nothing offered. He became increasingly curious to know why nobles of such standing visited Spanuto in this wilderness, from Paris and Sedan. The mention of a courier from Spain also pricked his incredulity into interest. However, he could not push fortune too far.

"Another dozen bottles between us?" he suggested, when their repast was done.

"No, enough is enough," and Duguet refused more wine with a sigh of repletion. He let out a roar at his lackeys, who were in a far corner of the room, to get the horses saddled, then looked at Bellegarde.

"How say you? Will these rascally burghers make another attempt, think you?"

"No. My men will be along any minute now. I owe you inestimable thanks, *monsieur,* for your quick action! I shall never forget it. Perhaps I may see you at Tours ere long."

"Good! I'll be at the Licorne Inn—an excellent place," said Duguet, and rose. The two exchanged bows, and. Bellegarde accompanied the other to the door. There, he made Duguet a second and very sweeping bow, with laughter dancing in his gray eyes.

"*Au revoir!*" he said, as the others passed out. And under his breath he added: "And when we meet again, you'll tell me more!

"For that I shall give you a proper hanging."

A pox on me, if I don't learn enough to question you more shrewdly the next time!"

Then he swung around, glanced at the inn-keeper, and crossed to where Jean le Borgne sat tied. He drew up a chair, took out his long poniard, and fingered it, his head cocked on one side, listening. After a moment there came the clatter of hoofs as Duguet and his riders passed out to the street.

"GOOD! THEY'VE gone." Bellegarde met the one glaring eye of the man before him, and smiled. "So you thought to poniard me?"

"You are not Florio; you lied to them," said the one-eyed man hoarsely.

"Right. Good thing you kept quiet about it, too." Bellegarde reached forward, cut the cords that held the man in his chair. "Do you know these clothes, this gold chain? They belong to Raoul de Gisy. He sent me to find you here. Come over to this table and—host! Half a dozen more of this wine, and food for Jean le Borgne! Quick about it!"

Bellegarde leaned back, laughing heartily at the utter amaze-

ment of the inn-keeper who thus served his hostler, and the
mingled emotions of Le Borgne.

"Come, come!" he exclaimed gayly. "I know everything; they
saw me riding into town with one of Spanuto's men, eh? And
you made a terrible mistake, eh? Diable! I've a black and blue
spot between my shoulders this minute! Well, let it pass; forget
it entirely, Le Borgne. I've good news for you."

He glanced around, found the inn-keeper out of hearing,
and leaned forward.

"Your master is safe and well. Florio is dead. There is money
to pay men, understand? Plenty of it. And that rascal Spanuto—
well, are you cured of your hurts?"

"No, *monsieur*," said Le Borgne, staring at him. "I can ride;
but as you saw, I have no strength, I cannot fight."

"Then, *pardie*, you'll ride! Gisy tells me you know every inch
of this country. I need you. Get cleaned, shaved, dressed, and
join me in an hour's time at that smithy I passed coming into
town. My horse has a loose shoe to be fixed, and I must purchase
a few small articles. Agreed?"

The other grinned suddenly. "I'll send word to the smithy,
then," he said. "It was thence that I learned of your coming."

"Oh! When I asked about you—I see!" Bellegarde chuckled.
"I am the Sieur de Bellegarde; but best not mention my name.
Spanuto thinks I'm a friend of his."

The one eye glinted. "And is it true, *messire*, about my master
having money—"

"And friends, aye. Are there men here whom I can raise to
follow me?"

"No," said Le Borgne. "These townfolk hate Spanuto's men,
but on their own behalf; they do not love my master. However,
I know of two rascals here who were talking this morning of
taking service with Spanuto. They would as lief take service
against him. They are Germans who have been in the guard of
the Duke of Savoy for two years past."

"None better," said Bellegarde, and passed a gold coin across the table. "Hire them out of that, in my name, but say nothing of serving against Spanuto till the time comes."

He passed out into the courtyard, after paying for the meal, sharply disappointed; he had hoped to ride away with at least a dozen men behind him. Still, two good ones were worth a dozen poor fighters, so he had not entirely wasted his time. And much as he wanted to read the letter in his pocket, he refrained. Raoul de Gisy should break that seal, for luck.

He rode slowly along the streets, aware that men stared blackly after him; news of the affray in the Arms of Navarre must have spread far and wide. But when he came to his goal, the smith grinned and took his horse and fell to work, so Bellegarde knew that Jean le Borgne had sent the promised message.

Bellegarde sought out the nearest shops, brought bread, cheese, meat, and when he returned to the smithy, his horse awaited him. Le Borgne was coming, also, mounted on a sorry nag, with two stalwart, half drunken Germans riding at his stirrup. Bellegarde saw at a glance that they were exactly the men for him. As he himself came from Lorraine and German was native as French to him, he greeted them in that tongue and their faces lighted up.

"Where from? Hesse!" he exclaimed. "I knew your landgrave well; served a year with him in Hungary! Follow me."

"*Ja, mein Herr,*" they chorused. They were brethren. Arnulf and Herman Breiter, flaxen-haired, well muscled, hardened rogues. Bellegarde mounted and beckoned up the one-eyed man, who was now shaved and shorn, decently clad, well armed, and showed a shrewd, intent visage.

"Here is food; divide it for carrying. You know the gallows of Gisy? An hour after sunset we meet your master there."

"A long time to go that distance, master," said Le Borgne.

"Do you know of any other men we can pick up?"

"By the score, aye; but not men to trust. Stay! There is Jules Casteau, who left us before I got my hurt; he had a shot through

the thigh, and went to his farm. It is not far out of our way, on
the hill road that goes to Gisy from the north. And he is a good
man, if recovered by now, as he should be."

"Every man counts," said Bellegarde, with a nod. "Lead the
way."

So Le Borgne rode out in front, Bellegarde following, the
two Germans in the rear.

LEAVING THE highway altogether, the one-eyed man
struck off by trails through a thick stretch of woods, for in this
direction lay the Forest of Vivierres, adjoining an ancient royal
château burned during the civil wars. In this forest bode only
charcoal burners and broken men, wild, hunted creatures outside
the law, who shunned the light of day and were no better than
beasts.

"A refuge for your master, at least, if worse comes to worst!"
observed Bellegarde, but Le Borgne crossed himself hurriedly.

"The saints avert the omen, *monsieur!* No, those animals are
like wolves, and go in packs. If he sought refuge there, they'd
tear him to pieces for his clothes alone. They live in trees and
in hovels underground. Sometimes they steal a woman from a
lonely farm; if they catch a horse, they eat it straightway.
Escaped galley-slaves, branded men, those out of their wits,
may join them, but no others."

"Is there none to ride them down and root them out?" asked
Bellegarde, wondering.

"And who would do it? No, *seigneur,* so long as they leave
his lands unharmed, the king's lieutenant in Tours cares naught
for what passes here. Nay, it would require an army!"

Bellegarde shrugged, and eyed the deep recesses of the trees
with no great love.

They saw no living creature for an hour or more, passed from
the forest and came to a road that wound among pleasant hills
strewn with vineyards. Now they were within the jurisdiction
of Gisy again, though not on its lands proper. They came
through a little hamlet, whose folk scattered like a covey of

quail at their approach, bolting doors and shutters in haste, vanishing completely, and so on again among the hills.

"A quarter-league from here," said Le Borgne, "is the stead of Jules Casteau. You had best let me ride ahead, and you follow more slowly. Armed men riding are shunned like the plague by these poor devils. You have only to follow this road and not turn off at the fork going to the left."

Bellegarde nodded. The other put spurs to his horse and rode on at a gallop, being out of sight in no time.

After a little the three came to a fork, or rather to the junction of a road that bore in from the left. As they approached this, one of the Germans spoke suddenly.

"A glitter among the trees, lord! On that road to the left."

Bellegarde drew rein, put fresh priming in his brass pistols, and waited. Then he, too, caught the glitter, saw dust rising, and a moment later two riders drew out of the trees, lackeys in a livery of blue and silver, followed closely by a light coach and four horses, and two postilions. The equipage halted, the riders staring at Bellegarde; then the coach door was swung open and a woman looked out. A mask of crimson velvet half concealed her face.

Bellegarde advanced, astonished at finding such travelers on such a road. The woman beckoned to him. He drew rein, dismounted, swept her a bow, and came to the coach.

"Well met, *monsieur!*" she exclaimed. "I fear that we have lost our way. For a league we have encountered no one, and the road is miserable!"

Bellegarde laughed a little. "Faith, I agree with you! Being a stranger in these parts myself, I cannot call it a hospitable region, and the roads are unmarked. You seek Courcelles?"

"Courcelles?" she repeated in surprise. "Heavens, no! I never heard of it!"

She looked at Bellegarde with obvious approval, and he at her with open admiration. She was dark, laughing, vivacious, and of such striking beauty as to draw his instant attention.

Despite the mask, in her quick and lively smile he discerned a swiftly uncertain temper that smacked of authority. Her jewels, her flowered satin, the rich appointments of her coach and the coat of arms painted on its panel, all spoke of wealth and birth.

"Well," said Bellegarde whimsically, "you're a long time, *madame,* telling me where you want to go!"

"Oh! Why, to the Tour de Gisy, of course! To find—"

"The devil!" exclaimed Bellegarde, staring sharply.

"Not at all, *monsieur;* one Captain Spanuto, or rather, a relative of mine who is now a guest with Spanuto. You know the captain, perhaps?"

BELLEGARDE BOWED very gallantly. He needed time to think. Divining that she was not altogether indifferent to him, he came close to the coach and smiled into the eyes that glittered behind the crimson mask.

"Faith! Now it seems that everything is altered, my whole destiny changed!" he exclaimed. "I am the Sieur de Bellegarde. Ten minutes ago I was traveling, although somewhat lazily, for Italy and the wars in Hungary against the Turk. Now, devil take Turks and Hungarians alike! Upon the honor of a gentleman, I shall remain in France."

She broke into quick laughter and extended her hand, upon which jewels glittered.

"Why not, indeed? Stay by all means, *monsieur!*"

"Alas, *madame!*" Bellegarde pressed his lips to her hand, with ardor. "Duty and desire pull different ways—still—"

"I can promise you hospitality, entertainment, and pleasant conversation at Gisy," she went on, "and perhaps I may have need of a sword to serve me there."

"You might find a worse blade than mine, then. Who is your relative there?"

"M. Praslin," she said, after a second of hesitation. Bellegarde changed countenance.

"Praslin!" he echoed. "Why—impossible!"

Her brows lifted in a charming grimace.

"How so, *monsieur?*"

"Why, *madame,*" said Bellegarde hastily, his fingers clasping hers in a momentary swift pressure, which was returned, "that fellow Praslin is a rascal! And you are an angel."

"He is a rascal, certainly," she returned coolly. "But how know you what I am, when you cannot see my face?"

"I do not need to see it," exclaimed Bellegarde. "I can feel it. Your angelic presence cannot be hidden by a mere mask."

"Come," she said softly, "will you not ride with us to Gisy, *monsieur?* It will please me."

Bellegarde recollected himself. He let fall her hand and turned, beckoning to his two Germans, who advanced at once.

"Ride on," he ordered, "and see if you can find that scoundrel of a guide who ran away! If you get him, stop and await us. I shall accompany this lady, until we encounter you."

"And," added the lady swiftly, leaning a little out of the window, "take your master's horse with you, for he rides with me. Enter, *monsieur!*"

Bellegarde gestured assent to his men, and opening the door of the coach, stepped in. She addressed her own men.

"Follow those two, but slowly." She turned to Bellegarde, who found a place opposite her among her baggage, and her eyes danced through the holes of her mask. "Upon my word, *monsieur,* I begin to think you yourself don't know where the Tour de Gisy lies!"

"*Touché,*" admitted Bellegarde cheerfully. "Our guide slipped ahead, presumably to inquire the way, of which he was uncertain. I can ride with you only until we find that man. I have most urgent business in this neighborhood, but to-morrow I may rejoin you. Spanuto only this morning asked me to visit him."

"You know him, then?" He could feel her gaze searching him, as the coach lurched forward.

"I met him; that is all. Not having been in Paris for some

three years, I know of little that has chanced there. I am a mere provincial recluse, a country boor—"

"You?" she broke in with a laugh. "Come, the truth! I know a soldier when I see one."

"Well, my princess—for you must be a princess at the very least—I recently killed another gentleman who had the misfortune to misunderstand my friendship with his wife. As he was a relative of a great noble, I started hurriedly for Hungary."

"Indeed! And do you not feel a certain awe," she asked merrily, "at being so close to a princess?"

"Not in the least; for she is masked, and I see only a woman."

"And your friendship with this lady of whom you speak, was purely platonic?"

The gray eyes widened with mock solemnity. "*Madame!* Nothing else would be possible, I assure you!"

She lifted her hands in assumed horror.

"What, *monsieur?* You would dare confess—"

AT THIS instant the coach dipped suddenly into a deep rut. It gave a violent thrusting lurch, and she was pitched headlong into the arms of Bellegarde.

He caught her adroitly, held her close, and pressed his lips to hers. With the movement, the strings of the mask were broken, and it fell away. In a sudden, astonishing access of strength she broke from his hold, but the sight of her unmasked beauty quite overcame Bellegarde, who could only stare at her in such obvious admiration that her anger melted.

"*Monsieur!*" she cried sharply. "Is that your idea of a platonic relationship?"

"Thank God, no!" said Bellegarde, replacing her in her own seat.

She burst into a peal of laughter. "Then you do not recognize me?"

"That were impossible. I have never been so lucky as to see

you before; but it is true that I have been with the army for three years past, my princess. Are you indeed a princess?"

"Would a lady of that rank be riding among these lonely hills?"

"Well, since meeting you I am a firm believer in miracles—"

As she met his dancing eyes, laughter rose anew to her lips—and then suddenly quenched. Her face changed. The blood drained out of her cheeks, and against their swift and terrible pallor her black eyes burned and blazed. They were fastened upon his hand.

"*Monsieur*—where did that come from?"

Her low, urgent voice went into him like steel, made his pulses leap as though a deadly peril were upon him. He twisted off the ring he had taken from the dead Praslin, inwardly cursing his folly in wearing it.

"This diamond?" he said coolly. "Faith, a pretty stone, eh? I had it at dice two nights ago, from a fellow in a tavern, and had his horse to boot—"

"You lie!" she cried out. "It belongs to Praslin! I gave it him myself!"

Bellegarde gave her a glance of stupefaction, then spoke rapidly. In her eyes sat a look he had seen only in the eyes of men whose swords were reaching for his life.

"Then, my princess, allow me the honor of returning it to you and beseeching your forgiveness for my unwitting fault in displaying it. All this is very strange!" he added thoughtfully. "Spanuto recognized the horse this morning. Apparently it had been stolen from him; perhaps the ring as well. He was in hot search of that rascal, too."

Her gaze devoured him with stabbing suspicion, as he placed the ring on her hand, but her face cleared before his merry, unconcerned look. Her fingers tightened upon his.

"I promise my forgiveness if you come to Gisy," she said, her voice very soft, thrilling, richly vibrant. "Please! I must see you again. I may need your—your help there—"

A slight shiver, entirely involuntary, seized upon Bellegarde; but he smiled into her eyes and returned the pressure of her fingers in assent. At this moment the coach came to a halt. One of the two Germans clattered up and stopped at the door.

"*Monsieur!* Arnulf has caught the guide, there; holds him tight, lest he run off again."

With a swift farewell to his charming companion, Bellegarde again took horse and spurred on with the German to where Le Borgne awaited him.

"You have found the man you came to find?" he asked.

"Awaiting us, *monsieur,*" said the one-eyed man in a strange voice. "Will you come?"

"Gladly."

But, as he gave his horse the rein, Bellegarde glanced after the departing coach, and his thoughts were very far from the work in hand.

He was soon recalled to reality, however.

CHAPTER V

CRUCIFIED

THE ONCE neat cottage had not been burned; it had
been wrecked, as by some vandal blast of fury. And, nailed
to the door by great spikes driven through hands and feet,
hanging in an attitude of contorted agony, was what remained
of a man.

"By God!" cried Bellegarde. "Who did this?"

"Ask of the pretty lady who visits the Tour de Gisy," said Le
Borgne with a sneer.

Bellegarde turned. The one-eyed shrank suddenly from his
look of icy rage, crossed himself, recoiled a pace. Then Bellegarde's hand left his dagger and he made a curt gesture.

"Bury him, the three of you, and leave me alone for a space."

He strode apart from them, walking among ruined vine-stubs
that had been hacked to the root.

No jest, then, what Praslin had cried out, about Spanuto
nailing him alive to a door! No use asking who had done this;
Jules Casteau had been left as a warning to other followers of
Raoul de Gisy.

"Where is any possible connection between Spanuto and
the Prince of Sedan?" pondered Bellegarde, frowning as he
paced between the vineyard rows. "Duguet comes from Sedan;
he brings that Italian rat a letter from the prince. Why? And
he goes to Tours, awaiting a courier from Spain. Why? Well,
we'll know more in due time. Decidedly, there's something more

to all this than the mere seizure of Raoul de Gisy's estate! And that woman knew Duguet well. Curious!"

Undoubtedly the masked lady was of the court. That singular court of Henri IV was half Huguenot, half Catholic, yet so gaily licentious, so bravely and arrogantly in search of pleasure alone, as to revive the almost incredible days of François I. She had lied about being a relative of Praslin; she had coolly agreed that Praslin was a rascal. No, she had nothing in common with that fellow. She was no idle waster of time and money and men. She was a woman with a purpose in all she did. And if she gave herself, her beauty, with a free hand, there was a purpose in this as well. Who was she, then?

Some love-flame, seeking to keep Spanuto company? Not she. Those hot and eager eyes of hers held far more than passion. The diamond ring—which she had given to Praslin! She was some great lady, and could be nothing else. Perhaps Praslin had been her lover, perhaps not. Was she a messenger? Possibly; yet she was a strange sort of messenger. No, it was all a dark and tangled skein, impossible to comprehend.

"But why did I shiver when she spoke of seeing me again?" wondered Bellegarde. "Something passed over me. I know not what. She attracts, yet repels. A pox take me if she hasn't sent many a man to hell ere this! And two more gentlemen coming to join Spanuto—for love of him? Devil a bit of it. For love of her, more like—ha! Was she luring me on to join him, then? Is she gaining recruits for him? No, no. And yet her kisses—good God, how they were sweet! And her very soul was in them; I could read it in her eyes. She was drawn to me, as I was to her, all in a moment—"

His head drooped, and he came to a halt.

To his mind recurred a smooth, shadowed face with violet eyes, a cool yet passionate voice whose passion was not from sensuous impulse, a woman whom he could scarce visualize, yet whose quick wit and impetuous temper had lingered with him. Something emanated from her that this gracious court beauty lacked—some quiet strength beyond sex. A species of shame seized upon Bellegarde, as though he could feel the scorn of that cool, angry voice leaping at him.

"*Diable!*" he thought. "I'm a fool! Well, I'm warned; if I see this fine lady again, she'll lure me as far as she likes, but I'll be on my guard. Eh? What is it, then?"

"*Monsieur,* time has passed," said Jean le Borgne, who had approached him. "Poor Jules is buried. We had best be moving on, if we're to reach the gallows by sunset."

"An hour past sunset," corrected Bellegarde. "At sunset, halt a while and eat. The place of meeting is at the gallows."

"I know the place, yes; my master has used it before this. It is a little thicket of ancient oaks, just below the gallows." Le Borgne shrugged. "Shall we start, then?"

Bellegarde nodded and strode back to the horses. In two minutes they were continuing their way.

SUNSET FOUND them halted beside a brook, almost within sight of the Tour de Gisy, in a covert of trees below the road. The horses cropped the grass as the four riders ate, washing down their repast with cold water from the stream.

Then Bellegarde rose. "Let us ride on and be the first to arrive," he said to Le Borgne. "I have nothing to fear if we encounter any of the Italian's men. They deem me a friend."

The other assented, with a nonchalant gesture.

Mounting, they rode on again. The sun was just vanishing in the west, twilight was creeping along the valleys with purpling shades. As they came to the crest of a hillock, Le Borgne drew rein and pointed off to the right.

"There lies the Tour, up that valley, hidden by the hill between us," he said. "And yonder is the gallows."

It lay almost straight ahead, on a little rise above the road—a great gibbet, upon which were three twisting things moving endlessly in the wind. Below it and across the road stretched out ancient oaks, huge, gnarled, widespread, part of the Forest of Vivieres.

Bellegarde urged on his horse in silence, seeing the look that had come into the face of Le Borgne. The man's one eye glittered at the restless shapes swinging from that gallows—shapes of men who had been his comrades, hung there in chains. So they rode down until the chains were creaking above them, when Bellegarde turned aside among the oaks and drew rein.

"Tether the horses," he said to the three, "then spread out and keep watch. If any speak you, the word is Gisy. We have a while to wait. It is still far from dark."

He himself, drawing away from them, went out and strode down the road, seeking to stretch his legs after the long day's ride. And, as he came out into the open beyond the trees, he was aware of a single horseman coming up the slope toward him. At first he thought it Raoul de Gisy, until he perceived it to be a more slender, lissom figure.

Then his heart leaped and he strode out into the center of the road, laughing, his sword out for a salute to the newcomer.

The rider drew rein, but presently came on, staring at him, and he saw it was indeed Angele, clad in man's garments of gray as he had first seen her, now wearing a yellow mask. But she did not recognize, in this splendid figure of scarlet and gold, the ragged, bearded man of the other day. Seeing that he stood as though to block her way, she drew rein before him and reached out a pistol.

"Make way!" she exclaimed sharply.

"Devil take me if I do!" answered Bellegarde. "Not for the devil himself, much less for an angel!"

"Eh?" She frowned down at him. "That voice—who are you, *monsieur?*"

Bellegarde swept his plume in the dust with a low bow.

"Is it not a pretty name, Angele? Guardian of secrets, guardian of my one friend, guardian of this rendezvous! Bellegarde, indeed, and at your service whole-heartedly. Dismount and walk with me. Ho, one of you rascals! Come and take this cavalier's horse!"

Forth of the trees came Jean le Borgne, with a salute to the lady, who called out his name in recognition. She dismounted.

"GISY'S NOT here yet; I told him an hour past sunset," said Bellegarde. "Come, comrade! Of God's grace, I beseech you, take off that accursed hat and mask and let me see what you look like! Since our first meeting, your voice has haunted me, and when Raoul told me your name, that gave reason enough."

"You! I can scarce credit it," she made answer. "What has happened?"

"Plenty!" and Bellegarde laughed gayly. "I met Spanuto this morning, cheated a courier who bore a letter for him at noon, and rode with one of his guests this evening; I've been learning things. But not enough. To-morrow I visit him at the Tour."

She caught her breath, staring at him.

"*Monsieur!* You—you cannot do that! You're not in earnest?"

"But I am! Faith, I talked with Mendoza to-day, and he knew me not."

"No wonder," she said dryly.

"Well—the hat?"

With a careless shrug she removed the wide-brimmed hat and her mask, and Bellegarde saw her small, well-shaped head, massed with golden hair, her pert, laughing face, instinct with alert intelligence, and caught the twinkle of her violet eyes in the gathering dusk.

"Are you satisfied?" she asked.

"Far from it! The cloak next, and then—"

"A truce to your gallantries!" she exclaimed, and the swift anger in her voice thrilled him again. She pulled the wide hat over her head once more. "I know your kind, *monsieur*—"

"But you do not," said Bellegarde, suddenly grave. "You do not, upon my honor—"

"Honor!" she cried out in scorn. "A word to cloak your ruffling swagger, your lechery, your lies! A mask behind which crawls a maggot of dishonor! I know what you court gallants are; I've heard my father tell; I've met your kind before. Be a friend to Raoul de Gisy, and I honor you for it—but your honor and mine are different things."

"Perhaps not," said Bellegarde, who had turned a little pale in the twilight. "My dear, there is a devil in your tongue, as I have said before, but I love you for it. Nay! I'm a soldier, not a court gallant. Play not the shrew with me, then. Why treat me like an enemy? Either you like me and feel shame to show it, or—"

"Like you, a stranger? Feel shame?" she cried fiercely. "Heaven forbid!"

"Well, I like you, and may Heaven further it!" and he laughed lightly. "Or else, as I was about to say, some trouble weighs heavily upon you."

At this she stopped short, trying to scan his face in the gathering obscurity.

"You are a strange man!" and she changed the subject abruptly. "Do you know that between us we must give of our best to help Raoul de Gisy? He's a dear, sturdy fellow, who would beat out his brains against the wall unless he were aided."

"One can't deny his faults," said Bellegarde, "but he has the gift of winning affection. And why? For his honesty, simplicity, bravery. Few men are like him. But tell me, comrade; whence comes your interest in Raoul de Gisy?"

"Whence comes yours?"

"Friendship. Also, we seem to be embroiled together in this mysterious affair. I think there's more to it than appears on the surface. Be frank! Art in love with him?"

"No. Good Lord! Because a woman seeks to help a man, must she be in love? No! We were children together. He has been set upon most foully, heaped with unearned dishonor, dealt with treacherously. Until now, he's been alone, driven ever into more desperate straits. I did not know you would be a man to stand by him. That is why—"

She fell silent, checking her speech.

"Something worries me," said Bellegarde quietly. "I heard to-day that Spanuto seeks to wed some one near here. Do you know anything of it?"

She made no answer, but he heard the catch of her breath.

"So?" he went on. "It's a desperate combination, then, of both against the Italian. Good! Count me in as a third. I'm most deeply involved myself, it appears; but our first task is to make head against Spanuto, clear him out by force of arms. Then, discover what's behind this whole affair. He and I must fight for our lives, then for our honor. Here—quiet! There are hoofs on the road—"

He caught her arm, listening. Then the voice of Le Borgne reached them, answered at once by a bluff, hearty greeting.

Raoul de Gisy had arrived from the upper road.

PRESENTLY THEY were seated, all three, under a huge gnarled oak whose ancient roots upcurled around them. The darkness was now complete. The massive boughs overhead were like a tent, shutting out the starlight. They could see nothing, not even each other.

"Well, Raoul?" inquired Bellegarde. "Anything happened since we parted?"

"Yes, a marvelous thing!" said Gisy with enthusiasm.

"Good; our luck's turning. What was it?"

"In Marcel's cellar I found fifty bottles of old Médun, of the '85 vintage."

Bellegarde broke into laughter. "In that case, let Mlle. de Chanlay tell why she has summoned us hither. I think she has found something better than wine."

"I have," said the young woman in a somewhat disdainful voice. "*Mon Dieu!* That you can talk of wine, at such a moment!"

"Courage!" Bellegarde reached out to pat her hand reassuringly. He found the boot of Gisy instead, and withdrew his arm. "Wine has its uses. Continue."

"My cousin, the Vicomte d'Aurilly, is a relative by marriage of M. de Rosny."

"And Rosny rules France," muttered Gisy. "The sour old Huguenot!"

"At least, the king is guided by him," she proceeded. "My cousin has talked with Rosny, who believes the charges against you both were false. Also, Bassompierre is a true friend, the most intimate companion of the king, and is working in your favor."

Bellegarde laughed harshly. "The most upright of ministers and the most profligate of courtiers! With these two advocates, Raoul, we should go far. But we need help closer at hand."

"You shall have it," she said quickly. "Under certain conditions, Aurilly is bringing forty men to Tours, within two weeks, and will place them at your service."

"Thank God! My ankle is cured this moment," said Gisy. "Forty men! That is a miracle."

"You spoke of conditions," said Bellegarde softly.

"Yes." She hesitated, then went on slowly. "Raoul, I thought you were alone, in desperate case. So was I, for Spanuto has—has made certain advances, offers, even threats. For some time past, Aurilly has sought my hand in marriage. Well, I have consented. My father has so written him—my father is in dread of Spanuto, also. For myself, as well as for you, this arrangement means—"

"This is glorious news, Angele!" exclaimed Gisy joyfully. "I know Aurilly. He is exactly the man for you. Wealthy, of splendid birth, very proud, a widower past the age of gallantry— What the devil! Who struck against me?"

"Your pardon," said Bellegarde, who had hit his knee viciously. "I could not see you in the darkness. *Mademoiselle,* you say he comes to Tours in two weeks?"

"Yes. Until then, you must do nothing."

"And is this all your news?"

"Is it not enough?"

"At least it is definite. We meet Aurilly in two weeks at Tours. At some tavern?"

"By no means. He has a house behind the Hôtel de Ville."

"Good," said Bellegarde. "Now, just who is the Prince of Sedan?"

"Why, the Prince of Sedan, of course!" said Gisy. "Head of the Calvinists in France and independent lord of Sedan. As great a man as the king himself. He hates the king, plots against him, and would join hands with the devil to further his own purposes."

"Hm!" Bellegarde frowned. "Why is Spanuto surrounded by gentry of the court? Within a week or two he'll be joined by Vicomte de Theleme and one Count Solbeig, who's from Sedan—"

"Where he has commanded the guards of the prince. Theleme is a gentleman of the queen's household, also a relative of Sedan."

"Clear enough. To-day a gentleman named Duguet reached Courcelles, bearing a letter from the Prince of Sedan to our Italian friend. He goes to Tours, there to await a courier from Madrid. Therefore the Calvinist leader at Sedan, the court of Madrid and Concini's party at Paris are all somehow connected with this Giulio Spanuto—"

"Oh, the devil take it all!" cried out Gisy. "Never mind all this; it makes my head ache. Queen's party, king's party, Sedan, Spaniards—a pox on it! Get it down to simple facts."

"Easily," and Bellegarde laughed. "The king stands alone; France personified. Every jealous noble and grasping foreigner plots against him. They have joined hands. Spanuto is their tool."

"How do you know this?"

"I am guessing at it. Depend upon it, this is some devilish deep plot!"

GISY SMOTHERED an oath in the darkness. "In other words, all the rotten elements in France have leagued with her foreign enemies, against the king. I can understand that. To what end?"

"So far, we don't know."

"Then what the devil is the use of talking? I wish we had lived twenty years ago, when you cut down a man if he was of the other party or embraced him if he was of your own! Things were simpler then. Now they're too cursed complicated."

"Agreed," and Bellegarde chuckled. "One question more. Why should a woman, young, beautiful, obviously of rank and wealth, be traveling to Gisy without even a maid? I met her this evening and directed her aright. She claimed to be a relative of Praslin, which I doubt."

"Love makes relatives by wholesale. Who was she?"

"I do not know. She was masked."

"You have a penetrating eye," said Angele de Chanlay dryly, "to discern that a masked woman was young and beautiful."

"Oh, I took off her mask," answered Bellegarde, "for I was curious. By the way, her coach bore a coat of arms."

"Describe it," said Gisy.

"Impossible; it was quartered. The crest was a boar's head, argent; the device was '*Plus que toutes.*' That is all I can recall."

"Enough. *Mordious!* That was the coach of the Duchess of Maine."

"This woman, then, was the duchess?"

"Unlikely. She is a great lady of the Rohan family, who is said to have married the Duc de Maine before he died. The fact is disputed. The king was madly amorous of her, but she played him a trick that made him furious. She is devoted to the queen. What would such a woman be doing here? No, no. Perhaps the woman was her maid."

"I am certain she was the duchess in person."

"A moment ago you did not know her," said the voice of Angele, mockingly.

"One can always tell a great lady, as one can always tell an angel. To a discerning eye, they cannot be imitated."

Gisy was oblivious to all this thrust and parry.

"I believe," he said with conviction, "you have hit upon something. This duchess is more familiarly known as La Fleche, from an estate near that place; she holds lands in Flanders and is very intimate with the Spanish ambassador. And we have Duguet, awaiting a courier from Spain, bearing a letter from the Prince of Sedan. Ah, my friend, what a chance you missed! If only you had obtained that letter!"

"It is in my pocket."

"What? Do you jest?"

"No. Duguet took me for Florio, because of the commission I took from Florio's body. Now, I promised to deliver the letter. And as you very well know, I am in the habit of keeping my promises. I propose that we open the letter carefully, learn its contents, and then I will deliver it to-morrow. I met Spanuto this morning and he pressed me to visit him."

"You met Spanuto!" repeated Gisy in a choked voice. "And he lives?"

"Assuredly. So do I, thank the Saints! He had six men with him."

"To open a letter and reseal it," said Angele quietly, "requires finesse, and a seal."

"This letter," and Bellegarde chuckled, "is sealed with a Venetian ducat; a shrewd move, as golden ducats of Venice are rare, and less easily counterfeited than an ordinary seal."

"Eh?" exclaimed Gisy. "A Venetian ducat? Why, devil take me! There were some among those gold pieces you pocketed this morning!"

"Exactly. Here is one. Here is the letter. We need only fire, a light, and a hot blade to neatly part the seal. Can we build a fire here safely?"

"A little deeper in the wood, yes. Call the men."

WITHIN HALF an hour a small fire was built, a knife point heated, and the seal of the letter neatly parted without the slightest injury to the paper or even to the wax itself. The letter bore no superscription, no address, no signature; merely three lines of writing in Italian, which Bellegarde translated by light of a blazing ember.

> On September tenth the château will be occupied. The first stag will be the last.

"Come! We have a riddle!" exclaimed Gisy, as Bellegarde set down the brand and produced a golden ducat, which he laid beside the embers. "M. de Sedan intends to occupy a château?"

"He would not write of his own intentions," said Angele. "This is the twenty-fifth of August."

"Precisely," assented Bellegarde. "On September tenth, something occurs in connection with a château; that is to say, in about two weeks. A courier is expected from Madrid within two weeks. Theleme and Solbeig join Spanuto within two weeks. And, within the same time—"

"M. d'Aurilly reaches Tours with the men for Raoul," said Angele in a low voice.

"True! Before then," went on Bellegarde, "we must try to understand more of what is going on. We have a fortnight before us. In that time, it will go hard if we cannot raise a score of good men, to add to the forty Aurilly brings."

"Why seek to understand all this intrigue?" objected Gisy.

"We're on campaign, *mon ami!* And we must know the enemy's objective. Spanuto has your castle, is in full possession, and you are now out of his reckoning. He will turn his attention to the real purpose of his presence here, and that of his friends. When we learn what that is we shall be in better position to act. I propose, therefore, to go and visit him in the morning, while you take Le Borgne, return to the White Horse and await word from me."

"When?"

"Perhaps to-morrow, perhaps next day; who knows? I may come myself. Then we go to Tours together."

"Good!" exclaimed Gisy. "And on the way, gather men!"

"Perhaps. At Tours, I shall renew my acquaintance with the Chevalier Duguet. Agreed?"

"With all my heart."

"Then our business is finished." Bellegarde took up the hot knife, touched it to the seal, and pressed this down with the ducat so that the former imprint was obliterated and the letter showed no trace of opening.

"And where do you and your men go to-night?" asked Angele.

"Under the stars."

"No. Ride back with me. There is a farm where you will receive good quarters."

"Gladly!"

Bellegarde called up the men, the horses were brought, and all mounted. Gisy shook hands and departed with Jean le Borgne for Santour and his hiding place. Bidding the two Germans follow, Bellegarde rode away beside Angele.

"And now," he observed gravely, "there is something I wish to discuss with you."

CHAPTER VI

FOREST ATTACK

"AH!" SAID her voice, cool and piercing. "You are about to become gallant?"

"No. I wish to draw your attention to my name, once more."

"Useless, *monsieur*. I fear you agree with the Greek maxim: First secure a handsome income, then practice virtue!"

"That maxim applies only to ladies. Consider! Bellegarde—a significant name. Above all at the present moment. You trust yourself with me; why?"

"Because I have no one else to trust," and in her voice Bellegarde detected a sad finality, as though she had abandoned her half-mocking banter to speak the truth.

"We have the same cause, the same enemy," he said quietly, gravely. "Are you the woman whom this Italian honors with his attentions?"

"Yes."

"You have a father—"

"Who is powerless. The Spaniard, Mendoza, spent several days visiting my father. In the course of his stay he corrupted our servants with gold. He was good enough to lend my father his own valet, an admirable man, who has quite won my father's heart with his attentions."

From her words, from the bitterness in her voice, Bellegarde understood much that was unuttered. Chanlay, he reflected, must be a singularly weak and helpless person.

"Let us be explicit, sweet angel! Your father, I understand, approves the match with M. d'Aurilly, and no doubt regards it as a thing settled. How, then, can he look complacently upon the Italian?"

"He does not know. Spanuto stopped at our château for a day, when he first came; he bore letters from the queen and from the Guises. When he looked at me—I knew then. I could see it in his eyes. Lately, he has sent me gifts by the hand of that valet, his spy."

"I see. And having a spy, he will doubtless know of Aurilly?"

"Of the marriage, of the betrothal for which Aurilly comes, yes. Not about the men for Raoul. I wrote Aurilly myself and told him to use a certain word in writing to my father, which would give me the information. Now do you comprehend?"

"Everything," said Bellegarde. "Spanuto will dash Aurilly aside like a leaf, and will not delay doing it. He'll come to the château and demand you by force of arms, if necessary."

"How do you know that?" she exclaimed in alarm.

"Because I would do it if I were in his place. Allow me to suggest that for the next day or so you take these two Germans of mine, who will watch over you faithfully. If you have errands or messages, use them; their service costs you nothing but their food, and I'll have no need of them at Gisy. Rather, they would hinder me there."

"But how would I explain their presence, to my father even?"

"Oh! That is very simple. Arnulf! Join us."

After a moment the massive figure of the German loomed beside them.

"Arnulf, I am going to lend you and your brother to attend Mlle. de Chanlay for a day or two, until I have need of you. Watch over her safety and obey her orders. Do not mention M. de Gisy to a soul; if any one tries to bribe you, accept the money, say yes to everything, and get all the information possible. Do you comprehend?"

"Perfectly, *mein Herr.*"

"You will follow *mademoiselle* to the château, ask for the

Comte de Chanlay, and tell him that you serve the Sieur de
Bellegarde, who brings him letters from M. d'Aurilly. Unfortunately this Sieur de Bellegarde met with an accident which
detained him in Tours—"

"It had something to do with a lady, doubtless," put in the
voice of Angele.

"By all means! A lady, Arnulf. He is following in a day or
two. That is all. Dismissed!"

The German saluted and fell behind again.

"My very honorable gentleman," said the voice of Angele,
with a hint of scorn, "how do you expect to issue forth from all
your lies?"

Bellegarde uttered a gay laugh. "Faith, my dear, lies are like
men-at-arms; either brave and faithful servants in a pinch, or
cursed dishonest rascals and cowardly. Mine serve, since I have
no men-at-arms, in place of better aid, and to a good end."

He heard a faint, fluttering sigh.

"Very well; I suppose you are right," and she fell silent.

THE END of this ride was that Bellegarde found himself
made welcome by an honest couple, tenants of Chanlay, who
gladly took care of him and his horse for the night at the request
of Angele. But when Bellegarde would have said farewell to
her, Angele had mounted again and she rode off into the darkness without answering his call.

He went to bed in a fairly bad humor. Her voice, her face,
lingered in his dreams; but he saw her always as a man. This
irritated him, even in his slumber.

With morning, he was up early, broke his fast, gave the good
couple a coin, and set forth upon his way, but by no means
blithely. It occurred to him that the masked lady, whether
duchess or not, would certainly tell Spanuto of having met him
with two servants. She would find that Praslin was dead and
suspicion would flare up anew because of that accursed diamond.
And now, if he appeared without any followers—

"*Diable!*" he exclaimed, drawing rein in some dismay. He had covered half a league, and was within sight of the gallows of Gisy. "Decidedly, Angele was right; my tongue will get me into trouble yet. No, I'd be a fool to risk it there. Much better to ride on, pick up Raoul, and make for Tours at once."

As he came to this decision he suddenly discerned a group of horsemen, just coming into the road from a bypath a quarter-mile ahead. A glitter of helms and breastplates told him that his decision had come too late. With a shrug he pricked on his horse.

A moment later, dismayed conviction grew upon him. Beyond a doubt, that figure in black, leading the dozen riders— yes, Spanuto himself! Bellegarde uttered an oath; then, with a shrug, he waved his hand in greeting and rode on.

"Well," he called cheerily, as the others drew near, "did you get your man, *monsieur?*"

"I did not," said Spanuto very pleasantly, in his liquid accents. "But did you find yours?"

"Aye, and with a vengeance!" Bellegarde broke into a laugh. "I found those rascally lackeys and lost them at once, for a friend borrowed them. Poor Duguet! Damme if I didn't drink him under the table—"

"Duguet, did you say?" interrupted Spanuto, his dark eyes watchful.

"Aye. I've known the chevalier of old; and he knows you, by the way. He gave me a letter for you, being anxious to return to Tours in company of my men, for he was somewhat hurt by a fall he had received. Where the devil is that letter?" Bellegarde began to search through his clothes, conscious of a sharp tense-ness in Spanuto's features, a quick anxiety.

"And I met the most charming person in the world, too," he went on. "Did she tell you of our encounter? Faith, it was a pity to let her go on alone, but I had promised to hand over those lackeys to Duguet—ah, here it is!"

He was immediately aware that the importance of this letter banished everything else from the mind of Spanuto.

"Yes, yes," said the latter negligently. "*Madame* is at the Tour now—but you will pardon me, *monsieur*. This may contain news of importance."

He impatiently tore open the missive. Bellegarde noted that his hands were slender but very powerful, gleaming with jewels. When he had glanced at the writing a gleam of joy darted into his eyes, and he thrust it away. Then he extended his hand with a quick, eager smile.

"Come! You bring me luck to-day, if not yesterday!" he said cordially. "I hope you are bound for Gisy? Good! Then ride on, I pray you. I shall return later in the day. Did Duguet give any other message for me?"

"None, but he saved my life from those rascals of townfolk, who took me for one of your friends—a devilish ticklish compliment, it seems!" Bellegarde laughed heartily. "But I'll not detain you longer, *monsieur*. To tell you the truth, I have not seen so charming a person in years—"

Spanuto smiled enigmatically. "Well, she expects you. I'll send back a man for guide." He called up one of his men, told him to act as guide, and to commend Bellegarde to the hospitality of Mendoza, who remained in charge of the Tour. Then, with a courteous salute, he went his way with his men.

"YOU ARE the gentleman Stuart guided, *monsieur?*" asked the soldier as they rode.

"Yes. Did he get home safe?"

"Oh, a rarely draggled bird, drunk and wenched and God knows what!" and the other laughed. He was a Gascon, a reckless, fuddle-headed rascal who had been with Spanuto on the previous day. According to him, it had been a hard ride and a bootless one, for the man in leather clothes had not been located.

"*Capandious!* We had action on the way home, though, and sharp it was!" he went on. "We came through that accursed forest—Vivieres, they call it—and struck some of those out-lawed animals. The saints preserve me from meeting them again! Two of our men were hurt, but we cut down a dozen of the ungodly creatures. One of their women was a beauty, too," he added with relish. "I did my best to catch her, but the cat had a poniard. I had to put my sword into her."

"Why doesn't your master clear out that nest?" asked Bellegarde idly.

"*Mordious!* He swears he'll take four days to it next week. One of their arrows went into his horse, poor beast! Aye, the captain's furious enough—"

As they talked, they came presently to the great stretch of ancient oaks, with the gallows on ahead. Here a lesser road branched off and ascended toward the Tour de Gisy and the village just beyond the castle. For some distance it passed through the thick growth of oaks, which was a portion of the Forest of Vivieres.

Suddenly, a little after they had entered the trees, the Gascon drew rein.

"*Monsieur!* Did you see something flicker in those trees ahead?" he exclaimed. "Damme if it didn't look like a glint of steel—"

A quick, furious oath burst from him. Bellegarde turned, to see a rope that had dropped about the man's neck and arms.

At the same instant something scraped his own body—another rope, dropping on him from above. The noose drew taut. He had a swift glimpse of the Gascon, lifted bodily out of the saddle, roaring great oaths—then felt a tremendous jerk at his own body.

With an unearthly scream, a horde of tattered, incredible figures, men turned very beasts, appeared all about the two men. The Gascon was hurled to earth, and they flooded over him, knives stabbing, axes flashing. Bellegarde clutched at his poniard, but the noose had his arms fast. Already he was out of the saddle. His frightened horse plunged, and with a crash he went headlong to earth.

The swirling tide of screaming things broke above him like a wave of horror; with the fall, the senses were stricken out of him.

CHAPTER VII

IN SPANUTO'S STRONGHOLD

BELLEGARDE OPENED his eyes upon a gray room, whose stone walls and floor were partially concealed by tattered tapestries and strewn rushes, respectively.

That last hideous scene leaped into his mind, then passed. He was lying in bed, beside a window whose casements were flung open. Turning to it, he looked down into a courtyard where a few men idled in the warm afternoon sunshine, and past this showed a garden. A glitter on the walls pointed out sentinels. Was this the Tour de Gisy, then?

A soft hand touched his forehead. He turned and looked up into the face of the woman from the coach. In her regard was a tender solicitude that startled him. Hurt, then?

"You are awake—good!" she exclaimed. "Keep quiet, *monsieur.*"

She sat down beside him and patted his hand gently. Jewels shone in her hair, at her throat. He tried to move, and felt stiffness in his head and shoulders.

"You!" he breathed. "Then—then I am—"

"In the Tour, yes," she said. "Those unspeakable animals had been seen by the sentries. Half a dozen men rescued you, barely in time. Their weapons had not penetrated your shirt of mail, but you were badly bruised. You slept all day yesterday like the dead—"

"What the devil!" cried Bellegarde, suddenly. "Have I been here two days?"

"Have mercy!" muttered the
Spaniard. "Where am I?"

"Almost; it is afternoon. Here is broth. Let me lift your head
a little—"

She suited action to words, and as she raised him Bellegarde
was aware of subtle perfume. She slipped pillows under his
head, fed him the broth, then ordered him to lie quietly for a
space and slipped out of the room.

Bellegarde flung back the covers and came to his feet. Except
for a cotton shirt, he was naked, and he regarded his body
curiously. It was much marked with bruises and was extremely
stiff and sore; bandages were about his arms and hips, proving
that not all the weapons had missed him. Still, there was no
great damage done.

When he looked about for his clothes they were nowhere in
sight. The first stiffness passing with exercise, he perceived a
tall armoire in one corner of the room, and wrenched open the
door. An exclamation of satisfaction broke from him at seeing
his garments neatly arranged, his rapier and baldric on a hook,
even his mail-shirt. He examined this and found not a break
in the fine steel links.

"*Diantre!*" he muttered, as he slipped into his clothes at cost of certain grimaces of pain. "Evidently I owe my life to these people. But two days! That is too much, by far. Those accursed forest dwellers were hanging about to take vengeance on Spanuto, eh? As usual, the innocent suffered with the guilty. There!"

Whether from his stupor or long sleep, or the incidental letting of blood, he felt entirely himself and mentally alert; still, there was no denying the stiffness and soreness of his whole body.

Laughter and voices from the courtyard drew his attention as he finished dressing. He went to the casement and looked out. Below, men were thronging with loud jests about a cart and a rickety horse; a swarthy fellow was displaying wares. Bellegarde gave a start of recognition; it was the peddler he had seen at the White Horse Inn.

Then, at a sound, he turned.

I N T H E doorway was an old man, regarding him with astonishment and holding a tray bearing cups and wine. At his belt hung an enormous bunch of keys, each key of sufficient size and weight to fell a man. A long beard, pointed and straggling, came down to his waist, and nothing could be seen of his face except a mass of gray hair, from which jutted a bulbous red nose flanked by watery eyes.

"Eh! *Monsieur!* You are dressed?" he exclaimed, closing the door carefully.

"As you see," and Bellegarde laughed. "What's that, wine? Excellent!"

"Those are pretty clothes, *monsieur*," said the old man, coming forward and setting down his tray on the stand beside the bed. "And a pretty gold chain, too. I have seen them before. I am the seneschal here, and am named Auguste."

"Oh!" said Bellegarde, remembering. "Yes, yes. Faith, you'd recognize these clothes if any one would! I had forgot that. You have a brother named Michel."

The old man gaped. "Fat Michel? You—how know you that, *monsieur?*"

"He keeps a tavern."

"He does, he does!" exclaimed the other in a wondering tone.

"This tavern is named the White Horse, in the village of Santour."

The old man fell on his knees, trembling. "*Monsieur!* If this is magic—"

"Michel is faithful to his master. You serve your master's enemy. Is it not so?"

Something in Bellegarde's voice, in his manner, banished the fear that had seized upon Auguste. He stared up for a moment, then came to his feet with an effort.

"Oh!" he said in a low voice, peering intently from his bleary eyes. "Now I begin to understand. You have been there, you have seen fat Michel!"

"Precisely," assented Bellegarde.

"And he gave you those clothes. He took them from here."

"Where is Captain Spanuto?" demanded Bellegarde, with a gesture of caution. He heard a creak outside, as of a board under foot. "Is he here to-day?"

"No, *monsieur*," said the old man. "Yesterday he rode to Chanlay; to-day he is gone to chastise those canaille who live in the forest."

Chanlay! Spanuto had been riding to Chanlay yesterday morning!

"He is a good master?" asked Bellegarde mechanically.

"None better, *monsieur*, if a body obeys promptly."

The door opened, and La Fleche stepped into the room, stopping short at sight of Bellegarde. Auguste seized this opportunity to depart.

"Dressed!" she cried. "You should not have done this—lie down, I beg of you! Why, you should not be standing, *monsieur*; here, sit and rest!"

She caught the arm of Bellegarde, who allowed himself to be pressed back to the couch. He could think of but one thing; Spanuto had gone to Chanlay the previous day. He knew what this must mean.

The woman, who was indeed La Fleche, pressed his hand.

"Ah, you have done wrong! You are feverish, *monsieur;* your eyes look strangely!"

Bellegarde came to himself. He was aided by a tremendous outcry rising from the courtyard, a tumult of laughter and shouts, through which pierced the screams of a man. Turning to the window, he looked down.

The peddler had been trussed up against his own cartwheel, and one of the soldiers was laying a whip on his back, while others thronged around. Directing the work was a small man with one arm still in a sling, and Bellegarde recognized him.

"Your friend Mendoza is humorous," he observed, turning back. He passed his arm about the slender waist of the woman at his side and smiled into her eyes. "Alas, princess! You know all too well the real cause of my fever!"

A light blush suffused her cheek.

"*Monsieur,* do you know to whom you are speaking?" she asked in a low voice, looking into his eyes. "Do you take me for a country girl?"

"No; for then you would not be so cruel," said Bellegarde. At the back of his mind was now only one thought; to get out of this place and reach Chanlay, find if Angele had need of him. "I have never met any one so cruel among the Turks, nor in Vienna—"

"Oh! So you've been in Hungary! I thought you were bound thither!"

"Returning there, my princess. And, since you disdain me, I need not stop here at Gisy—"

"But I may need you, *monsieur!*" she replied. "Yes, that is true. I have found that my relative, Praslin, was basely murdered here. Yet not basely; I should say, unfortunately. You see, not far from here there lives a gentleman who is out of his head, a madman—"

She paused musingly, no doubt to concoct some story. To his amazement, Bellegarde saw that she spoke in the deepest earnest, with an appearance of sorrowful gravity.

"This poor madman," she went on slowly, "cannot be blamed for his actions, perhaps, but he must be restrained. I shall prevail upon Captain Spanuto to put him under lock and key—"

She had all the air of imposing a confidence, of imparting a great secret. Despite the apparent absurdity of her words, Bellegarde divined that he was on the verge of learning something of the highest importance. At this instant, however, came a hasty step at the door. La Fleche freed herself and was on her feet as the door was flung open.

MENDOZA CAME into the room, passionate fury contorting his bruised features. His arm was out of the sling; in both hands he held a leather doublet—the same discarded by Bellegarde and sold to the peddler at the White Horse.

In a flash, Bellegarde perceived the frightful truth. Mendoza had learned whence the peddler had obtained these garments; unless stopped at once, he would send men to the White Horse and inevitably discover Raoul de Gisy.

"*Madame!*" burst out Mendoza. "I have discovered everything—that wretch has confessed—"

"One moment!" Bellegarde rose, with so stern an air that the Spaniard's rush of words was abruptly checked. Whipping out his rapier, Bellegarde held it up to display the hilt of gold and gems. "Look at this! Do you see it?"

His words, his mysterious manner, centered the attention of the others.

"Yes, *monsieur*," said Mendoza politely, panting a little. "But I regret that—"

"Stop!" commanded Bellegarde. "I am not jesting, *señor*. I had this sword-hilt from the Aga of the Janissaries himself, when he was dying outside the walls of Belgrade. It is not mere cold metal, but was made by a sorcerer among the Moslems. When one utters certain mystic words and then holds the hilt close to the ear, thus," and he pretended to listen attentively, "the most secret thoughts of those around are imparted to his mind."

He perceived instantly that he had judged his man aright, by the superstitious flash in the Spaniard's eye. But Mendoza had more important affairs on hand.

"That is interesting, *monsieur*," he replied. "However, what I have to say will not wait—"

"Allow me to tell you what you are about to say."

"Oh!" returned Mendoza, with a thin smile. "If you can do that, *monsieur*, I shall readily admit that you are the greatest magician in the world!"

"You were about to speak of this leather garment in your hand."

"Naturally."

"It was offered for sale by the peddler in the courtyard. You recognized it."

Mendoza started slightly. "As my own, perhaps?" he said with a slight smile.

"No, *señor*." Bellegarde affected to listen again. "No. As that of a man whom you saw and met, three days ago—or is it four? I am not certain. If you will examine one sleeve of this doublet, you will find a hole in it which was made by your own sword. Am I correct?"

The Spaniard stared at him, gulped hard, recoiled a pace. Pallor had leaped into his features. From the corner of his eye, Bellegarde saw the woman cross herself hastily.

"You were about to say that you have located this man," went on Bellegarde calmly, "whom you have been seeking in vain. The peddler informed you that he had bought this leather doublet at a village inn. The name of that inn—ah! The White Horse."

Mendoza shrank, his eyes bulging from a ghastly face.

"*Sí, sí, señor!*" he croaked in Spanish. "But—the foul fiend is in this!"

"No, merely the magic of the Moslems," and Bellegarde surveyed Mendoza with a grave air. "But there is something else, *señor;* a warning, a terrible warning! Yes, I hear it plainly. This, however, is for your ear alone. Two weeks from now—ah! Yes, yes. Perhaps *madame* will leave us alone for a little?"

Bellegarde turned with a bow as he spoke. The woman's piercing eyes held a certain fear, and she, too, had become very pale. Without a word she inclined her head and then left the room, closing the door behind her. Bellegarde waited, listened for the creak of the plank, then turned to Mendoza, who was also making the sign of the cross in terror.

"Danger is to befall you in two weeks," he said with a somber air.

"Yes!" faltered the Spaniard. "In this place?"

"I am not sure. It comes from Tours."

"Oh!" Mendoza straightened a little. He was looking at Bellegarde with a certain crafty glitter in those soft eyes of his. "*Monsieur,* I am positive that I have heard your voice somewhere before this, even before our meeting yesterday!"

BELLEGARDE KNEW that his little game was played out. He would now learn nothing from this man. He advanced a pace.

"Listen," he said, holding up the rapier hilt. "Listen for yourself, my friend—"

Mendoza leaned forward. As he did so, Bellegarde struck him with the golden hilt, above the ear. Under the crushing force of the blow, the Spaniard fell in a crumpled mass.

With his poniard, Bellegarde slit up the leather doublet, bound Mendoza hand and foot with the strips of leather, crammed others into his mouth and tied them securely, then rolled the unconscious, gagged, helpless figure beneath the couch, disregarding his injured arm.

Barely had he done so when there came a step outside, a heavy knock at the door.

"Enter!"

The Scottish soldier, Stuart, opened the door and saluted with a smile.

"Ah, *monsieur,* a happy surprise to find you up! I am seeking M. Mendoza."

"He was here, but was very much disturbed," said Bellegarde. "He said something about having made a terrible mistake, and that he was going to make his devotions."

"Devotions will not run this castle," said Stuart. "There is a man below seeking you, and I must have authority to let him enter."

"I authorize it," said Bellegarde quickly, "and assume full responsibility. Send him here."

"At once, *monsieur,*" and with a salute, Stuart departed.

Bellegarde hastened painfully to the window, saw a saddled horse below, but no rider. He was forced to wait until steps sounded at his door, and another knock. At his command, Stuart entered, showing in Arnulf Breiter.

"Thank you, *monsieur,*" said Bellegarde to the Scot. "You may leave us."

The door closed. "Well? What has happened? You have a message?"

"Yes, *monsieur,*" said the big German. "Yesterday, Captain Spanuto came to Chanlay."

"I know that. Go on! Was there trouble?"

"Yes, but I know little about it, except that M. le Comte came out of the room from their talk looking like a dead man. Spanuto and his men remained until afternoon. After they had departed, M. le Comte was taken to bed with a seizure. He wrote a letter and sent it off, but I know that it went nowhere, for certain of Spanuto's men had orders to watch the roads about the château. They told me so. Well, this morning *mademoiselle* informed me that M. le Comte was certain to die. At noon she ordered me to ride here and tell you he had died."

"He is dead!" exclaimed Bellegarde. "Then she is alone—"

"Yes, *monsieur*. She told me to come here and so inform you, and to remain with you. My brother remains with her. To-morrow M. le Comte will be buried. To-morrow night she leaves with my brother and goes to a certain inn you wot well, named the White Horse. You and I are to meet them there. That is all, *monsieur*."

"Good. You have a clear head," said Bellegarde. Chanlay dead! Spanuto would hear of it at once, but Spanuto was away to-day. This changed everything. There was no pressing need to leave here, since this German would serve to warn Raoul de Gisy.

"Listen well. The White Horse is in a village called Santour, at some distance from here. You'll have the best directions I can give you, but will need better; do not ask any one here, however. Mount and ride to this village instantly. Go to that inn." Bellegarde took the golden chain from his neck and handed it to Arnulf.

"Give this chain to the inn-keeper, a fat man named Michel. Say you come from me, and ask for M. de Gisy. Tell this last that everything is known, and that to-night or to-morrow Spanuto will certainly come to kill him. You and he both must leave that inn without delay. Tell him to take our money with him. Both of you go to Chanlay to-morrow night. He cannot appear there, but you can. Reach there, you understand, in time to keep *mademoiselle* from going to the White Horse! She would not leave until after dark, I fancy. You might even meet her on the road."

"And once there, *monsieur*? Or once we have met *mademoiselle?*"

"Meet me at the gallows. The others will know the place. I shall be there some time after dark to-morrow evening. That is all. Can you remember it?"

"Perfectly, *monsieur*."

And the stalwart German, with another salute, turned and strode out. From the window, Bellegarde saw him swing into the saddle and ride away. The peddler and cart had gone, too.

POURING WINE, Bellegarde drank it with a sigh of relief. After all, things were not so bad; but he must either poniard Mendoza, a deed from which he recoiled, or else he must remain in this room and keep his victim quiet. What with the bonds and gag, he reflected, Mendoza would be insensible, numb, perhaps dead, by morning. So much the better.

"Good! I remain here and match wits with Spanuto," he thought. "That man will return ere dark, will learn about the peddler and the leather garments, will guess everything. Some one doubtless heard the peddler say where he bought those garments. Good! Spanuto will ride out on the instant to catch his man, as he thinks. That Italian will be saddle-galled ere another day breaks!"

And he laughed a little as he sank down on the couch and took off his rapier, doublet and the steel-linked mesh, of which he had no more immediate need. Searching the armoire, he discovered other garments, among them a clean linen shirt which fitted passably.

"Luxury!" he observed, as he donned it. "So much clean linen bodes me no good. Now, if that razor I bought in Courcelles is still in my pocket—"

Light broke suddenly upon him as he rubbed his chin. This two-days' beard had no doubt jogged the memory of Mendoza; this, and his voice. He whistled softly and fell to work with the razor, managing a very fair shave.

He had scarcely finished when there was a tap at his door and the duchess entered.

"What, magician?" she exclaimed. "Not resting, surely?"

"Aye." Bellegarde sank back on the couch. "I am exhausted, upon my word!"

"Then it is safe for me to enter," and she regarded him merrily, yet with a certain half-hesitant gravity. He smiled.

"Yes, your highness."

"Oh!" She started, searching his face. "How do you know—"

Bellegarde had already perceived that, while this woman might be frightened by his asserted magic, she did not believe in it. And it occurred to him that Angele de Chanlay might have believed in it, but would not have been affrighted. He smiled at the thought.

"You, *madame*," he said quietly, "are far too clever a woman to credit my nonsense about magic, as that fool Mendoza did."

Her dark eyes warmed. This flattered her instantly, far more than any other words could have done. She came toward him, sat beside him, still searching his face.

"Who are you, *monsieur?* How did you know? How long have you known?"

"Mendoza has told me everything," he said. "That is to say, nearly everything. Come! A little while ago you were on the point of confiding a secret to me, I think."

"Who are you?" she repeated, suspicion in her eyes. Belle-garde made a negative gesture.

"You know my name. I am a soldier. I have eyes and a brain, like you. I can be of service to you; but only if you trust me. I am not a man to be cajoled, I assure you."

She instantly assumed a naïve warmth, and a caress stole into her eyes.

"I know that, *monsieur.* That is why I was about to tell you the truth, when we were interrupted. But tell me—how did you impose upon Mendoza?"

"By knowledge," he said, and shrugged. "I had already met the man, if you remember, as that diamond on your finger proves. Enough of this! We were discussing a madman?"

"But yes." She immediately abandoned her questioning, as though the statement that he could not be cajoled was a challenge to disprove it. She gave him a languishing smile, then appeared to recollect something.

"Oh! But first, I must tell you that I am departing for Tours shortly—"

"Where Duguet is now engaged with a lady?"

Her eyes flashed. "He does not concern me, *monsieur!*"

"I think he does." Bellegarde sat up, and his gray eyes flamed suddenly at her. "Do you desire my help? Then tell the truth—everything! Mendoza is a crafty fool. Spanuto is a rascal, who is now endeavoring to carry off a nobleman's daughter from the next estate—"

"What?" She leaped up. "A lie! He would not dare—it would endanger everything—"

"I think Spanuto would dare a good deal; he is now waiting until you are gone, is that it? I see it is. Well, make your choice! If you desire to trust me—"

"If this is true, then by Heaven I will trust you indeed!" she exclaimed in a passionate outbreak of fury. "He is now running down those forest canaille. I'll find out the truth the instant he returns. If this is so, come to Tours! Ask for Madame La Fleche, at the Moor's Head Inn."

To Bellegarde's amazement, she turned and ran from the room. He was certain that, as the door slammed, he heard the sound of an oath trailing on the air behind her.

"Pleasant creature!" and he grimaced wryly. "The secret, however, remains undiscovered."

CHAPTER VIII

A WHIRLWIND

T O H I S vast astonishment, Bellegarde found that he had precipitated a whirlwind.

Twenty minutes later he was looking out at the courtyard when Spanuto and thirty men came riding in, bringing some wounds and four wretched prisoners. The first person to greet them was La Fleche. She accosted Spanuto with obvious anger as he dismounted.

Although Bellegarde could not hear what was said, the attitudes of the two were eloquent. La Fleche was furiously accusing. Spanuto drew back a pace in evident confusion—then she suddenly struck him across the mouth. The Italian merely bowed, wiped his lips, and regarded her with murderous but silent visage.

Five minutes later her coach was being prepared. Another ten minutes and, ignoring the pleas of Spanuto, she was whirled out of the courtyard. Bellegarde stretched out on his couch again and whistled softly, in some consternation.

"Decidedly, this woman is more dangerous than I thought!" he reflected. "She does not receive orders from Spanuto; instead, it is he who obeys her! Well, she is a duchess for one thing, and there are only eleven in all France. Apparently, Spanuto's project of marriage has put a spoke into her wheel; he meant to keep it from her, eh? She strikes him, and he cringes. Hm!"

He could not recover from his surprise at her furious impulse; in everything she did, this was evident. When she left this room, she had meant to go to Tours within two days. Then she spoke with Spanuto, flew into a fury, and departed straightway. True, she had left Bellegarde with a rendezvous.

Once she had gone, however, Spanuto must have learned about Mendoza's discovery, for his voice rose in shrill excitement. Bellegarde, recollecting his victim, rose and pulled aside the bed-hangings and inspected the hapless Spaniard. He was delighted to find that Mendoza had undoubtedly fainted from pain, but was breathing regularly.

"I should be sorry to become a murderer," muttered Bellegarde, rising, "so if he merely dies from his suffering, it would save me that pain. Ah—this must be our worthy captain!"

His door was flung open, and Spanuto appeared on the threshold.

The Italian was extremely pale, and was trembling with anger. He became calm at sight of Bellegarde, and bowed.

"I rejoice that you are safe, *monsieur*," he said. "Your pardon; has M. Mendoza been here?"

"Some time ago, yes. He departed very quickly, after speaking with *madame*."

Spanuto snarled, as though this word stung him.

"We found your two lackeys at Chanlay, *monsieur;* they told abominable lies and had never heard of Duguet. I should like to understand this!"

"Faith, so should I!" said Bellegarde. "One of them arrived here; the man was drunk, and I dismissed him from my service. I gathered that they had tried to rob Duguet, who gave them a sound thrashing."

Spanuto's face cleared slightly. "Oh, very well. I must find Mendoza! You will excuse me, I am sure. I shall return to-night. If you lack for anything, the seneschal has orders to serve you."

"He has already spoken with me, thanks."

Spanuto withdrew. Presently Bellegarde heard his voice in the courtyard, and looked out. The Italian and half a dozen riders were just departing—no doubt for the White Horse.

"Well, so far, so good!" Bellegarde relaxed with a sigh. "La Fleche has gone to Tours. Spanuto is mystified, but suspects nothing definite. Mendoza is safe. To-morrow night I meet Angele and Raoul—hm!"

Drowsiness had come upon him, and he yielded to it without resistance.

WHEN HE wakened it was in swift alarm, for a hand was stripping off his shirt. Then he lay back, seeing old Auguste was standing at one side, while the soldier Stuart was laying him bare. The lean Scot grinned at him.

"Repayment, *monsieur!* I'm about to rub you with an oil this old rascal has provided, which he guarantees will have you hopping nimbly about in the morning. Lie quiet, now, and let me get at your neck and shoulders. *Diable!* You're bruised, sure enough, in more places than one."

For the ensuing half hour, Bellegarde was well anointed, while old Auguste stood back and grimaced at him, evidently trying to convey some meaning, but without success. Not until Stuart had finished his task and departed, with the thanks of Bellegarde, did Auguste voice what was in his mind. Then he came close to the bed, leaned over, and spoke hoarsely.

"D'ye know what's happened, *monsieur?* The foul fiend hath been here! Aye, in broad daylight, and flew away with that Spaniard in his arms!"

A low and stifled groan came from beneath the bed. With one startled cry, old Auguste turned, darted to the door, and fled. Laughing, Bellegarde rose, locked the door, then came back to the bed and flung himself down. He was asleep again in two minutes.

It was sunset when a hammering at the door wakened him. He rose and opened, to admit a man with his supper. Chuckling, the soldier told of how the prisoners taken by Spanuto in the forest raid had been hanged and now decorated the gallows on the road below. Bellegarde got rid of him, glanced at his prisoner, and found Mendoza unconscious. Having eaten, he locked the door again, dragged out the hapless Spaniard and cut him loose. By this time darkness was falling fast.

Relieving the captive of a poniard, he laid him on the bed, tethered him wrist and ankle to the bedposts, blindfolded him, then poured wine into his mouth. When Mendoza came to himself with a sputter, Bellegarde's fingers clamped about his throat.

"Silence! You feel this?" The poniard touched his neck, pricking his skin sharply. Mendoza tried to nod, and Bellegarde relaxed his grip.

"Mercy!" muttered the Spaniard, "Where am I?"

"In the torture chamber, fool!" muttered Bellegarde, and poured more wine into his mouth. "Spanuto has confessed everything. The Duchess of Maine has been seized; she also has confessed. Solbeig and Theleme are arrested; Duguet is dead. Speak! You have this one chance to join your confession to theirs, or be put to the question. Yes or no?"

The breast of the wretched man rose and fell in quick breaths. Still in agony from the bonds, which had left his hands and feet swollen and inanimate, probably tortured also by his recent wound, just wakening from repeated faints and uncertain of what had happened or how much time had transpired—at hearing these names mentioned, a low and terrible groan burst from Mendoza. He was in no condition to use his wits, and these names shattered him.

"I will speak! I will confess!" he cried frantically.

"Speak, then!" said Bellegarde in Spanish. "Hold, inquisitors! Take down his testimony, scribe! Speak, you scoundrel!"

Mendoza trembled with terror.

"The signed agreement comes to Tours from Madrid," he cried out. "The queen is to become regent. The king is not to be harmed—merely kept a prisoner—"

"Liar!" exclaimed Bellegarde. Thunderstruck though he was by this intelligence, he drove in his words. "La Fleche has confessed that the king was to be murdered!"

"It is a lie!" Mendoza writhed desperately in his bonds. "Spanuto was to hold him closely guarded here—that is why we needed this place, why we invented the other plot and cast blame upon Gisy and his friend—"

"Upon the Marquis de Brisac, with your forged letters!"

"Yes, yes. The frontier cities are to be turned over to Spain, who places troops at our disposal. A Calvinist state is to be erected with Sedan its capital, the prince at its head. Fifty thousand crowns are to be paid us. No harm to the king, no harm! They will seize him at Tours—Duguet is arranging it with one of the royal equerries. While he is hunting! Spanuto does that, and brings him here. When everything is signed—"

"Then he would be murdered."

"No, no! It is a lie!" Mendoza's voice rose to a shriek.

Swiftly Bellegarde clapped down his hand and shut off the cry. The Spaniard struggled. Foam flecked his lips. Then he relaxed abruptly and lay motionless, breathing heavily. He had fainted.

BELLEGARDE TRUSSED him up anew, rolled him back beneath the bed, then stretched out to consider this astounding confession. His thoughts were chaotic, whirling about the nub of what he had just learned, but gradually they settled.

In a flash, he had the meaning of the mysterious accusations against Gisy and himself—they had thought him safe in Hungary, out of the way. Gisy had been destroyed: first, because Spanuto desired vengeance; second, because this castle afforded the very place the conspirators needed to effect their scheme. It was ideal to their purpose.

But all this mattered little. Bellegarde's brain flew past and forgot it in the more amazing news. The king! There was the great thing, the supremely important thing. After all, he might have anticipated some such objective to the plot, had he dared fly so high. There was no doubt whatever that Mendoza had spoken the exact truth. Bellegarde whistled softly as he thought of the mysterious letter from Sedan.

"A mystery no longer, eh? That letter was to inform Spanuto that on the tenth of September the king and his retinue would occupy the royal château at Tours. And the first stag, that is to say the first hunt, would be the appointed time. Which means, the eleventh of September, for the king is too devoted to the chase to miss a day.

"*Diable!* What a plot it is, too! Spanuto and his riders waiting. A traitor among the equerries. The king seized. If not killed, he is brought here, where everything has been carefully planned beforehand. His presence would never be suspected at this isolated spot. The Italian party of the queen joining hands with the Spaniards, bartering them a part of France for money and power in what remains of the country.

"More of France carved off with Sedan to make an independent power. How desperate the Spanish must be to agree to erect a Calvinist state! Still, they can always knock it down again later. France looted of land, cities, territory, in order that these devils may swim in gold and power—no, no!"

He rose, paced up and down the room restlessly. The gigantic scope of the whole thing had dazed him at first. Now it terrified him. He perceived what La Fleche had been on the point of proposing—the "unhappy madman" must have been the king, and she had been about to bring Bellegarde into the ranks of the plotters. Then, fired with fury at Spanuto, she posted off to Tours, knowing or believing that Bellegarde would follow.

"No wonder she was furious!" reflected Bellegarde. "This arrogant madness of the Italian might well endanger everything, as she said. If he became embroiled with Chanlay, if he did anything illegal, all eyes would be turned on him; and their whole game was to get him securely established here, but quietly, without noise. And what will La Fleche do, now that she has found that I speak the truth? Will she trust me, as she promised—ha!"

After all, the thing resolved itself very simply in his mind, as he cooled to it. He, and he alone, knew this whole affair; and he must reach Tours, drop everything else, and warn the king. If he could find Bassompierre, that would be sufficient, for Bassompierre would most assuredly be with the royal party at Tours.

So absorbed was Bellegarde in these thoughts, so wholly intent upon them, that he did not observe a slight scratching, scraping sound that came from beneath the bed in the darkness.

He was still striding up and down when he caught harsh voices, saw the glitter of torches outside, heard the massive gates creak open. Into the courtyard rode Spanuto and his few riders; but more came than had departed.

IN SUDDEN anxiety, Bellegarde leaned at the window, peering down. Two prisoners, fast bound, showed in the torch-light. One was fat Michel, keeper of the White Horse. The other was Arnulf Breiter, the stalwart German whom Bellegarde had sent with his message. He saw Spanuto dismount, go to the two and shake his fist at them.

"An hour from now you'll talk!" cried the Italian hoarsely. "Take them to the torture room! Has any sign of Mendoza appeared?"

Bellegarde drew back.

Deliberately he went to the bed, picked up the poniard he had taken from the Spaniard, and half reached underneath to drag out his victim. This rat must die; he did not doubt that Mendoza was a prime mover in this whole plot. Let the man waken, come to himself, and he would remember having talked, having been tricked. Therefore, he must die.

"Why did I not kill him at first meeting? Fool that I was, even as Angele called me!" muttered Bellegarde. "Aye, fool. But I cannot do it now. There must be some other way; I might leave him here. Or I might do it the last thing. I cannot deliberately put the steel into a helpless man!

"Yet, if the king's life hangs upon it, and the welfare of France—"

Yes, he must do it. He saw clearly that there was no other

recourse, no other way. Well, at least let it wait awhile! No hurry about it. He dropped the dagger, and it fell on the stone floor with a tinkle of metal.

Again Bellegarde fell to pacing up and down. That oil had taken the stiffness out of him; he felt himself again, able to do anything. And what he must do, took form and shape before him in the darkness. There was no haste. Spanuto had not caught Raoul de Gisy; he meant to eat, drink, rest a little, and then put his two prisoners to the torture.

Once more, Bellegarde dressed himself, donning the mail-shirt with his doublet over it. He buckled on poniard and baldric, then went to the window, waiting, watching those in the courtyard, whistling softly under his breath. He did not hear slight sounds that came from beneath the bed. He was waiting, watching.

Presently he discerned the figure of Stuart beneath the torches. He leaned forward.

"Ho, Scot!" he called loudly. "Stuart! Send me the seneschal with a light and with wine!"

The Scot turned, glanced up, and while he could not see Bellegarde against the dark wall, recognized his voice and waved a hand.

"Aye, *monsieur*, at once!" he replied cheerfully.

Now befell one of those curious and unforeseen chances whose incidence may swing unexpectedly the entire history of an individual or of a nation.

Giulio Spanuto had returned weary, close to exhaustion; but he was a very courteous person, and mindful of his guests. As he sat at meat in the hall of the castle and quaffed a great flagon of wine, he bethought himself of Bellegarde and beckoned one of the men who stood at the door. The old seneschal was not to be found, at the moment.

"Take a lantern to the tower room," he said, "in case M. de Bellegarde is awake and has need of a light. Most like he has been forgotten."

The soldier saluted and departed in search of a lantern.

Bellegarde, meantime, crossed to his door, opened it, and looked out; for as yet he had not left this room. He found himself upon a winding stair, where a thin taper burned in a wall niche below. Several steps down he discerned another door, which stood ajar, and he descended to it.

Before him was a small and bare room, on the opposite side of the tower. He took the taper from the niche and turned into it, passing to the window. Opening this, he discovered that he was in the very tower which gave name to the whole castle—an immense and obviously very old circular structure which defended the entrance.

He looked out. On this side, in the starlight, he could see the winding approach, the thick masses of trees beyond, and the outspread countryside. He peered down, swiftly reckoning the chances of escape from here. To leave this place by the gateway, after doing what he had in mind, would of course be impossible.

WHAT HE saw caused hope to spring within him. The window was small and was crossed by a single bar of iron, designed to make more difficult any entry from without; but a man might easily squeeze past this. The ground outside was no more than twenty feet below him, and there was no ditch or moat outside the walls, for the hillock fell sharply away from the building.

"Good!" muttered Bellegarde, so intent upon the ground as not to be aware of a figure with a lantern passing outside the doorway. "These blankets from the bed can be slit up to form a rope, and fastened to this iron bar; or, if left double, can be slipped away once we are down. Then no trace will remain to show how we left."

He drew back and glanced about the little room, but this was quite empty. Still, the blankets from his bed would do admirably. They must be made ready now, however, and the strips knotted together, against the moment of need. For that moment, as Bellegarde foresaw very clearly, would admit of no delays.

So thinking, he picked up the taper again, went out to the stairs, and replaced it in its niche. As he did so, he caught a sound of sharp, surprised oaths from his own room. Looking up at the door, he found it ajar and discerned a glint of light within. Auguste had arrived, then.

Unhurried, he mounted to the doorway—then paused, inexpressibly startled. Not Auguste stood inside there, but a soldier; and with him, talking rapidly, was Mendoza, just freed from his bonds. On the floor was set a lantern.

They had heard the stair creak under Bellegarde's foot, and turned. The soldier whipped out his sword; Mendoza, with a cry, swooped for the dagger on the floor. But already Bellegarde was in the room, his long rapier out. As the soldier uttered a shout and slashed at him, he knocked the blade aside with an angry exclamation—but it was too late now to use his wits. Mendoza was flying at him from the side, shouting furious oaths, calling for Spanuto. Both of them hurled themselves upon him.

Cursing the over-quick thinking of this soldier, Bellegarde retreated to the doorway; then, poised for an instant, he suddenly flew at them. Mendoza shrieked out as the rapier pierced his throat. His voice failed and died; but Bellegarde staggered, for the blade of the soldier struck him over the heart. The steel shirt saved him once again. Turning, he beat the man back and an instant later stilled his cuts and thrusts with a lunge through the body.

The soldier staggered away and collapsed. Then he half rose. Bellegarde, panting, was leaning on the long Ferrara blade, staring down at Mendoza. With one final, convulsive effort, the man lifted up his sword and hurled it, hilt first, and fell in a sprawled heap of death.

Bellegarde looked up from the dying Mendoza. As he did so, the heavy sword-hilt struck him squarely across the eyes.

He was knocked backward as though by a thunderbolt. A cry of agony was wrenched from him. He caught at the door, saved himself from pitching out and down the stairs, then the senses fled from him. He fell in the doorway, his legs on the stairs, his rapier still in his hand.

It was thus that Auguste found him, when the old seneschal came stumbling up the stairs with a light and a bottle of wine.

CHAPTER IX

TORTURE CHAMBER

IT SO chanced that, after calling down to the Scot in the
courtyard, Bellegarde had drawn the casements shut. Thus,
no cries or other sounds of that fight had reached any one below.

Setting down his wine and light, old Auguste muttered shrill
oaths in his beard, stepped into the room, peered at the two
figures there. Mendoza was not quite dead. He lifted himself
a little, uttered a choked, incoherent cry, motioned with his
poniard. Auguste clutched at his great bunch of keys and swung
them down into the Spaniard's face, with no more emotion
than if he were beating out the brains of a mad dog.

Mendoza spoke no more.

Hobbling across the room, Auguste opened the armoire, took
out the flagon of oil that had been left there, and returned to
Bellegarde. He sat down on the steps and fell to work. Bellegarde wakened to his ministrations, and to sharp pain that drew
a low groan from him. Everything was dark. Blood and oil
covered his face, his eyes were puffed and swollen; when he put
up a hand and touched them, he groaned again.

"Quiet, *monsieur!*" came the voice of Auguste. "Quiet, for the
love of Heaven! I finished that dog of a Spaniard—he, he! I
finished him," and his shrill laugh cackled out. "I had a word
with Michel; no one knows that we are brothers. He told me
to find you. Quiet, and let me rub in this oil. It will reduce the
swelling presently."

Bellegarde relaxed.

"So that accursed Mendoza was here all the time, eh?" went on Auguste. "I knew there was something queer about his disappearance. Oh, I'm a sharp one, I am! I saw them fetch in fat Michel, and I got a word with him. Here, *monsieur,* drink this wine—"

Bellegarde obeyed, and sank back again.

"I am blind," he said in a low voice. "Are my eyes destroyed?"

"Well, that is hard to say," came the response. "Your face is gashed, and your forehead, and all wondrous bruised; no, the eyes are only swelled, *monsieur.* Here, let me wipe away the oil and blood. That's better! With a bandage to keep the blood out of your eyes—"

He was working deftly as he spoke, twisting a bandage about the cut forehead and making it secure. Bellegarde presently pried open his right eye; as through a mist of blood, he could see the light, the old goat-bearded seneschal. With an effort, he could keep the eye open a little.

"Faith, I thought my sight was gone!" he said, and laughed shakily. "That was a shrewd blow."

"Well, you look like a different man, beyond question. *Monsieur,* what is to be done? My brother implores you to save him. If he is put on the rack, he says he cannot keep from talking, for he cannot endure the torture."

"I have a plan," Bellegarde said. "There is a torture room here?"

"Aye, and it has been used of late."

"Can you get me there unseen?"

"Possibly."

"Bring me the two blankets off my bed in there."

Auguste rose, with creaking joints, and presently reappeared with the blankets. Bellegarde sat up, leaned against the wall and drew his poniard. After a little he had slit up the blankets, and Auguste knotted the strips.

"Take them into the little room yonder. Tie one end securely to the window-bar, and leave it."

Mumbling crankily to himself, the old seneschal caught up the rope and went. Bellegarde came to his feet, but immediately sank back again, stifling a groan. Then he rose, stood erect, and cursed softly. After a moment the pain subsided. The prompt application of the oil had somewhat taken out the soreness. He could now see fairly well out of his right eye, and a very little with his left.

To have this mishap come at such a moment, when everything depended on prompt action, was maddening.

OLD AUGUSTE reappeared, clawing at his long beard, and surveyed Bellegarde with his bleary eyes. He uttered a cackle of laughter.

"*Diable!* You look scarcely human, *monsieur!* Is it your plan to return here and leave by way of that window?"

"Precisely. You will have to act as guide. I know nothing about this place."

"Then you will have to go easily, *monsieur.* There is plenty of time; they will not begin the torture yet awhile. I have no mind to be caught. I have lived a long time, but only by not being hurried. I do not intend to have these rascals practice on me with their weapons. Do you understand?"

"Perfectly. But if we can release those two men now, before the torture begins—"

"Impossible. They are in a dungeon. Although I have the key, six of Spanuto's men are in the room through which we must pass; others are in the guard-room close by. Once in the torture chamber, it will be a different matter. There will be only two torturers and Spanuto himself. With luck, we can go there now and you can hide yourself there."

"Very well," assented Bellegarde. The other shook a skinny hand at him.

"You need not expect me to remain, *monsieur,* I warn you! It is none of my business. I will help you, but I'll stay outside. If you are killed, as I think likely, I want to know nothing about it."

"Agreed. Lock the door of this room—wait!"

Bellegarde turned into the room again, stooped painfully, and retrieved the sword that had so nearly finished him. He took the poniard from Mendoza's relaxed hand, and picked up the lantern. Then he came back on the stairs, while Auguste closed the door, turned the key on the outside, and placed it on his great bunch.

"Follow, *monsieur*."

Bellegarde came after him down the stairs. The door of the tower opened directly on the courtyard; here Auguste halted and peered forth cautiously, then, with a gesture, strode forth. Instead of crossing the open, he followed the wall to a door entering the buildings at the left, held it open, then closed and locked it.

Bellegarde saw that they were in a passage

"Praise be to the saints, none saw us!" ejaculated the seneschal. "Instead of going by the usual way, *monsieur*, I shall take you through the cellars. Guard your light well, and remember how you go. You may have to retrace this road alone. This door at the right, you perceive—it conducts to the cellars."

Not a door, but an open arch, with steps beyond. Bellegarde descended, every faculty on the alert. A door at the bottom, then the dim expanse of a huge cellar, in which were piled provisions, powder barrels, wine casks, disused furniture and every manner of object conceivable. Through this confusion Auguste threaded an assured course, which Bellegarde noted without difficulty. The pillars that upheld the structure above were squat, monstrous things, obviously of very great age.

Auguste paused before a massive door, inserted a key from his bunch and turned a creaking bolt. Then he paused and turned to Bellegarde.

"This leads directly into the torture chamber, *monsieur*," he said gravely, "but no one knows of its existence; why, you will observe in a moment. I must return to Captain Spanuto, lest

my absence be observed. Farewell! And if you do get out, tell
Monsieur Raoul that I have done my best."

"Aye," said Bellegarde, and clapped him on the shoulder.
"Farewell."

He pulled open the door and stepped into blackness.

HOLDING UP his lantern, he glanced around. The
chamber where he now stood was large. The wall through which
he had just come was of wood, and to the beams were affixed
various instruments of torture. When he closed the door again,
it fitted into place between two of these beams, so closely as to
be unsuspected.

The other walls, like the floor, were of stone. Opposite Bellegarde was a low arch with a thick door—the usual entrance,
obviously, since there was no other. A rack stood on his left.
Near it were chairs; a fireplace was at one end of the chamber,
manacles were fastened into the stones, and a pillar bearing
chains was clearly used for flogging—and had been so used not
long since, as spattered bloodstains testified.

Looking about, Bellegarde perceived only one possible place
of concealment, and advanced to it. This was an enormous
cupboard near the rack. One door stood open, broken on its
hinges; the other was in place. It was quite empty. Stepping
into this cupboard, he found that he could stand upright within
it and be entirely hidden from view of the room.

Drawing his own rapier in case of need, he blew out the
lantern and shoved it into the depths of the cupboard, then
followed it, holding the sword and poniard in readiness. Again
he cursed the wound across his eyes, for sight was by no means
easy; at moments a red mist floated across everything.

He waited there, immobile, for at any moment the ancient
wood creaked dismally.

Minutes passed; not many of them. Then came a rasp of bolts
and the door flew open, with the voices and steps of men breaking the silence. Light filled the room, as smoking flambeaux
were brought in and placed in the cressets.

"*Diable!*" said a voice. "I'd like to see that fat rogue on the rack! Why the devil does the captain want no one else present?"

"Ask him, and not me," said another voice. It was that of Stuart. "All right! Bring them in! Place the fat one on the rack. Strip him."

"And the German?"

"His turn later. Let him watch the business."

A momentary silence. Then came the blubbering tones of fat Michel uplifted in terrorized pleadings, until the sound of a hearty slap that silenced him was drowned in noisy laughter. A firm, steady voice broke the silence.

"A pleasant hostelry, this!" said Arnulf Breiter. "Why not let me go first, comrades? It'll give you more fun. The fat rascal won't last ten minutes."

"You in your turn," said Stuart. "Stand there, against that cabinet."

The broken door of the cupboard was obstructed by the stalwart figure of the German, his crossed wrists bound behind his back.

"Tell the captain all's ready," exclaimed Stuart. "And clear out, the rest of you."

Amid ironic farewells and scrape of feet, Bellegarde ventured a forward step and looked past the figure of Arnulf. Stretched on the rack, stripped, hands and feet outspread and bound, was the enormous nakedness of fat Michel. Beside that bed of torture stood two of the soldiers, arrant rascals by their faces, stripped to the waist. Stuart waited beyond the sight of Bellegarde.

"This fat lump will pull out wrists and ankles the first turn," observed one of the two torturers. "Should have made fast to elbows and knees, comrade."

"Bah! With his ankles out," said the other, "put the boot on him and he'll squirm, I can tell you! Here, draw up those cords at your end."

The winch was turned, pulling taut the quivering, heaving

wretch. Under cover of the clatter, Bellegarde spoke under his breath.

"Arnulf! Back against the cupboard."

An instant later the German backed a little, until he was against the opening. Bellegarde reached out with his own rapier and drew the razor edge across the cords. Almost at once they parted. Arnulf stood motionless.

"Attention!" exclaimed the voice of Stuart.

A QUICK, firm tread, the slam of the heavy door, and Spanuto was in the room. He came to the chairs, swung one around, and his piercing, birdlike gaze flickered about the place as he seated himself. The Scot saluted.

"Captain, have I your permission to depart?"

"Remain," said the Italian curtly. "You have taken Florio's place as my lieutenant; do as he would do. You, there! Give this fat rogue a few turns—wait! One question. Come, fat one! What do you know of M. de Gisy? Was he hiding at your tavern?"

"No, *monsieur*," came the quavering accents of Michel. Spanuto leaned back and twirled his mustache.

"Very well. Go ahead with it."

Bellegarde thrust sword and poniard into the hands of Arnulf, gave him a push and a sharp word.

"Guard the door!"

Coolly, Bellegarde stepped out of the cabinet as the German moved over to the door. Spanuto leaped to his feet with a shout of surprise. Stuart turned, whipping out his rapier. The two torturers halted and stood gaping.

"Have I interrupted your pleasure, my honest Giulio?" said Bellegarde lightly. "That is a pity. However, this fat rascal happens to be a very good friend of mine—"

"Name of a devil!" cried Spanuto. "Bellegarde! What means this—*mon Dieu!* What a face!"

Arnulf, a grim smile on his lips, was in front of the door. But all eyes were upon Bellegarde, who swept the Italian a bow.

"A truce to further masquerade, captain," he said briskly. "Here's the end of your chase. I am the Sieur de Brisac, friend to M. de Gisy. It was I who killed Florio and Praslin, and who am now about to kill you. Out with your sword, and—"

Spanuto, a deadly pallor leaping into his face, recoiled a pace. "You!" he cried out. "You!"

Bellegarde leaned forward and with his poniard cut loose the two feet of Michel. A wild oath burst from Spanuto, then a sharp order.

"At him! Down with him—quick, fools!"

The two torturers sprang forward, Stuart circled in from the side. Those two had no swords, but one held the iron bar from the rack, the other a heavy maul. Bellegarde retreated, a smile on his lips.

"Careful, Scot!" he exclaimed. "Your new position is most unlucky, I assure you! Stay out of this, if you value life—"

The man with the iron bar swept a sudden terrific blow at Bellegarde's knees. Leaping over it, the long Ferrara blade flashed from Bellegarde's hand, and that man clutched at his throat as he fell, and the iron bar slithered and clanged on the stones. Stuart drove in a vicious lunge from the side, but the Ferrara met it, warded it off.

The second torturer crept around, approached Bellegarde from the rear, and swung up his maul. A frightful cry burst from him; the glittering blade of Arnulf Breiter stood out a hand's breadth from his chest, then was jerked loose.

Stuart pressed his attack in dour, determined silence. All this while Spanuto stood as though stupefied, but now he quietly bared his own rapier and circled. Bellegarde saw his intent, knew that he could run the German through and get out of the room in an instant.

"Arnulf!" rang his voice, as he kept the Scot's blade in play. "Cut Michel loose. 'Ware of the Italian! I'll take the door—"

And as the German leaped toward the rack, Bellegarde retreated deftly, until the door was at his back. Now he had Stuart before him and, over on his left, Spanuto. The latter drew in, catlike, awaiting an opening.

"Scot, I love you—but I must kill you," said Bellegarde, parrying a hot attack. "Say an Ave, man, quickly!"

THE EYES of Stuart widened on him, the man's face, flushed and strained, drained of blood as he met that icy gray gaze so steadfast upon his own. Suddenly, as he drove in a low thrust that missed Bellegarde completely and fastened his steel deep in the oak door, a gasp escaped him. He had transfixed himself on the Ferrara.

And, as he fell, dragging the rapier from Bellegarde's hand, Spanuto rushed in with a deadly, venomous attack.

Agility saved Bellegarde then, agility and the long poniard in his left hand, after the prevalent vogue. Spanuto pressed him close, a murderous flame in those black eyes, drove him back and back, while the poniard desperately engaged his steel.

"To me! *Au secours!*" blared out the Italian's voice.

Bellegarde's foot struck something. Swift as light, he stooped, caught up the maul that the torturer had let fall. He balanced and flung it, and the heavy object struck Spanuto squarely in the forehead.

The Italian went down like a pole-axed bull.

Disregarding him, Bellegarde leaped for his rapier, plucked it from the body of Stuart, flung himself at the door. From the other side came shouts, questions; there was no way of barring the door on the inside, however. Nor was any key in the door.

"Back!" shouted Bellegarde, his lips at the keyhole. "Let no man enter!"

"That was not the captain's voice!" he heard some one exclaim, but already he had turned.

Michel was on his feet now, Arnulf was waiting. Bellegarde gestured to them, and darted across the chamber toward the concealed door. He found it, shoved hard on it.

As he did so, some one threw open the other door. In the

archway showed a mass of fierce faces, half questioning, half hesitant. Stuart came to one elbow, pointed to Bellegarde.

"At him! Get him—get—"

The Scot fell forward again, but a wild, shrill yell went up. The soldiers flooded into the place. Bellegarde watched them coolly; Michel was gone, Arnulf was following. As the crowd surged forward, he himself stepped back through the opening.

Arnulf slammed the door in their very faces; Bellegarde found and turned the key in the lock.

"A pretty trick, master!" and the German laughed softly.

Bellegarde saw to his surprise that they were not in darkness. A light burned dimly across the cellar; he realized that old Auguste must have left it. A tremendous hammering began at the door.

"Follow!" said Bellegarde, striding out. A piteous cry came from Michel.

"*Monsieur,* I am naked!"

"Your wedding night, fat frog!" jested Arnulf coarsely. "Move!"

Auguste had left his light near the exit door. As he reached it, Bellegarde extinguished the light. The others were close upon his heels. A rending and smashing sound arose; the door of the torture room was going down.

"Follow me, and quietly," said Bellegarde, his voice very calm. "Michel, if we get out of this place, we must make for Chanlay, find Mlle. Angele. Arnulf, you got the message to Gisy aright?"

"Aye," said the German. "But I lost my way and they were hard on my heels. M. de Gisy hid in the pigsty. They caught me."

"Eh? Was Gisy drunk?"

"No, *monsieur,*" said Michel plaintively. "He had not had above a dozen bottles of my old Medun."

With an oath of anger and dismay Bellegarde plucked open the door before him, just as the cellars reëchoed with wild yells as the other door went down. The three passed through into the corridor and Arnulf locked the door behind him.

Down the corridor, and now at the outer door, which was ajar; here Bellegarde paused. The whole castle seemed to be in wild uproar, voices resounding from every direction, and the flare of torches was rising.

"Risk it," he said, and stepped out. He broke into a run, the others pounding after.

A SHOUT arose, then a shrill yell, a clash of weapons, and suddenly men were pouring upon them out of the courtyard. The opening of the tower loomed ahead; no door here, but an archway with the stairs winding upward. Bellegarde halted.

"Up the stairs, Arnulf," he said, panting a little. "The open door on your left. Throw out the line that is already prepared. When Michel is down, call to me. I'll hold them."

"Right, *monsieur;* and you go second," said Arnulf calmly. "Move, fat one, move!"

Michel bleated in fear and pounded up the stairs. Arnulf followed him closely.

Bellegarde waited coolly, rapier and poniard in readiness. The first wave of the attackers paused uncertainly as the torchlight illumined him, and drew back. Then a man came shouting that Bellegarde had slain Spanuto, and with a wild snarl of rage they rushed forward. Bellegarde drew back within the arch, so they could not reach him from the sides, and his rapier darted out as the fierce faces broke in upon him.

The foremost man fell. The long poniard dashed up two blades, the Ferrara drove the life from a second man. They came pressing in, three abreast; one slipped in the blood, another took the point full in his face and screamed wildly.

Then he had a moment's respite, while they ringed in the archway, shouting for pikes and pistols, and more men came running to join them. From up the stairs he caught a wild roar of rage, and Arnulf's voice drifted down in curses.

"The fat fool has stuck—"

Bellegarde suppressed a groan. Michel was stuck in the window, then! But now the wave of men came swirling in again upon him.

At this instant he was aware of a panting breath, a sword that flashed past him, and here was Arnulf at his side, hurling himself into the packed throng like a madman, cutting and stabbing. Again the circle of faces drew back, leaving dead men and wounded at the foot of the tower.

"He is through—on his way down," panted Arnulf, wiping sweat from his eyes. "Go, go, *monsieur*—"

A pistol exploded. The ball struck Arnulf in the breast as the weapons came sweeping in again. He threw himself forward headlong, gripped one of the leaders, and then was down beneath the feet of the others, stabbing. But almost at once he had disappeared.

Bellegarde turned; a pike hooked into his clothes and dragged him down, blades leaped at him. Up again and free, the Ferrara licking those fierce faces with bitter tongue. Now another pike caught hold and jerked him off balance.

He stabbed a man above him, thinking of the irony that he and Arnulf alike must die to let fat Michel escape. His poniard sank into flesh, and a man screamed. Then something hit him over his hurt head. In a blaze of stars and agony that ended in blackness, Bellegarde relaxed and lay quiet.

So they flooded past and over him, up to the room above, just in time to see a white naked shape fluttering away into the forest depths like a grotesque pale bat.

CHAPTER X

BELLEGARDE'S FATE

DURING SIX days Bellegarde saw nothing and no one, except the guard who came twice a day with food and water.

At first he lay half in stupor, suffering all the agonies of blindness, until he discovered that he was not blinded in the least. Instead, he lay in a dungeon cell evidently below the castle, for steps came down to the grating that served as door, but no light whatever.

A heap of rags was his only furniture, and he was stripped to shirt and breeches.

When he sought for speech with the guard, he encountered only a stony impassivity. Once Stuart entered, heavily bandaged, to inspect him, but refused all speech. The dour Scot regarded him as the guard held up a lantern, and then departed in silence.

Bellegarde had no idea when the chains had been shackled on him. Wrists and ankles; he had freedom of movement enough and to spare, but the chains were there to stay, an ominous sign. By feeling, he could tell there was no padlock. An armorer had done that work.

That there must be some reason for this singular treatment he was well aware, but the explanation baffled him. The only thing certain was that Spanuto was in ignorance that he had learned anything about the plot, for Mendoza would assuredly tell no tales.

This was not highly comforting; through the long dark hours

the knowledge in his brain was an unending torment. He was helpless, gyved, and beyond question doomed. Meantime, the conspiracy was moving merrily to its appointed end.

Everything that had so puzzled him was now bitterly clear. This Italian was merely the apex of a far-spread triangle, the head of a spear clutched by divers hands and thrust into the very bowels of France. Sedan, Madrid, the Italian party at court, would rend the unhappy country apart. The plot must infallibly succeed, also. Henri IV was a fatalist, notoriously careless of his life, and when hunting was absolutely carried away by this sport.

It was not the thought of his country that tormented Bellegarde. To him, as to most noblemen of the period, allegiance was a personal matter; Henri of Navarre was like a legendary hero of chivalry. Quite literally, the king was France. This very fact made the success of the plot more certain. With the king hidden away, government was paralyzed until the regency of the queen was accepted by Parliament; and by then, all would be lost.

Not the plot against the king alone; he had also gained full knowledge of more personal affairs. In his hand, thought Bellegarde, had been the rehabilitation of his friend, of himself. Once the lesser members of this conspiracy were seized, they would confess everything, as Mendoza had confessed. The names of Gisy, of the Marquis de Brisac, would be cleared completely. Signed agreements coming from Madrid—why, those documents alone would be sufficient for everything!

And thanks to a fat inn-keeper, the one man who might have saved everything now lay ironed in a dungeon, his knowledge entirely unsuspected. The bitter irony of the whole thing preyed upon Bellegarde. He cursed fat Michel, cursed his own folly. He should have made certain of escaping himself, bidding others to the devil.

In his heart, none the less, he knew this would have been impossible.

He had entirely lost track of time. It seemed that a month

The bandaged Scot regarded Bellegarde in ominous silence.

must have run its course while he lay here in darkness. When he slept, rats wakened him with their teeth; when he woke, they were ever about him, squeaking or frisking about in horrid silence.

Despair dragged at him ever more surely.

Then, abruptly, came heart-hurrying words.

HIS GUARD had come and gone. Bellegarde sat in the darkness, munching a crust, when he heard a slow step. There was no light, however.

"*M'sieu,* are you there?" came a husky voice.

"Aye," said Bellegarde, astonished.

"It is Auguste. No noise; do not cry out. Here, take this wine and meat."

Bellegarde could scarce repress the eager joy that beat at his lips. He clawed his way to the grating, took the wine and food, fell upon the latter wolfishly. Presently, hunger appeased, he took a draught of the wine and bethought himself of the seneschal.

"Gone, Auguste?"

"No, *m'sieu.*"

"*Pardieu!* How long have I lain here?"

"Hm! It was three days before I learned where you lay; another three days before I could open an ancient door, walled up, that led into this passage. Six days in all, *m'sieu.*"

"What has happened in that time?"

"Nothing."

The one word came with a shock. Impossible!

"Why am I here?"

"Because you were fool enough to fight, instead of running."

"Devil take you, I know that! Why didn't they kill me?"

"Because Spanuto desires to do that himself. Again you were a fool, not to kill him when you had the chance. He was much hurt, but now he is better. He'll be on his feet to-day, and will hang you before long."

Bellegarde's laugh was harsh.

"Did your brother get away?"

"Fat Michel? Yes. I have heard nothing from him, at least."

"Well, if you got here, why can't I get out the way you came?"

"You could, if you were here in the passage, *m'sieu.* But your door is of iron, old but strong; it cannot be broken. And they have the keys to it, not I. That Scot keeps the keys himself, for he hates you bitterly, and as he is never drunk, I cannot get them."

"Make him drunk."

"He swears not to drink a drop of anything except wine until you are hung. And to make him drunk with wine is out of the question. After the tenth bottle, he grows sober."

"Bah! Put brandy in it."

"Well, that might be done," answered the old man. "Yes, it is possible. He's a good fellow, that Scot; we are friends, and he listens to my stories of the old days. I do not want to hurt him."

"Neither do I," said Bellegarde grimly. "But I want to get out of here. Have you heard any news from Chanlay?"

"Hm! I did hear something. Spanuto sent some men over there but they came back disgruntled. Something had happened; I could not find out what it was. Spanuto cursed like a madman."

This was more cheering. Bellegarde began to perceive that he had been tormenting himself with all sorts of imaginary occurrences, for nothing.

"Listen, *monsieur*," said Auguste. "I will help you. I will try brandy in the wine and say I have found some of that marvelous Beaujolais of '76; the Scot will believe it, because he knows nothing about wine. And then I will let you out. When, I cannot say; as the chance offers. I will come back with food and wine for you to-morrow."

"And a poniard," added Bellegarde. "A long one."

There was no response. If Auguste heard those words, he departed without saying so.

His repast finished. Bellegarde shoved the wine bottle under the rags and stretched out, a thousand fantasies and wild conjectures running through his mind. At the worst, he reflected, he might somehow convey a message through Auguste that would reach the outside world, perhaps to Bassompierre, who would certainly accompany the king to Tours. Upon this cheering if rather uncertain possibility he dropped off to sleep.

HE WAS awakened by two soldiers prodding him, and came dazedly to his feet, the light of their lantern dazzling his darkness-blinded eyes.

"Up!" growled one of them. "Move quickly! You're about to be introduced to the justice of this seigneury, rascal!"

"And may you have joy of it," added the other, with an oath. "By the saints, I'd enjoy swinging your long carcass to the gibbet when the time comes!"

Bellegarde inferred that he was not popular with Spanuto's men.

Presently, if he entertained any doubts in the matter, they were quite set at rest. The two guards shoved him from the cell and urged him up stone stairs; presently he came into a chamber filled with men and lighted by two small windows. This was the guard room. To the unaccustomed eyes of Bellegarde, the morning light streaming in these windows was blinding. He could see little or nothing.

Jeers and oaths hurtled at him from every side. Many of these men were Italian or Spanish or German; he gathered that they had liked Florio. His guards urged him through the midst, and onward. A moment later he entered that same torture chamber whence he had rescued fat Michel.

The ruddy light of torches was easier for him to bear, in here.

Spanuto, booted and spurred, a hat pulled over his eyes and hiding any traces of his late indisposition, sat talking with Stuart. Two of his men stood at one side, awaiting orders. The countenance of the Italian was lit by a contortion of vivid hatred as Bellegarde was brought in before him, while the Scot eyed the prisoner with a dour, hard eyed glare. At the Italian's side was girded the long Ferrara blade with its glorious hilt.

Unshaven, half naked, face still discolored from its hurts, Bellegarde was a sorry object, but his gray eyes looked out with a calm and poised regard.

"Welcome, M. de Bellegarde," said Spanuto softly. "You enjoy our hospitality, I trust?"

"It is admirable," said Bellegarde. "But yon know my name, I think."

"Ah, you told us something about a M. de Brisac, which I disbelieve." Spanuto showed white teeth in a smile. "You are the Sieur de Bellegarde, having indeed a passport to that effect. So you killed poor Mendoza, and my honest Florio, and M. de Praslin to boot! May I ask why?"

"On purely personal grounds," came the cheery response. "Being a friend to M. de Gisy—"

"Precisely," intervened the Italian. "Who is an outlaw. Therefore you yourself are beyond the law, for having aided him. However, as you may guess, we are not dealing with avocats and courts of law and the personal rights of nobles. How did you come to bring me that letter from M. Duguet?"

"As a favor to him, of course," responded Bellegarde. "I met him by chance. He confided the letter to me, upon my promise of delivery, and posted off to see a lady."

He perceived instantly that no word had come from Duguet regarding his playing the part of Florio. Spanuto nodded quietly.

"And being in honor bound, you delivered the letter. You lied to me about those two Germans of yours—"

Bellegarde smiled. "Of course, in view of your attentions to a certain lady."

"Ah! You are a squire of dames, also!"

Bellegarde bowed with a mocking air. Stuart muttered a low word to his master.

"No, no," said Spanuto, leaning back in his chair. "I know these Frenchmen better than you, my good lieutenant. M. de Bellegarde, this honest Scot of mine insists that you be laid upon the rack yonder, and otherwise entertained."

"A rather absurd idea," commented Bellegarde. "Since I am quite willing to answer your questions, without torture."

"Oh, there are no questions; I quite comprehend everything," and Spanuto shrugged. "It is a matter of punishment, not of interrogation. You understand, the law would suggest that you be tied to four horses and pulled apart."

"A spectacle for Parisians, not for soldiers."

"I agree with you." The Italian's tone became silkily smooth. "I desire to punish you, *monsieur,* and I strongly doubt whether torture would have that effect; certainly, it would be rather silly to kill you and so end the punishment."

"Apparently we are entirely in agreement," said Bellegarde, smiling.

"There remains, however, the lash." Spanuto waved a hand toward the pillar and chains. "A sound whipping, say fifty lashes every day—"

"Oh! An excellent notion," said Bellegarde. "I very much doubt whether it would draw any expressions of dislike from me, however."

Spanuto showed his teeth in a mirthless grin. His voice exploded suddenly.

"Exactly. We are in absolute agreement. I do not intend to give you any chance to match your will against mine, you unspeakable dog! I know you French, you nobles! A proud, intolerant breed, full of arrogance; you'd like nothing better than to prove that you could stand up under any torture! It would be your way of showing yourself the stronger. Resistance can always beat aggression, is it not so?"

"It might be an interesting experiment," said Bellegarde reflectively. Spanuto laughed.

"Oh, we'll not try it! I assure you that I have a better way of breaking your pride, my fine nobleman—yes, yes, I know you accursed French nobles very clearly! I know your absurd loyalties, your ideas of chivalry! I have studied you, and you are all alike. My good lieutenant, order that man brought in here; the one whom you found on the road some days ago."

Stuart snapped an order at the two waiting soldiers, who departed with alacrity.

BELLEGARDE WAITED, ill at ease. He quite understood that this Italian possessed a diabolic sort of intelligence, an aptitude at torture which could pierce to the very quick. His first thought was that Raoul de Gisy had been captured; but he dismissed it, knowing that Gisy would be killed on sight by this Italian, never taken prisoner, never spared.

He perceived, too, that Spanuto meant to break his pride, disgrace him in some manner, cover him with shame and shatter his supposed pride. This brought a smile to his lips, but he suppressed it quickly. Spanuto's estimate of the French nobility was remarkably accurate, but it missed its mark where Bellegarde was concerned. He had come through a hard school of arms where vanity became confidence, arrogant pride was

transmuted into quiet dignity, and the usual preening ostenta-
tion was dismissed with a shrug and a laugh.

When the guards brought in a bound prisoner, Bellegarde
stiffened slightly. It was Herman Breiter, the second of his two
Germans, a bandage about his head. Spanuto laughed a little,
made a gesture of dismissal, and the German was led out again.

"Now, M. de Bellegarde, I wish to propose something," said
Spanuto softly. "I may set this pestilent fellow of yours upon
the rack, and let him suffer other torments, finally impaling
him below the gallows. And I'll do it! On the other hand, you
may not only save his life but give him his liberty."

"How?" demanded Bellegarde.

"By giving me your word of honor as a gentleman to obey
my orders for three days, no matter what those orders may be,
no matter what dishonor they may cause you."

"And after three days?"

Spanuto shrugged. "We'll talk of that when the time comes."

Bellegarde reflected swiftly. A week had passed. Another
three days and Spanuto would be departing for Tours. Therefore,
Spanuto meant to kill him before departing. The Italian's plan
flashed upon Bellegarde instantly. It was clear that Spanuto
attached no importance to this German and would spare him
as carelessly as kill him.

"It would appear," said Bellegarde slowly, "that you believe I
would keep my oath."

"Strangely enough, I do, *monsieur*."

"You are right. On the other hand, I have no belief whatever that you would keep yours. I will agree to your conditions,
provided I may have a moment's speech with this man, and
may see him ride off freely and unhurt."

"The latter, yes," said Spanuto. "The former, no. You shall
have no speech with him."

Bellegarde shrugged. "Very well. I agree."

"You understand, I shall in no wise spare you?"

"Understood," and Bellegarde bowed.

The Italian regarded him half frowningly, and a note of grudging admiration came into his voice as he turned to the dour Scot.

"You perceive, my worthy lieutenant, I was right about these Frenchmen. No torture can subdue their arrogance; but they will, from that same arrogance, submit to anything in loyalty to those who serve them."

"Right, *signore,* right!" said Bellegarde with a smile. "It is most singular how you should be thus acquainted with the character of a gentleman!"

A little color stole into the pallid features of the Italian, and the eyes became pools of venom. Then Spanuto rose.

"Bring this fellow to the courtyard. Have a horse saddled and let the German depart. But no speech between them, mind!"

"Wait!" exclaimed Bellegarde sharply. The other turned. "It has just occurred to me, *signore,* that during these three days you might be overtaken by a long-due fate, and perish; or the real Sieur de Gisy might drive you from these walls; or I might assume wings and fly away, as certain magic powers learned among the Turks would enable me to do. So, in any of these three cases, I hold myself released from the oath."

Spanuto broke into a laugh, and Stuart grinned at his elbow.

"Agreed, agreed!" said the Italian, and swaggered out, still laughing.

BELLEGARDE'S TWO guards urged him after, and presently he came into the courtyard where a horse was hastily saddled—a sorry nag, indeed, but still a horse. Breiter was freed, but now there was delay, and voices rose high.

Stuart came striding over to where the Italian stood, beside Bellegarde.

"Captain, the fellow refuses to go without orders from his master. He says he prefers to share the fate of M. de Bellegarde."

Spanuto's brows went up, and he turned.

"Come, *monsieur!* Give him the order, if you please."

Bellegarde nodded and lifted his voice in a sharp, clear call—but in German.

"Await me at the Moor's Head Tavern in Tours, and ride quickly!"

Breiter saluted and mounted.

Spanuto gave Bellegarde an amused glance.

"Await you in Tours, eh? You see, I also know German, *monsieur.* Well, if the fellow is faithful as he seems, he will grow old of this wait, I promise you! Gate guards—open the gates and let that man out!"

The gates swung open, and then closed again after Breiter rode out alone. Most of the Italian's men were gathered here by this time.

Spanuto faced his prisoner with a slight smile.

"On your knees, *monsieur!* Swear upon the honor of a gentleman to obey me."

Bellegarde came to his knees. "I swear."

"Very well." Spanuto motioned the two guards. "Strip him. Use your knives."

A moment later Bellegarde stood naked, as the remnants of his clothes were cut from him.

"Now, our stables here are very foul," observed the Italian. "I doubt if they have been cleaned in the past ten years, *monsieur.* Tools will be given you, and you will set to work at once." A laugh went up from the watching men, and Spanuto gave them a sharp word. "Have your fun—but mind you! No whips, no killing blows! At all events, not to-day or to-morrow."

At this, the laughter spread, and Bellegarde comprehended that on the third day he would suffer in body, whereas for the first two he must suffer only degradation. Such degradation as would have driven most men of his rank to sheer madness, to a blind and frantic fury of rage.

Bellegarde only bowed politely.

"It will be a great pleasure, *signore,* to show you how a gentleman should keep his stables!"

At this, Spanuto lost his head, struck him bitterly across the mouth, then turned and strode away. But the soldiers closed about Bellegarde, hustling him toward the stables, showering him with filth and petty cruelty.

So began his oath-keeping.

CHAPTER XI

INTO A TRAP

W HEN SPANUTO had descended upon the White
Horse Inn like a whirlwind, Arnulf Breiter, who had
repeatedly lost his way thither, had but recently arrived. He and
Le Borgne were trying to sober up the undeniably fuddled
Raoul de Gisy.

The storm broke. Le Borgne slew one of Spanuto's men and
was himself slain. Arnulf Breiter and fat Michel were dragged
away by Spanuto, and Gisy remained ignominiously hidden in
the pigsty. Later a hostler pulled him out, bathed him, sobered
him. About midnight, in bitterness of heart, he took the concealed gold, mounted a horse, and left the inn.

Gisy had only a hazy idea of the message from Bellegarde,
but headed for Chanlay.

As though his evil destiny were not yet finished with him,
he gained the Chanlay demesne toward dawn; then the horse
went into a hole, broke its leg, and Gisy lay senseless until two
honest peasants found and recognized him. They carried him
and his bag of gold to their farm and put him to bed. Then,
after long discussion, they sent word to Angele de Chanlay.

About the same time, fat Michel was bearing his naked,
briar-scratched paunch through the forest reaches, making good
his quivering escape.

Knowing every one in this entire district, Michel went painfully hobbling through the dawn and reached the farmstead of
a distant relative who held fief from Chanlay. Michel also went

to bed, with many a groan, but he remembered perfectly the message brought by Arnulf. He sent his relative to bear this message to Angele; adding that Bellegarde was now dead, and only God knew where Raoul de Gisy might be.

Such was the information that reached Angele, as they carried her father to his burial. Later, as she was in the church-yard, one of the thronging peasants muttered a low word, telling where Raoul de Gisy was lying.

At the château again, that afternoon, Angele took counsel with the one person she could trust; the German, Herman Breiter. Him she sent to find Raoul de Gisy. Ere he was well outside the château grounds, however, three horsemen appeared closing the road to him.

The end of this encounter was that one man died, but Breiter was stricken down. The other two carried him a captive to the Tour de Gisy. There, thanks to his wound and his wits, he told such a maundering, senseless tale that Spanuto had him flung into a cell and left, and sent off a dozen men under Stuart. The Scot had orders to invite Angele to the Tour, and to bring her by force if she refused.

They found her gone, and two horses with her.

An hour after nightfall, Angele gained the farm where Raoul lay, and he came forth to hear the evil news. All evil, from her father's sudden end to Bellegarde's death. When he had re-warded his hosts and sent money to those who were hiding fat Michel, he swung into the saddle and rode forth with her into the night, seeking the highway for Tours.

A bitter ride was this for them both, and evil luck had not yet run its course, for on the following day Angele lay ill with fever in the tavern that sheltered them and could not ride on. Gisy summoned a leech, and bleeding gave her relief; but for three days they needs must remain here idle.

Then the next morning they rode on, with Tours ahead that evening.

"WHAT WILL you do here, Angele?" inquired Raoul de Gisy with some uneasiness. "Where go?"

"I shall await M. d'Aurilly," she answered in a lifeless voice. "It does not matter. He will not be here yet. I cannot go to his house here. I just want to be alone, away from every one and everything."

"*De Par Dieu!*" he exclaimed. "You talk like a girl entering a convent!"

"If I had not promised marriage, I might do worse."

"A pox on such talk! Aurilly will be here in a few days; then all will be right. With the men he brings—ha! I'll strike the Tour and take that accursed Italian alive. I want to see the rascal drawn apart by horses or broken on the wheel."

"You will still be outlawed."

"Pouf!" Gisy laughed at that. "I'll go back to Hungary. Poor Brisac! The world will never be the same again, Angele; but you cannot understand, of course."

"No," she said in a low voice.

"It is impossible to think of him as dead. He was one of those persons who seem impervious to destruction, as though a guardian angel were always watching over them. It is true, his sword always gave the angel marvelous assistance. And how he was equal to any emergency! That was the wonderful thing. I am rather quick-witted myself, but Brisac was far ahead of me. I remember, he held an island in the Danube for three days against the whole Turkish army—"

"Enough of this, enough!" cried out Angele abruptly, in a stifled tone. "Where shall we go at Tours?"

Gisy gave her a look of astonishment, but she had turned her face away from him.

"Well, it is true you had not known him long. At Tours? Oh, that is simple," and he twirled his mustache, his spirits rising a trifle. The very thought of Brisac saddened him and at the same time filled him with a terrible thirst for vengeance.

"I know an excellent tavern there," he went on, "where you

can have a quiet chamber and be entirely safe until M. d'Aurilly appears, and where I'll be well bestowed likewise. It's in the Rue des Ursulines, a most convenient location, and it used to have some of the most remarkable Paulmy I ever tasted, of the '91 vintage."

"You should be very comfortable there," she said in a steely voice.

"Oh, naturally." Gisy gave her a perplexed look, then shrugged. "An admirable place, the Moor's Head, but a little out of date. In my father's time, I remember pilgrims always used to go there, but—"

"Well, it should serve our purpose," she cut in. "Please, Raoul—I want to think."

"*Bon Dieu!* In silence? Why, I remember Brisac used to say that most women could only think when their tongues were wagging—"

She threw him a glance, and he fell silent abruptly, cursing to himself and wondering what the devil he could have said to anger her. After an hour or so, however, she was herself again, smiling a little in her old friendly way when she regarded him, and Gisy forgot all else except the desire for vengeance that waxed ever more strongly within him.

He had fought well enough for his own sake, though with no great luck. The death of Brisac, however, had roused him out of himself and wakened something new in him. He looked older and graver; even his simple straightforward spirit was stirred, and as they came jogging slowly into the city, late in the afternoon, he was actually pondering stratagems wherewith to take Spanuto alive. With money and men, he meant to lose not an instant when Aurilly arrived, but to take the road of vengeance forthwith.

AS THEY were entering the city, a dust-streak behind them developed into a horseman riding hard, his mount flecked with foam. Dust-covered, weary, he passed them without a glance, but Angele suddenly drew rein, staring after him, sharp pallor in her cheeks.

"I know that man!" she exclaimed. "Raoul! He was with Spanuto at the château—one of his Italian followers! I remember noticing his queer scarred face—"

Gisy shrugged and quieted her swift alarm.

"Tours is a big place, my dear. He paid us no attention, evidently recognized neither of us. We'll not see him again."

"I suppose not. I wish I knew why that woman was at the Tour de Gisy!"

"Eh? Oh, the woman he—I mean, that duchess? La Fleche? I had forgot about her," said Gisy. He brightened perceptibly. "A remarkable woman, that; some very curious stories are told about her."

"I can well believe it. You have never seen her?"

"I was madly in love with her, yes." Gisy preened his mustache. "However, I will not lie to a comrade; I did not have any luck. As a matter of fact, I did not know who she was at the time. The court was at Fontainebleau, and I talked with her one night during a ballet, and she seemed extremely gracious—"

"Spare me the details; I am not one of your court ladies," said Angele coldly. "That gentleman from whom our friend had the letter—Chevalier Duguet—is here in Tours, remember. Perhaps Spanuto's messenger was bringing him some word."

"Very probably. Hm! At the Licorne Inn, Brisac said."

"Brisac!" said Angele softly. "So you knew him, Raoul; but I shall always think of him as Bellegarde."

"Oh, the devil!" exclaimed Gisy roughly. "Why must you bring him up? Why must you talk about him?"

"Eh? But a while ago it was you—"

"Well, that was different," said Gisy illogically, wrinkling up his face. "It was my mood, I suppose; and I've changed. Here in the city, with people all about us, it's different. I'll be lonely as the devil. I don't want to think about him, do you understand? Thank the saints, if the Moor's Head has any of that Paulmy left, I'll drink a dozen of it at dinner and drown out—well, you needn't look at me like that. By God, this thing has hurt me, Angele!"

"Poor Raoul! I'm sorry." She reached over and touched his arm. "I didn't understand. I'm hurt, too."

"Yes, yes; your poor father—I know," he said compassionately, but she drew away and wrapped her cloak more closely about her, and said no more.

So they came to the Moor's Head, with sunset still an hour away.

Gisy, who was actually in no danger here in Tours and who would have forgotten it in any case, stamped about like a great lord, was treated with huge deference, and upon finding that plenty of the '91 Paulmy remained, was greatly pleased. He obtained a retired chamber for Angele, and another not so retired for himself; and as Angele at once went to her room and decided to remain there until the morrow, Gisy bestowed most of his gold with her for safety's sake.

Then, ordering a tremendous dinner prepared for himself, he went forth to find the merchant upon whom his Genoa paper was drawn. In this errand he succeeded so well that he was back in half an hour with more gold, hid the most of it in his room, and then descended to the main room of the tavern to see about his dinner.

As he crossed the courtyard, he came to a sudden astounded halt.

A COACH had just entered, and he recognized it with a shock that held him speechless; also, he recognized the lady alighting from it, followed by her maid. Her eyes fell upon him, and widened. Instantly, Gisy advanced with a bow.

"*Madame!*" he exclaimed joyfully. "You, of all people! Decidedly, the angels have descended among us!"

"It is M. de Gisy, then!" she replied gayly. "What good fortune! Only the other day I was speaking of you with friends."

Gisy gave no sign that he understood this reference. He must not let her become aware that he knew anything about her visit to the Tour de Gisy, of course.

"But how does this chance?" went on La Fleche. "I understood you were—"

"Oh, that was a mere nothing," exclaimed Gisy quickly. "The king has done me the honor to pardon me; matters are being adjusted very happily. You are passing through the city?"

"By no means. I am waiting here, on certain business of the queen. You know, the court will be here in a few days. Here, however, I am merely Mme. la Fleche—remember it!"

"The court!" Gisy blinked at this information, so that laughter rose in her merry eyes.

"Well, the king at least—for the hunting," she went on. "So I'm stopping here. I've just been engaging a maid, having lost my poor Sophie to a guardsman."

"But I am also stopping here!" exclaimed Gisy. "And that reminds me; there is an excellent dinner nearly ready. If I might have the honor—"

"Bah! Good company is better than food," she said swiftly. "Have it served in my rooms in half an hour; you agree?"

"With all my heart!" cried Gisy, overjoyed. He pressed her hand, and the pressure was returned. Instantly he was in the seventh heaven. "In half an hour, then!"

He bowed again over her hand, and strode into the tavern, roaring out orders and calling for a bottle of Paulmy on the instant.

La Fleche, however, beckoned one of her outriders and spoke rapidly to him, in a low voice. In her manner was a certain tensity, an almost savage eagerness. The man bowed and strode away. La Fleche turned to the maid whom she had that afternoon engaged.

"Come," she said. "I am giving you the evening free; go back to your relatives for the night, after I have changed my garments."

"*Madame* is most kind!" exclaimed the maid joyfully, and they mounted the stairs together.

Raoul de Gisy was somewhat incredulous over his own luck, but this passed into expansive delight. In that swift hand-pressure, in those dark, glowing eyes, in the invitation itself, he had read all too plainly that happiness might be his for the asking. He discovered that *madame* had been here for some days, and occupied an entire quarter of the upper floor; she was regarded by the inn-folk as a princess at the very least, an opinion which Gisy solemnly confirmed. His air of mystery created a vast impression.

And the court coming to Tours! He had almost forgotten this, but remembered it as the bottle of Paulmy emptied. Well, that was not so good, for Raoul de Gisy; but he must let Angele know about it. With her father's death, she became a ward of the king, which meant efficient protection against Spanuto—and there was no doubt that the king would seize the chance to punish that Italian for having affronted her. Yes, matters were moving very well indeed!

"The luck's changed," thought Gisy, and ordered another bottle as he waited. "Aurilly will show up any day, and I'll take the forty men and clear out before the court arrives. *Diantre!* When luck changes, it changes! I'll find out what La Fleche was doing at the Tour, also. I'd better be damned careful about it, too; if she's connected with Spanuto, I'll have to use my wits. She's a sharp one—but I'm a match for her."

He sent some dinner and wine to Angele, and considered duty done.

MEANTIME, THE outrider returned to the inn with a cloaked gentleman, led him up the stone stairs that ascended from the courtyard, and so to the quarters occupied by the duchess. These quarters were most conveniently situated, being over the stables in the rear, and quite away from the rest of the establishment, with gardens on three sides.

Admitted by La Fleche, the gentleman disclosed the features of Chevalier Duguet.

"I am at your service, *madame*," he said, bowing. She spoke rapidly to him, and he whistled.

"You have outriders, postilions?"

"Bah! They are servants," she answered. "They would run if this man but looked at them!"

"I see," said Duguet reflectively. "Hm! He will have a lackey; decidedly, you give a person devilish short notice, your highness!"

She stamped her foot angrily. "Fool! Can you not remember that here I am only Mme. la Fleche? Will you risk ruining everything, as you did with that Bellegarde? To let him tell you he was Florio—"

"*Diable!* How was I to know?" and Duguet shrugged.

"And now Spanuto has him safe; and he proves to be Brisac, the Marquis de Brisac, do you understand? The one whose letters were forged."

"You seem somewhat put out about the matter," said Duguet shrewdly. "Did he trick you, also? Well, let it pass. About our man Gisy! Either I must do the work myself, and at once, or else take time enough to find the right man. I prefer the former plan."

"I do not," she said decidedly. "You are an excellent swordsman; but we need enough men to make certain. This must not be bungled."

"Very well. There is my cousin, M. d'Auvergne, exiled to his estates by the king, whom I have been visiting for the past two days. He lives three leagues from here. Then there are MM. Robert and Henri de Carpignac, whose estates join his. With those two brethren and Auvergne, whom I have gained over to our party, we have four. Four lackeys who can use their swords make eight. Are you satisfied?"

"Entirely," she assented. "Go at once. Kill your horse if you must!"

Duguet bowed deeply to her.

"Not one horse shall be killed, but eight, since there are eight of us. On return—"

"Come directly here to these rooms. Knock three times. I shall entertain M. de Gisy until you return."

Duguet took his departure.

As he left the stairs and crossed the courtyard, he observed a procession coming toward the stairs. There were at least a dozen servants bearing dishes and candles in the greatest profusion. Behind these were borne smoking platters. The host and his entire family, pressed into service, helped to carry the most delicate meats and pastries.

The cook held aloft a huge tray of polished copper, stacked high with sweetmeats; the rear was brought up by the sommelier, staggering under an enormous, dust-covered cubicle containing bottles. Curious, Duguet halted him as he passed.

"What is this procession? What sort of liquor is in those bottles?"

"*Monsieur*, it is the last of the famous Paulmy of '91. M. de Gisy has taken the entire lot for his dinner, which you see being carried upstairs."

Duguet perceived the figure of Raoul de Gisy approaching, and after one intent look at the other, drew his cloak about him and left the courtyard.

"So the fool does not even hide his name!" he reflected, and then smiled to himself. "With such a dinner, and such a companion to entertain him—*diable!* I need not hurry."

CHAPTER XII

GISY FIGHTS

BEFORE HIS memorable dinner drew to a close, Raoul de Gisy felt well assured that the conquest which had failed in Fontainebleau must succeed in Tours.

La Fleche did her best to ply him with wine, and he was nothing loath; but he did not become drunk in the least. For one thing, this vintage, which was a precursor of the later Vouvray but with a more subtle and delicate bouquet, was heady yet not strong; and for another thing, Gisy had been determined to keep his head this evening. He had, accordingly, drunk a flagon of olive oil before coming to dinner.

La Fleche, indeed, was astonished by his capacity, and was charmed by the effect upon him of the wine. Gisy flung aside his usual swagger and became his simple, unassuming self, a character so rarely encountered as to commend itself instantly to his companion.

This witty and lovely woman, accustomed to the rapier brilliance of the court, at first despised him; then she began to admire his utter simplicity. When he discussed his more recent experiences, abandoning braggadocio for a gentle whimsicality not unlike that of Bellegarde, she became interested. In a word, from the very attraction of opposites, Gisy exerted a fascination of which he was quite unconscious.

Still Duguet did not return.

Later, the outermost of the three chambers was abandoned to the servants, and the two retired to the inner room overlooking the gardens. La Fleche flung open the casements and looked out at the stars, while beside her Gisy reclined on cushions and softly fingered a lute. At one side burned candles in a huge wooden sconce against the wall.

"Was that a Hungarian love song?" she asked, as he ceased playing.

"Yes," said Gisy, and sighed a little at thought of Brisac.

He had mentioned the name, but she denied all knowledge of it. He had not thought to ask about Bellegarde. Nor had he extracted the least information regarding Spanuto, for she had parried his inquiries deftly.

"Why do you sigh, chevalier?" she demanded.

"For one who is dead," answered Gisy. "Poor Bellegarde—I mean, Brisac! At times, it is hard to believe that he is dead—"

"Bellegarde? Oh! Then he is Brisac—is that it? My dear chevalier, I had no idea they were the same! This is really curious!"

A delicious trill of laughter came from her lips. Gisy regarded her with a frown.

"I do not see what is so amusing about it," he growled angrily. "He was killed the other day by that accursed Italian friend of yours, who holds my lands."

"What nonsense!" she exclaimed. "Only to-day I heard otherwise. He is not dead at all; he is merely a prisoner at the Tour de Gisy."

"What?" cried out Gisy, dropping the lute. "Do you dare to jest—"

"Bah! I swear he is alive. What if Spanuto is a friend of mine? So much the better. I have influence with him. I'll send him word about your friend, do you understand?"

A furious joy overwhelmed Raoul de Gisy, as he recollected the courier who had passed him on the road. He knew this woman must be uttering the truth. He suddenly seized her fingers and pressed them to his lips.

"Ah! Ah!" he murmured incoherently. "You do not know—if

you will do this—devil take the Italian! I'll give up everything to him if he lets Brisac free—"

At this moment, from the door of the outer room sounded three soft knocks.

LA FLECHE started. She drew away with an abrupt movement and plucked a candle from the wooden holder. Gisy paid small heed, for all his thoughts were with Bellegarde. Then he heard her voice, and something in it startled him.

"It is my maid, perhaps," she said hurriedly. "I will see."

She started for the second room, whose door was locked. Gisy came quickly to his feet and followed. That curious note in her voice wakened in him a vague alarm, and he half stooped to pick up his sword, which lay near the lute he had dropped. Then, with a careless shrug, he abandoned it and hastened after her.

"Let me at least hold the candle," he exclaimed impetuously. "The wax will drip—"

"No, no!" She laughed and broke into a quick run, shielding the flame with her hand and throwing back a merry, rougish glance. This outer room, second of the three comprising her quarters, was vaguely illumined by the single flame, filled with shadows.

Evading him, she came to the door, turned the key, then flung the door back.

"Enter, enter!" she exclaimed.

To his stupefaction, Gisy perceived four men crowding into the room, with drawn swords.

With the same glance, he was aware that La Fleche stood to one side, holding up the candle so that he was full in its light. There was no surprise in her face, but only a fierce eagerness, a wild and furious expectancy that thinned her features and made her look suddenly like a Harpy gloating over her prey.

With a fearful comprehension, Gisy looked at the four men. One of them he recognized, and an exclamation broke from him.

"Ah! M. d'Auvergne! This intrusion—"

"Yield, M. de Gisy!" exclaimed Auvergne, stepping past Duguet and threatening the helpless man before them, who was armed only with a poniard. His sword flickered toward Gisy. "Yield! You are outlawed—"

"Bah!" exclaimed Duguet. "Kill him and have done with it."

"*Messieurs!*" Gisy drew back a pace, incredulous horror in his eyes. "You are gentlemen, not murderers—"

"Kill him!" spoke up La Fleche, her voice hard as steel.

"Let me have one word with you, Auvergne," cried Gisy imploringly. "One word in private—you see I am at your mercy—"

"Kill him, do you hear?" repeated La Fleche furiously.

Duguet took a step forward, but Auvergne halted him.

"Let me speak with him, as he desires. By the saints, I am a gentleman and not a butcher. Well, Gisy, what is it?"

He advanced rapidly toward Gisy, who had drawn a little back.

"Why should you kill me?" said Gisy in a low voice. "I have never harmed you, *monsieur.*"

Auvergne, his sword half lifted, regarded him gloomily.

"You are to die; that is enough. If you have any last request, speak it."

"Oh! One only, then," said Gisy, and leaned forward as though to whisper.

The woman closed the door and locked it.

Swift as light Gisy's left hand seized the extended arm of Auvergne. His right caught the sword-hilt, wrenched away the weapon as though he dealt with a child.

"My one request, *monsieur,*" he cried, and plunged the blade into Auvergne's body.

DUGUET'S SWORD was already darting at him. With incredible agility, Gisy leaped sideways and avoided the thrust;

this movement caused the rapier in his hand to break off in the body of Auvergne. He had, however, his own poniard.

"Fools! Finish him quickly!" cried out the voice of the woman. So terrible was its shrill fury that Gisy shivered. He glanced about; there was no escape except into the farther room.

One of the Carpignac brethren had glided around and now stood in this doorway, while the other and Duguet were coming at him.

Poniard in one hand, the broken sword—a sliver of steel a foot in length—in the other, Gisy retreated until he could engage the rapier of Duguet with his broken blade. Then he rallied so swiftly, so fiercely, that the other gave back before him. His poniard drove straight for Duguet's heart, only to slither from metal, and shatter in his hand.

"Assassin!" cried Gisy, in passionate fury. "You wear chain-mail—"

A leap saved him from Carpignac's blade. Duguet was still staggering from the force of that thrust, but gasped out a sharp word.

"From the left, Henri—"

"I have him," and Carpignac laughed, for Gisy was now in the corner, armed only with the broken weapon. "Hold the door, Robert!"

Coolly, Henri de Carpignac darted forward and slashed down with the edge. Gisy interposed his broken blade, and the poor steel shivered to the very hilt. Blood leaped on his shoulder as Carpignac's weapon wounded him.

Duguet was rallying to take him in flank. Gisy hurled himself forward. With his left arm he fended Carpignac's thrust, and his fist smashed into the man's face, knocking him backward. Duguet lunged, but his point only touched Gisy's hip without disabling him.

A roar of rage on his lips, Gisy charged for the doorway where Robert de Carpignac stood. The latter drove in his blade to meet the charge. Into his face hurtled the broken hilt; Gisy struck against him bodily and knocked him away. True, the rapier tore through the flesh of his left thigh, but the way was cleared.

"Fools! Fools!" shrilled out the woman's voice. "Oh, if I were a man—"

"He cannot escape," replied Duguet. "Our lackeys are in the garden."

This was true, as Gisy perceived. Panting, he caught up his own rapier and darted to the open window, to descry four figures awaiting below, steel glinting. He turned, as Duguet and the two Carpignacs advanced toward him.

"Apparently, you neglect nothing, gentlemen," he observed. "Luckily, I have now a better sword than the one we broke. It belonged to Florio; a soldier, and not a gentleman. I'm afraid poor Auvergne was a bad judge of steel. Who's first?"

The others paused. Gisy had the window at his back, the canopied bed at his right side, and the wall of the room at his left. He could only be attacked from the front.

Robert de Carpignac, wiping blood from his face where the sword-hilt had struck him, turned and disappeared abruptly.

His brother spoke to Duguet. "He knows the Italian method. So do you, Duguet. Engage him, therefore."

"Ha!" exclaimed Gisy, suddenly animated. "Duguet, eh? He who bore a letter from Sedan about a château and a stag!"

Duguet, astounded, lowered his sword and stared, blinking. "How do you know about—"

Gisy suddenly uncoiled like a steel spring, his gaze full upon Duguet as his rapier darted forward. He did not lunge at Duguet, however. His blade flickered past the latter and the point drove into the side of Carpignac, who stood just behind. Instantly, Gisy was back at the window.

"He has killed me!" cried Carpignac in a terrible voice. "Aside, Duguet—"

He shoved Duguet from his path and flung himself upon Gisy, who met his sword coolly and engaged it, fencing in the

Italian manner. For the second time his point entered the man's body; but now Carpignac dropped his weapon and pitched forward. He rolled over on his back and lay motionless, blood coming from his mouth.

"Two!" said Gisy, regaining his position. "Ready, M. Duguet—"

Duguet was already lunging, with a vicious oath. Behind, in the doorway, stood La Fleche, holding her candle aloft as though fascinated by the spectacle before her.

NOW GISY found himself meeting a rapier trained in Italian fence, a wrist more clever if less strong than his own, and a cool head. He comprehended at once that unless luck favored him he was a lost man. Behind Duguet he caught a glimpse of La Fleche, moving swiftly. She was picking up the sword fallen from Carpignac's hand. The silken robe fell from her shoulders; she shook it away impatiently and stood leaning forward, watching intently for a chance to dart in, the candle-light striking her lovely body into soft beauty. But her face was that of a devil.

Duguet lunged suddenly, and his point touched Gisy's throat—a mere touch.

"An inch farther next time!" he panted, seeing the blood spring. At this instant, the bed-canopies were parted and the face of Robert de Carpignac appeared there. Gisy did not observe it, for Carpignac was standing on the bed, above him and to his right. He attacked Duguet desperately, sent in two vicious thrusts that drove the other back, then heard a ripping sound as Carpignac caught down the bed-curtains.

Gisy turned his head. His eyes distended as he saw Carpignac in the act of throwing those draperies out above him. He stepped quickly aside, but put his naked foot upon the face of the dying Henri de Carpignac, and the teeth of the latter closed upon his instep.

A cry of agony, of terror, burst from Gisy. Blind and desperate with pain and fury, he dashed aside Duguet's weapon and caught hold of Duguet, just as the bed-curtains fell about them both, completely enveloping them. Carpignac stood poised on the bedside, ready to leap down. La Fleche stood watching, awaiting some opening for the sword in her hand.

Those two figures, enveloped by the curtains, writhed and struggled until the draperies seemed imbued with life. To tell which shape was Duguet and which Gisy was impossible. A low and terrible cry, half-muffled, came from the twisting folds. Then the two watchers drew back in startled alarm, as the double figure seemed to rise in the air, the curtains billowing up in fantastic outlines.

For one instant there was a glimpse of white flesh, of blood-smears—then a second cry burst from Duguet as Gisy flung him bodily through the air. A tremendous crash; his body struck the window, smashed out the casements, fell to the ground below.

Gisy swung around, sword in hand, just as Carpignac leaped at him. To avoid that leap was impossible; Gisy met it square-ly, with a furious bellow of rage, striking up the other's blade. The two crashed together and went reeling, Gisy clutching at the figure of Carpignac, whose poniard was out.

Then, like a terrible vision, he saw La Fleche darting in at him from the side, saw her weapon plunging at him as he reeled. Frantic, desperate, he swung Carpignac across his hip. The woman's sword plunged into the back of Carpignac, transfixed him, and the point scraped Gisy's breast. Putting out all his strength, he hurled the screaming man from him, hurled his body full at the slim figure of La Fleche, saw her borne back-ward by that frightful missile.

Then, recovering himself, Gisy caught up his rapier, darted to the window, and swung himself out to the ground eight feet below.

The four lackeys had just recognized, in the broken figure at their feet, the form of Duguet. In consternation, they beheld this naked, blood-streaming man leaping down at them, and they straightway scattered. One alone held his ground and lunged forward as Gisy came to earth, but his thrust missed its aim.

Then Gisy had him by the collar.

"Quick! Strip to the skin, or you die!"

The sword-point at his throat, the trembling lackey lost no time in obeying. When La Fleche leaned out from the window above, there were two white figures in the starlight. With an imprecation, she drew back her arm; but Gisy had heard her voice, and as the thrown poniard faintly glittered, he ducked to one side, then scooped up the lackey's garments. "

"*Au revoir,* fair lady!" he exclaimed, and blew her a kiss. "To our next meeting—and may it not be interrupted so soon! I'll give your love to Bellegarde."

Then he was gone, laughing, into the obscurity. His one thought now was to get a horse and make his way back to the Tour de Gisy. He completely forgot Angele de Chanlay.

CHAPTER XIII

BELLEGARDE REVOLTS

PELLANCOURT WAS a huge, uncouth Gascon, with enormous mustaches, a love for garlic, and all the swaggering braggadocio that had made his people famous. Bellegarde had been placed in his charge, and after a day and a half of acquaintance, Pellancourt was full of assurance.

Also, he had received private instructions from Spanuto. To the chains that kept Bellegarde a prisoner without hampering his movements, the Gascon had attached a cord, and keeping at a little distance, he would jerk at this cord occasionally, his voice ringing out across the courtyard.

"Regard me, comrades! *Mordious,* I am become an Egyptian with a monkey. Nice beast, kind creature, fling out the filth! Dance for the soldiers, little monkey!"

Invariably his efforts would be greeted by roars of laughter. When crossing the courtyard he would perform the same antics, to the huge amusement of his fellows.

For a day and a half Bellegarde had labored, naked and reeking, in the Augean stables of this hill-castle. Upon him, from all sides, were heaped taunts and jeers, all manner of filth, even blows. He paid no attention whatever.

He performed his work like a man in dream, but he was very far from being in dream. To save that faithful German from torture and death, he had bartered himself for three days, and he did not shrink from the bargain. Spanuto would have no satisfaction of it, on this he was resolved. If he could not master his own pride and angry resentment, he was a poor sort of fellow.

True, he had now become certain that the Italian would kill him on the third day, and two days had nearly sped, for it was mid-afternoon. On the following evening, he knew from the talk among the men, they would ride forth to be gone two or three days; whither, they themselves did not know.

Bellegarde, however, knew. Spanuto would ride to take his kingly game.

If the naked, shaggy, unspeakably dirty man in irons kept his head lowered to all jeers and insults, resented no blows or vile jests, and performed the despicable tasks allotted him without a murmur, his gray eyes remained cool and keen. All the while, he was awaiting what chance might offer him, alert, guarded. At the worst, he knew he could force them to slay him quickly, but he was not seeking death.

Old Auguste had not returned the previous night, promises to the contrary, and this was discouraging.

There were new witnesses to his humiliation this afternoon. The Vicomte de Theleme had arrived the previous night, with Count Solbeig and four lackeys; they stood now in the courtyard with Spanuto and watched as the Gascon oaths rang out and Pellancourt displayed his "monkey." Solbeig was a huge, brawny fellow who roared with laughter at the spectacle. Theleme, however, did not laugh at all. He was a thin, saturnine man of haughty mien, and Bellegarde guessed that the scene did not sit well with him.

The stables, however, were certainly getting cleaned.

Bellegarde was forking manure from its ancient nest into the court, with a two-tined fork, long and narrow. Pellancourt, who had been drinking not a little, thought to make his captive perform more strenuously for the benefit of the three gentlemen and the watching soldiers behind.

Plucking from the wall a long carter's whip, the Gascon

leaned back against a huge post that upheld the front roof of the stables, and cracked the whip with a roar of mirth.

"Ha, monkey!" he cried out. "Here, move faster! Lie down now, and wallow in that manure you've just pitched out! You hear me? Come, out with you!"

BELLEGARDE CAME from beneath the shelter, out into the sunlight. The whip cracked above his head, the Gascon jerked at the cord. Bellegarde moved forward until he was opposite the fellow—then he suddenly darted sideways. The fork lunged up and in. It drove into the huge post, gripped the neck of the Gascon between in two tines, and sank into the wood.

Pellancourt was held firmly, yoked like a beast.

He dropped the whip, and with both hands tore savagely but vainly at the tines; one of them had pierced the skin of his neck. His voice bellowed out frantic oaths of pain and fury. Bellegarde stepped back, caught up the whip, and began to lash the man with merciless deliberation.

A wild tumult of voices arose. Some of the watching soldiers burst into outcries of rage, others into peals of laughter, but all awaited orders from Spanuto. His pale features livid with fury, the Italian took a step forward. He was instantly halted by the Vicomte de Theleme, who addressed him with angry hauteur. Spanuto paused and bit his lip. It was clear that the nobleman, already deeply outraged by the treatment accorded one of his own class, was intervening; although Solbeig only roared with laughter.

At this moment a shout pealed from the sentries at the gate. The din of voices fell, as the men turned, staring. Spanuto made a gesture, and the gates swung open. Bellegarde drew back, seeking the cause of the abrupt cessation; only Pellancourt still twisted and struggled, his hoarse bellow unchecked.

A single horseman rode into the courtyard. It was Herman Breiter.

The German swung to earth, saluted Spanuto, and extended a folded paper, with a stolid and casual air. His gaze flickered about the courtyard and then came to rest on the Italian, who was frowningly opening the communication. He read it, and his face changed.

"*Per Bacco!*" he exclaimed, and looked at Breiter. "He gave you this?" Where is he?"

"Awaiting my return, *monsieur,*" said the German. "I cannot say where."

Spanuto's eyes narrowed, then he shrugged, rightly assuming that he would not get much result from torture. He turned to his two companions and extended the letter.

"From Raoul de Gisy," he said. "Read for yourselves. He offers to place himself in my hands if this fellow Brisac, or Bellegarde, is set free to-morrow at sunrise."

Solbeig, a bluff, hearty brute, clapped him on the shoulder.

"Faith, your exchanges are lucky, Giulio! When you get Gisy, you'll soon exchange him for a still better—eh? Oh, of course."

He nodded, catching a gesture of warning from the Italian. Theleme returned the letter.

"Apparently," he said, "this Sieur de Gisy is a very knightly gentleman."

A spasm of fury contracted the lips of Captain Spanuto, who glanced around, caught the watchful eye of Stuart, and beckoned the Scot to his side.

"Send a man up to the tower at once, to mark whither this German rides. Bid Giles le Bœuf and my own lackey Vittorio saddle and ride after him, at a distance; both of them are shrewd men, good at such work. Let them leave their arms here and act as leisurely travelers."

Stuart departed. The Italian strode over to the German, waiting beside his horse.

"Well, fellow! You are bold, to trust yourself here again."

"Why not, captain?" answered Breiter, mildly, looking him in the eyes. "A messenger has nothing to fear."

"Precisely. Tell M. de Gisy that his offer is accepted. At sunrise to-morrow your master will depart free and unharmed."

"Armed and clad," added the German, with a glance at the sorry figure across the courtyard.

"Agreed," assented Spanuto. "Where does M. de Gisy meet him?"

"He did not say, captain. An hour after my master leaves here, M. de Gisy will arrive, alone, to surrender himself."

"Very well. You may depart."

"One moment, captain," intervened the German. "When I was here before, I heard certain talk. Nothing definite. I seek news of my brother Arnulf—"

"He was slain when M. de Bellegarde tried to kill me," said Spanuto.

The German said nothing, but his face seemed to harden as he met those dark eyes. Then he saluted, turned, and swung up into the saddle. Count Solbeig came and caught Spanuto's arm.

"By the mass! You would take the man's word that he will surrender himself?"

"Yes," said the Italian curtly. Theleme, who had joined them, smiled thinly.

"Come, come, Captain Spanuto! Confess the truth. We are friends and allies, are we no?"

Spanuto regarded them for a moment, and broke into a laugh.

"And with the one purpose ahead," he added. "Is it likely that I would let yonder rascal go free, after he killed Mendoza, Praslin, and Florio? Hm! You'll see for yourselves. Now, I pray you, excuse me."

CHAPTER XIV

SETTING THE TRAP

STUART WAS approaching, his errands done. Spanuto beckoned him and strode over to the stables, where Bellegarde stood in stark dismay, having caught some of the talk.

"What means this insubordination?" snapped Spanuto. "You swore to obey me."

"You, by all means," answered Bellegarde. "But not this Gascon dog."

"Throw down that whip."

Bellegarde obeyed. The groaning Pellancourt was being released from his yoke.

"Your friend Gisy offers himself in exchange for you; it is accepted. To-morrow at sunrise you will depart free and unharmed. Stuart, take him back to his cell. In the morning have the armorer strike off his chains and bring him to me."

As he accompanied Stuart, Bellegarde was aware of a hard, dour look from the Scot.

"You are lucky, *monsieur*," said the latter harshly.

"Your luck is ended," returned Bellegarde. "You've recovered too soon. Next time, I'll give you three inches of steel instead of a scant inch."

Stuart laughed grimly.

Rejoining his two companions. Captain Spanuto led them across and into the garden of the castle, a sweet, well-watered spot thick with ancient trees. A table had been set out here, with seats, and old Auguste had brought forth his best wine.

Bellegarde was almost through
the ring when a pistol exploded.

Dismissing the bleary eyed old seneschal, Spanuto caught up a silver flagon and laughed.

"To success, my friends! We can talk freely; here are none to overhear us, and it is time that we set forth our plan."

"High time, meseems," said the Vicomte de Theleme, relaxing and sipping his wine. "This Arbois is excellent! I congratulate you. It is the king's favorite wine, also. But first—what about these two gentlemen, Gisy and Bellegarde?"

Spanuto smiled. "Don't worry about them. I have two superb trailers riding after that accursed German. By sunset, we'll know where Gisy's hiding. An hour later, or perhaps by midnight, we'll have him here. Unless he's killed first."

The vicomte made a gesture of distaste. "Well, it is your affair. The plan?"

"We take thirty men and ride for Tours. At the village of St. Vecin, close to the forest where the king hunts, the equerry who is in our pay will meet us with word of the next day's hunt. Knowing the direction, the rest is simple. Each of us takes ten men; we separate, we wait, and seize our prey when he appears."

"If he is not alone?"

"We have weapons, *per Bacco!* As you may know, however,

he usually outdistances all the others. At most, we'll have only one or two grooms to deal with, or a huntsman."

"Very well." Count Solbeig leaned forward, frowning. "But as yet, no signed agreement has come from Madrid! And I understood that—that a certain lady would be here."

"She was here, and went on to Tours."

"Tours? But that was left to Duguet."

Spanuto shrugged. "This Mme. La Fleche is of uncertain temper," he observed. "If she changes her mind, not St. Michael himself can prevail against her. And she changed her mind."

"Well," and Theleme nodded, "if she's at Tours, everything there will go perfectly, be assured! Banish your frown, M. Solbeig. I drink to your health, future Marshal of France!"

"And to yours, future duke and peer!" returned Solbeig, laughing. "You've prepared a chamber for his majesty?"

Spanuto glanced up at the round tower by the gate.

"Aye, and of the best," he responded significantly.

So they jested and talked of the future, this Italian and German and Frenchman, whiling away the afternoon very pleasantly until the sun began to lower in the west. And Bellegarde, meantime, lay in the darkness of his cell, cursing the chivalric folly of his friend and his own helplessness.

Then, to the three in the garden, came sudden interruption.

THE LANK, powerful Stuart appeared striding toward them, and at his side was one of the two men who had followed Herman Breiter.

A cry of joy broke from Spanuto. "Ha, Giles le Bœuf! What luck?"

The man, who had donned cloak and hat for his ride, grinned evilly. "All luck, master! We ran him down to a pretty farm not four miles from here—a place that we have missed heretofore, since there are no girls about. Gisy was there. We remained among the trees, out of sight. Vittorio is waiting there to make sure our game doesn't depart. In that case, he'll leave word beside a big stone we marked."

"You hear that, Stuart?" exclaimed the Italian. "Order a dozen men to saddle instantly. I'll take charge, and we'll have that rascal on the gallows ere darkness fall—"

He fell silent, staring. A shout from the walls, then another. Stuart lifted his voice and had quick response.

"A man riding hard. Blue and silver livery of that lady who was here—"

"La Fleche!" exclaimed Theleme. "She herself, perhaps!"

At an imperative gesture from Spanuto, the lean Scot turned and ran for the courtyard, shouting an order to open the gates. Spanuto handed Giles le Bœuf a coin and dismissed him, and the three eyed one another in frowning silence.

Presently Stuart appeared with a staggering figure in blue and silver, and the Italian nodded.

"One of her men, aye. What the devil has happened?"

Solbeig leaped up, filled a goblet with wine, and shoved it at the messenger as he came up to them, exhausted and covered with dust. He seized it with thanks and gulped the wine, then straightened up.

"A letter, my lord," he said. "Also a verbal message. Here—"

Spanuto seized the letter, tore it open, and a startled exclamation broke from him. He turned to Stuart and dismissed him with a curt order.

"This is incredible!" he exclaimed. "Here, I'll read it—it's from her, of course."

> "You should have caged the falcon Gisy instead of playing with doves. Duguet is dead; so are others. Gisy was here and is gone. The courier from Madrid has just arrived. I have the signed agreement and will follow with it. Will meet you *en route* or await you at Gisy."

"What the devil!" exclaimed Solbeig, astonished. "Where does she think we'll be, then?"

Spanuto made an impatient gesture, and continued reading:

"Everything is changed. The king arrives here earlier than expected. More by word of mouth; you may trust the bearer."

The only signature was the hastily scrawled arrow—La Fleche.

"Well?" Spanuto turned to the messenger. "What word do you bring?"

"That you must reach the village of St. Vecin by noon to-morrow, *monsieur*," said the man.

"What?" cried Theleme. "Thirteen leagues before noon to-morrow?"

"That is nothing; it can be done before sunrise," snapped the Italian. "Continue, fellow!"

"My mistress said to tell you that the work must be done to-morrow. The man you know will be at St. Vecin at noon or before. The stag will be hunted in the afternoon. She is making all arrangements. The king is arriving to-night, almost alone, having left the court at Blois. That is all."

"*Pardie*, it is enough!" exclaimed Solbeig with energy.

One would have said that he was delighted by this sudden burst of action. Not so the Italian, who stood with a dozen conflicting emotions reflected in his face. Then he lifted his head.

"Go; rest and sleep," he said to the messenger, who bowed and departed. He raised his voice. "Stuart! Eight men to hold the walls in case of need. The others, saddle and arm; we leave in ten minutes. Food and wine for three days. No spare horses."

HE TURNED to the other two, a flame in his eyes.

"The moment has come; everything is clear, *messieurs*," he said quietly. "This devil Gisy has upset things. Fortunately, La Fleche was at Tours to take hold. Stuart and ten men will ride out and bring in Gisy, holding him with the other against our return. Thirty men will leave with us. To-morrow at noon we shall be in St. Vecin."

"All of us?" queried Theleme dryly. "When there are no spare horses?"

Spanuto made a gesture of reassurance.

"Of our thirty men, perhaps six will be unable to keep up," he said. "They will have money; they will obtain extra horses and await us. Three men from here will bring on the spare horses, slowly. Once the work is done, we shall have fresh mounts as we need them."

"But not for all of us."

"For enough of us, at least. Remember, there will be no immediate pursuit."

Theleme nodded and sank back in his seat, satisfied.

"The king is playing into our hand," went on the Italian, with kindling ardor. "By leaving the court at Blois, he is as usual probably designing to visit some lady in Tours. No one will know what has become of him. For a day or two, there will be no anxiety; and then it will be too late."

"Good," exclaimed Count Solbeig. "Let me understand aright. We leave now, and do not pause until we reach St. Vecin. Some time to-morrow afternoon we leave there and return here—"

"By the following sunrise. Two nights and a day of hard riding, with an occasional rest of an hour."

"*Herr Gott!* By then, we shall be dead, if the horses are not!"

"What? Is your marshal's baton not worth a ride?" exclaimed Theleme, laughing.

Solbeig grunted, and reached for the wine. "Bah! I'll outride both of you. Agreed!"

"Then," and Spanuto turned, "leave your lackeys here to augment the garrison, get what things you need, and join me in the courtyard. The Scot will hold the place until we return."

The Italian mercenary was as good as his word. Within ten minutes he and his two companions rode forth, thirty men clattering after them, perfectly armed, equipped and mounted. The spare horses would follow more slowly, in a couple of hours.

Barely was the last rank clear of the gates when Stuart and ten troopers clattered out in the other direction, with Giles le Bœuf riding beside the Scot, to run down and seize Raoul de Gisy.

Some little time later, as Spanuto came to the crest of a long hill, he drew rein and glanced back, searching the country behind him. The other two paused.

"You have seen something?" asked Solbeig.

A smile touched the Italian's lips and he lifted his arm. "Yes. Do you see it?"

"Nothing except a distant smoke."

"Which signifies that Gisy is taken and the farm that sheltered him is destroyed."

And turning his horse, Spanuto drove in his spurs.

CHAPTER XV

LA FLECHE CONSPIRES

IT WAS quite true that Duguet was dead, for his neck was broken in that fall from the window to the garden below.

Midnight found the Moor's Head at Tours and indeed the whole quarter in great commotion, with provosts, archers of the guard and curious residents thronging about.

The royal lieutenant himself was summoned from the château, but when he came face to face with Mme. La Fleche he started, and then bowed very low. Ten minutes later the commotion was at an end.

Since there was no law against duelling, and this was clearly the aftermath of a duel, nothing could be done about it.

Duguet's lackey accompanied his master's body back to the Licorne tavern. Scarcely had sunrise broadened into morning, however, when he returned to the Moor's Head, with two gentlemen who had arrived in search of Duguet. One came from the south, one from the north; a Spanish cavalier and a gentleman from the court at Blois. Both greeted Mme. La Fleche with profound respect and displayed no reluctance in treating with her instead of with the defunct Duguet.

Within half an hour one of her equerries saddled and mounted in hot haste, and rode forth alone with her message for Spanuto. The others ordered her coach prepared and her horses brought out.

Angele, meantime, learned of the murderous events of the night from the maid who brought her breakfast. Before she had finished dressing she discovered that Raoul de Gisy must be the person most involved, although his name had not entered into the affair. He was missing from the inn, however, his room unused.

Summoning a hostler to attend her, Angele set forth on foot to the house of M. d'Aurilly, and when her name was made known the servants in charge received her with sorrowful deference. To her consternation, she learned that Aurilly was dead.

Word had come only the previous day from Blois. Aurilly, there with the court, had died very suddenly of the plague.

Hearing this, she sat frozen for a long moment. Unutterable relief and sharp dismay seized upon her at the same time. True, she was now free of her promise to marry him, but the assistance promised by Aurilly was non-existent, and there was no other place to turn in search of new aid. Bellegarde was dead. Gisy had vanished. Here in Tours she was alone and friendless. The court lay at Blois, and there she might turn to the king for protection; but she did not seek protection for herself.

Presently she was walking back again with the hostler. The world seemed ruined around her. Aurilly was dead, Bellegarde, her father; and now Gisy had disappeared. No doubt, she thought, he would be searched for down here in Tours as an outlaw. She still had his money safe, however.

So she came into the courtyard of the Moor's Head and sent the hostler to see if there were any word from Gisy. Her eyes fell upon the coach that was being made ready; she saw the device upon its panel, and remembered the conversation beneath the gallows. So this woman was here—this duchess who was called La Fleche!

From the outside stairs that ran up along the wall of the building came voices. Angele lifted her eyes and saw La Fleche descending, elegantly costumed, glittering with jewels, and beside her a cavalier, who was gazing down in astonishment. This gentleman was the king's lieutenant, who had visited at Chanlay two months ago and had known her father well.

Upon reaching the cobbles he bowed low to Angele; but, as she still wore her man's attire of gray, did not venture to address her. He spoke for a moment with La Fleche, then took his departure. Angele felt those dark, brilliant eyes upon her, as the hostler returned with a shake of his head; then La Fleche was coming swiftly to her, hand outstretched.

"YOU ARE Mlle. de Chanlay? I am Mme. La Fleche; I have heard of you from the Sieur de Bellegarde—"

The name smote Angele like a blow, and the sharp dark eyes perceived her confusion.

"What?" exclaimed La Fleche quickly. "It is not possible that you know him?"

"Yes," murmured Angele.

She knew that this woman was somehow connected with Spanuto, was a duchess, was probably fully cognizant of the plot against Raoul de Gisy. Suspicion and distrust filled her heart, a certain hatred hardened her violet eyes.

La Fleche did not observe it, for her active brain was already seizing on this meeting, seeking to turn it to advantage. Here before her was the woman for whom Spanuto had been ready to jeopardize everything. Possibly a spy; more likely, a simple provincial noblewoman who might be of use. A hundred possibilities flashed before her mind's eye. She went on speaking, with the winning grace and charm which she could assume at will.

"My dear, you are a friend of that gentleman? Then—"

"And of M. de Gisy," said Angele, looking her in the eyes. La Fleche started slightly; she caught sight of her maid, who was approaching, and motioned the girl toward the coach, whose liveried outriders were now waiting.

There recurred to her mind the exclamation uttered by Gisy the previous night, about that letter from Sedan, whose contents he had so clearly known.

"Good!" she exclaimed warmly. "I, too, am a friend of M. de Gisy—"

"*Madame,*" and Angele drew herself up coldly, "I do not believe you, and I refuse to regard you as a friend. I know that you are not what you say, but a great lady of the court. I know that you are a friend of the Italian, Spanuto—"

La Fleche broke into a laugh, leaned forward, laid her hand on the arm of Angele. Her eyes were eager, brilliant, alive with light. This country girl was clearly a dangerous equation.

"Listen! That is true; but there is more you do not know," she said rapidly. "You are aware that under the name of Bellegarde is hidden that of—"

"I happen to know that M. de Bellegarde has been killed by your friend Spanuto!" snapped Angele defiantly. The eyes of La Fleche widened.

"You also think that! But it is not true! Gisy thought the same thing; in reality, our friend is a prisoner at the Tour de Gisy. I swear it! I am his friend. It is true that I have certain business with that Italian; but business alone. I am endeavoring to clear up the good name of the Marquis de Brisac, and to refute the terrible accusations made against him and M. de Gisy, who is my very good friend also. Only last night, when men came to kill him, I enabled Gisy to foil them and escape—"

Angele scarcely heard all this, scarcely listened to the convincing story poured out by the woman before her.

"Wait!" she broke in. "You say that Bellegarde is not dead? How do you know this?"

"A courier from Spanuto came to me late yesterday. When I told Gisy, he leaped in the air like a boy; I think he has gone riding back to the Tour, for he was carried away by joy. Ah, my dear, let me help you!" and La Fleche took Angele tenderly in her arms. "Realize that I am a friend, that my sole aim is to help and not hurt!

"Shall I confess it?" she went on, with a well-assumed confusion. "Perhaps you have guessed my interest in M. de Brisac— an old friend, a more than friend! There; I have opened my heart to you—"

Angele pushed her away gently.

"Please—let me think!" she exclaimed. "You say that Gisy escaped—"

"Yes. There was a fight, but thanks to my warning he got away."

I T W A S well that the sharp eyes of La Fleche could not read the thoughts burning in the brain of the girl. Even had intuition failed her, Angele would have known that La Fleche lied; for Bellegarde was certainly not an old friend, had not even known who this woman was until Gisy identified the arms on the coach.

But—Bellegarde alive! Oddly enough, she believed this intelligence where she disbelieved everything else that La Fleche said. She rallied, summoned all her forces, realizing that she must meet La Fleche on her own ground. A tremulous smile came to her lips, and she put out her hand to that of the other woman.

"Then I was mistaken about you—"

"Poor dear! I don't blame you," said La Fleche with sympathy. "I have heard, too, that this upstart Italian has dared to annoy you with his attentions. From this moment you are under my protection. Let him dare to so much as address a word to you! Your family—"

"Alas, I have none," said Angele mournfully. "My father died; I fled from the château and came here with M. de Gisy, for there I was not safe. And now I do not know what to do."

"Your château is not far from the Tour de Gisy? Ah, that explains everything! Come let me offer you protection, friendship, aid!" and again she took Angele in her arms. "I am going now, this instant, to the Tour de Gisy; I shall settle matters with that Italian mercenary, bring him to terms. And I shall also take up your quarrel with him. Come, there is room in my coach. Return to your own place, my dear, in the assurance that you'll be safe there! We shall see about M. de Brisac, or Bellegarde if you prefer that name. I am not without power, and if I order it, Spanuto will certainly release him."

She kissed Angele, who felt a cold repulsion at the touch, but endured it.

"It is true; I had best return to the château," said Angele musingly. "But you will have no room for me; there is your maid to carry. And I have a horse—"

"Devil take your horse! One of my outriders can lead him. The maid will sit outside. If you'll accompany me, then make haste! I'll reach the Tour de Gisy sometime to-night; these horses of mine are fast, the coach light. Thirteen leagues is nothing to them."

"Good! In ten minutes I'll be ready," and Angele hastened into the inn.

Now, the inn-keeper was an honest fellow. Upon visiting Gisy's empty room, he had found the gold concealed there; and knowing that Angele had been in company with Gisy, he spoke to her of it. She at once turned over to him most of the gold she was holding for Gisy, so that the man stared at it in dumb amazement, but promised to keep it safely. On the previous night Gisy had taken his horse, but had neglected everything else in his hot haste to be gone.

Within the promised time Angele was back in the courtyard with her few belongings. Her horse was saddled and taken in leash, she entered the coach with La Fleche, and with cracking of whips they rolled out of the inn yard on their way.

La Fleche said nothing about her courier, who had preceded them by a good two hours with orders to reach Spanuto ere sunset, at any cost. For, on this same night, the king would arrive at his château from Blois, where the plague was raging. And on the morrow he would certainly hunt in the forest.

As they rode, Angele talked merrily, but now and again she surprised a swift, strange light in the dark eyes opposite her, and behind her own apparent simplicity was an unwonted guile, a wary alertness. She suspected all that La Fleche said and did, but she gave not the least sign of her feelings. Bellegarde was alive! This fact, which she no longer doubted, remained like a song in her heart. If Bellegarde lived, then not everything was lost.

ONCE OUTSIDE the city they made high speed along the paved highway, until they struck off into the hill roads to regain the remote district of Gisy. La Fleche probed deftly and deeply, to discover how much this girl with the violet eyes and man's attire might know; Gisy's remark about the letter from Sedan had aroused all her suspicions.

Angele, however, while accepting her protestations of friendship with the warmest gratitude, evaded every effort at probing. This was the easier because she actually knew nothing of the plot itself. La Fleche presently wearied of the game, becoming convinced that Angele was after all nothing more than a pawn who might be useful. Angele did not conceal that she had hoped to meet her cousin at Tours, instead meeting news of his sudden death.

"Oh! I knew M. d'Aurilly well!" exclaimed La Fleche. "Dead of the plague? That is only too likely, for it is raging both at Paris and at Blois, as it usually does in midsummer. The whole court is in confusion, they say, and may return to Fontainebleau. Well, my dear, I'm going to get a nap."

Sleep she did, and looked lovely in slumber as do few women. Angele regarded her peaceful beauty, wondering how much of the tale related about Gisy's escape of last night had been true.

At noon they halted for an hour to bait the horses, then sped on. The afternoon was hot and dusty, the road extremely rough for a coach; but La Fleche made no complaint over jolts and bounces, continually urging the driver to greater speed in cruel disregard of the horses. As the sun drew toward the west, Angele realized that they would make Chanlay a little after dark, and urged La Fleche to halt there.

"Spanuto's men will be gone," she said, "and in any case I would have nothing to fear if you are present. Why not break your journey there, take fresh horses, and go on later to-night to the Tour de Gisy, if you must?"

La Fleche nodded. "Thanks, my dear. You say well that there is nothing to fear. If that swaggering Italian dares but look at you again, I'll say a word to melt his ardor! You'll take your rightful place at home, without further trouble."

And well rid of the minx, she thought. Angele's quiet simplicity had palled upon her, and she began to think the girl might be worse off than in the arms of Spanuto, after all. Perhaps that astute Italian might be in need of a check-rein or a bribe, later.

THE SUN was at setting, and Angele had just proclaimed that they were not three leagues from Chanlay, when the coach came to a halt. La Fleche put her head out of the window with an angry inquiry.

"Men approaching on the road, *madame*—a troop, apparently."

"Oh!" Instant excitement appeared in the eager countenance of La Fleche. She opened the coach door and leaped out. "It is he!" she cried, then recollected herself and turned quickly to Angele, who was peering forth. "Stay there, keep out of sight, my dear! It is that rascal Spanuto. Let me handle him."

Angele obeyed.

Spanuto it was, riding hard for Tours with Baron Solbcig, Theleme and his troopers. At sight of the coach beside the road, and the woman awaiting him, he waved the others on, and brought his horse to her side, dismounting swiftly and bowing with scant courtesy.

"*Madame,* you are magnificent!" he exclaimed. "The courier reached us in the nick of time. Gisy is trapped and awaiting my return. We'll be at St. Vecin ere noon to-morrow—"

"Not so loudly, if you please!" La Fleche gestured toward the coach. "No need of my servants learning everything."

"Right. You have the agreement from Madrid?"

"Yes. Unopened; I've had no time or opportunity. In the

morning I'll send on the copies to Sedan and Paris. Undoubtedly the Spanish treaty for him to sign is here, also. That will
go back to Madrid as soon as signed."

"He will claim fraud."

"Before he can claim anything," and La Fleche laughed
shrilly, "its provisions will be in force. All now depends on your
stroke."

"It will not fail," said Spanuto, with energy.

"You'll need fresh horses—"

"Enough will be provided. Some are following us, others will
be gathered and brought on. Why the devil was everything
changed so suddenly?"

"The pestilence has broken out at Blois. The king will plan
on spending some little time at Tours; everything is in confusion."

"Good! The gods favor us!" Spanuto's dark face lighted up.
Then he bowed. "Farewell! I must rejoin my men."

"May luck attend you!"

He mounted, drove in his spurs, and departed after his troop
at a gallop.

La Fleche waited a moment, to subdue the fierce exultation
that flamed within her, lest she reveal anything to Angele. Then
she turned and came back to the coach. Angele, who had caught
those first hasty words, gave her a glance of inquiry as she got
in.

"What did he say about Gisy?"

"He thinks he has trapped Gisy, but did not explain; he is
riding toward Tours and will not return for a day or two. I gave
him a sharp admonition about leaving you alone, so fear not.
I'll go on to the castle—"

"You'll help them? Gisy and Bellegarde?"

"Of course. If they are there, I'll have them free in no time;
or at least beyond harm."

La Fleche did not stint her promises, which cost nothing

and might keep Angele appeased; but she promised so much that Angele clearly perceived the woman was lying.

The coach went on again over an extremely rough stretch of road. Darkness was now approaching rapidly; on either side the road was the stretch of thick ancient woods that one encounters just before reaching Chanlay—the Parc de Chanlay, as it was ironically termed.

A cry of warning from the outriders; a lurch of the coach, then a crash and it all but overturned as one wheel was smashed in a mudhole. La Fleche, who faced forward, was hurled from her seat with the greatest violence, and struck headlong against the side panel as the coach toppled down. There came a shriek from the maid outside.

ANGELE STARED down at the woman, who lay on her back on the floor of the coach, senseless. For an instant she thought La Fleche was dead. Then she saw her bosom rising and falling, for in the fall the straps of her bodice had burst. She perceived something else, also—a packet, heavily sealed, and addressed in Spanish script to Duguet.

In a flash Angele remembered that Duguet had been awaiting word from Madrid.

"Are you hurt, *mesdames?*" The alarmed maid appeared at the door, opening it. "Oh! *Madame* is injured—"

"She has fainted, that's all," said Angele, and scrambled out over the prone figure of La Fleche. As she did so, she deftly caught up the packet and put her hat over it as she alighted. "What has happened?"

"A wheel smashed, *madame*," answered one of the postilions.

"Give me my horse," said Angele. "My château is not far. One of you ride on with me—or better, wait here and guard *madame*. I'll send a coach at once."

She brooked no protests, but as her horse was brought up, sprang into the saddle. The packet was by this time safe beneath her doublet. Promising to send aid immediately, she struck in her spurs and was gone into the gathering obscurity.

When the coach was out of sight she halted her horse and examined the packet. In the darkness she could make little of it; but apparently the seal in the wax was the royal crown of Spain.

"What does it mean?" she thought. "This is evidently the message Duguet was awaiting. She has had it from him, is going to the Tour de Gisy. Why did she not give it to Spanuto? There's a good deal here I don't understand; but it must have some connection with Raoul and Bellegarde. This is not paper, but vellum, and therefore of importance."

Was Bellegarde really alive? Was Raoul really trapped? She hesitated, then went on in a desperate state of mind. Somehow she must reach the Tour de Gisy, at all costs, and see for herself. This packet might be of the greatest consequence to either or both of those men, for it was clear enough that some intrigue was afoot. Yet La Fleche had lied so consummately that after all she might have lied about Bellegarde too.

Angele pressed on. She was leaving the woods behind now, and had a mile of open meadow road before coming to the side way that led to Chanlay..

Her mind was flitting ahead. Spanuto might have swept off all her horses, but some of her farmers could provide a few—enough for a coach, at least. The servants would be at the château; her own servants, not those placed in charge by Spanuto. If that accursed valet remained, he should be whipped off the place at once. Yes, she was mistress there, and if she sent out for La Fleche, the woman would learn as much upon arriving.

Suddenly Angele drew rein, startled. From the darkness ahead, faintly pierced by starlight, came the crashing hoofbeats of a horse at gallop, approaching rapidly. No shelter here. It was one of Spanuto's men, beyond doubt.

She drew to one side of the road and waited, hoping he would pass without a second glance. She could see the figure in the starlight, the horse thundering down the road at breakneck speed; but the rider could see her as well. A startled oath broke from him, and then he was upon her, drawing rein sharply, a rapier leaping out at her.

A startled cry broke from the girl.

CHAPTER XVI

ESCAPE

BELLEGARDE, AS soon as he was back in his cell, raged against the folly of Raoul de Gisy in sacrificing himself; but exhaustion claimed him and presently he slept.

He wakened to find a man shaking him.

It was one of the soldiers, who held a lantern aloft, and cursed him in a maudlin voice as he sat up, blinking. Bellegarde saw bread and wine at his side, and the soldier produced a bottle from under his belt.

"Come on, rascal, eat and drink!" hiccuped the soldier. "Devil take me, this lieutenant of ours has good wine in his room! I'll just finish this bottle while I'm here. Take charge, he says to me, and forgets that he left his private tipple in sight. I'll take charge, all right! Aye, with a will—"

He set the bottle to his lips. Bellegarde glanced around, rose slowly. The soldier was alone, and there was no need to ask his story, after what he had just said.

"That has body to it, that wine!" and the man lowered the bottle for breath. The lantern waved wildly in his other hand. He leered down at Bellegarde. "Ha, rascal! Lucky thing I stayed here instead of riding with the captain, eh? Hell bent for Tours, there and back, and plague take horses or riders who don't keep up! Going to the village of St. Vecin, too. I know it well, that village. Was born near there. The king comes to the inn there when he's a-hunting—they have the wine he likes."

A swift thrill shot through Bellegarde. The king! Spanuto had gone, then!

"Your captain wasn't going till to-morrow night, fellow," he said.

"Oh, indeed!" The soldier leaned against the wall and laughed. "A lot you know! Courier from Tours—one of those jackanapes in livery, with the fine lady who was here. And the Scot posted off to catch your friend Gisy—"

"Let me set down that lantern before you smash it," said Bellegarde. He reached out and took the lantern. The half maudlin soldier made no resistance, but grunted and lifted his bottle again. Had Auguste prepared that wine for Stuart? There was no knowing, but here was a chance given by the gods, not to be missed.

As the soldier emptied the bottle, iron hands caught him about the throat and pulled him down.

"Auguste? Bah! I can't count on that doddering old fool," thought Bellegarde, as he peered at the senseless figure under his hands, and then rose. "The village of St. Vecin, eh? And Spanuto has gone there to get his prey? Well, one man can go faster than thirty. By the saints, I'll manage it somehow! Only a handful of men left here—hm!"

He drew out the soldier's blade—a heavy, two-edged sword meant for stout work. And stout work he gave it now, hacking at the links of his chain until the soft forged iron yielded to the tempered edge. The manacles about wrists and ankles could only come off by hammer and chisel; but they could remain without hurt.

When he had finished, a short length of chain remained fastened to his right wrist; he could not get rid of this. However, he was now unhampered, free to act. His first move was to strip the soldier, already snoring from his liquor, and array himself in the man's clothes. Then he shoved the fellow back among his own rags, so that to a casual glance he seemed the half-naked prisoner, and stepped out of the cell, lantern in hand.

The door clanged shut.

NO TIME now to wait for Auguste or try to find the old
seneschal's hidden door. Bellegarde had one purpose, and one
only—to get out of here with a horse, and ride to St. Vecin.
Haste was imperative; every moment counted. No time to seek
some secure way of slipping out. Rather, he must use audacity
to the uttermost!

The thought of Raoul de Gisy tormented him. Stuart had
gone to trap Gisy; had probably done so by this time; might
return at any moment. His hesitation was brief. Gisy, he knew
well, would be the first to bid him go on his errand. More hung
on this than the life of a man, and Bellegarde had already jeop-
ardized everything; he had learned his bitter lesson, and must
pay for it.

"Folly!" he groaned, as he followed the upward steps to the
passage beyond. "We learn through folly, aye; what a fool I was,
to let fat Michel buy the life of a king with his own worthless
hide! Now to remedy that and all else."

Daylight showed ahead. He was astonished to find that it
was no more than sunset.

An open door on his left. Ahead, a burst of voices, men
gaming and drinking—the guardroom, no doubt. He turned
in at the open door and found a large, comfortable room, whose
window opened on the garden. Now he knew where he was,
and orientation came swiftly. This must be the lieutenant's room,
occupied by Stuart, where that maudlin guard had found the
wine.

Bellegarde extinguished the lantern, glanced swiftly around.
He shed his ill-fitting garb, donned stout garments of half-
leather, picked up a steel cap, selected a poniard and long rapier
from a rack of weapons—not without a sigh for his own Ferrara,
whose golden hilt now adorned Spanuto's hip. Crossing to the
water basin in the corner, where hung a bit of silvered glass, he
worked swiftly with soap and razor. Presently he was himself

again, hard-jawed, clean. Leather boots from the corner, cruel Spanish spurs—ready!

He crossed to the window, opened the casement, and next moment was in the garden.

No one was in sight; the place seemed empty. Striding swiftly into the courtyard, Bellegarde turned into the long stables, then whistled in sharp dismay. Empty, indeed; in the gathering twilight only four animals stood there.

For the past two days he had been working on this very spot, among these horses. He knew at once that three of these beasts were unfit for his purpose, but the fourth might serve. It was a rangy, powerful bay, the same Spanuto had ridden into the forest, and the animal's neck bore a half-healed knife wound.

With a shrug Bellegarde caught down saddle and bridle and turned out the big bay. In five minutes he was in the saddle. Now he must chance everything on the men at the gates; boldness, defiance, the voice of authority, might well surprise them into obedience. If not, so much the worse for them all. Most of the men remaining were no doubt in the guard room.

He touched in the spurs. The sun was well gone, shadows were gathering as the bay went clattering out across the courtyard. Three or four men by the gate turned in astonishment, but Bellegarde gave them no time to ask questions or to see his face.

"Open, open!" he shouted, hurling a volley of oaths at them. "Captain's orders, you fools! Open!"

Leaderless, not recognizing him for either friend or foe, they quickly obeyed his command, and the gates swung out a little for him to pass through. He urged the bay on, and next instant was outside. A yell broke from one of the men, but Bellegarde laughed, drove in his spurs, and sent the big horse down the slope.

Free!

HE BROKE into a gallop, but not for long. His eye caught a glitter, a moving mass, ahead and below, by the gallows. Rec-

ollecting the lean Scot and his party, Bellegarde drew rein with
a curse, then swung to earth and led his horse in among the
ancient oaks, at the very spot where that ambush of the forest
dwellers had pulled him down.

Gripping the nostrils of the bay to prevent any whinny, he
waited grimly. Soon Stuart and his little group of men came
into sight in the gathering darkness. Bellegarde noted the three
empty saddles. Then his gaze fell upon the two prisoners in the
midst, and he stiffened. There rode Herman Breiter, bound, and
beside him Raoul de Gisy was drooping in his saddle, apparently hurt.

"We've not seen the men with the spare horses," remarked
one of the troopers.

"They went around by Courcelles, to pick up a few beasts
there if possible," answered another. "They'll come back into
the highway about where this accursed road branches off, five
leagues from Tours."

Bellegarde trembled as he listened to them, saw Gisy jerk
up in his saddle. The blood ebbed out of his face; he glared from
his covert, grim and gaunt, tortured by the thought of riding
deliberately away, of venturing nothing to save this man who
had ventured so much to save him.

Yet the power of the driving urge within him would not be
quelled. In one scale lay Gisy, in the other the king. And the
latter was weighed down, too, by the fact that success there
meant vindication for himself and Gisy.

No, he must go on at any cost, give ungrudgingly of his wits
and effort toward the one great objective! Everything else must
go by the board.

Yet temptation drove furiously at him. Stuart and seven men,
two or three of them wounded; no more. One bursting yell, a
rush of headlong attack, and it would be queer if he did not
scatter them, or at least give the two prisoners a chance to break
clear!

Bellegarde uttered a low groan in the torment of his thought.

He saw the men glance around, catching the sound. One or two hurriedly crossed themselves; the pace was quickened. And with a frightful grip of self-restraint, Bellegarde let them ride on.

When they were gone he led out his horse, swung into the saddle and spurred as though the devil were after him.

He knew perfectly where he was, and there was no danger of losing his road. How long the bay would last at this pace was a question; but somewhere, somehow, he would get another mount. A good thirteen leagues to Tours, but something less to St. Vecin. Perhaps not above thirty-five miles. No, the poor brute would founder long ere that was covered!

Desperate at this certainty, Bellegarde spurred the harder. Stars were out, but a haze of clouds obscured half the sky and intensified the darkness of the night. Chanlay was close now; though, as he had not been there, Bellegarde was uncertain of its position.

Then, abruptly, he caught at his reins. As he came thundering down a gentle incline he sighted a dark figure ahead in the road—one of Spanuto's men, perchance. Well, at all events, there was a spare horse for him! He plucked out his rapier, uttered an oath as his horse slipped, then was reining in sharply.

A frightened cry came to him in a woman's voice.

"The devil!" he exclaimed. "Your pardon—I did not know it was a woman—"

A queer laugh rang in his ears, half hysterical, half of unutterable relief.

"Bellegarde! Bellegarde! Is it really you?"

ASTOUNDED, HE leaned forward, peered at her, then sheathed his rapier and brought his panting horse beside hers. His hand went out to her.

"Angele! By the saints, what a meeting—you, of all people!"

"We thought you were dead," she exclaimed, clinging to his arm. "Ah, Bellegarde—if she had not told me—"

"She?"

"La Fleche. Your duchess. I came from Tours with her to-day."

"Devil take it all! You—with that woman! Why, she's the life and soul of the whole accursed thing! She's the one actively behind it all—"

"Behind what?"

"Oh, I forgot you don't know. The plot. I must have your horse, Angele! I know the whole thing. They're planning to seize the king to-morrow. Spanuto is doing the work. He's gone on, and I must get ahead of him with warning—no time to think, no time to talk! This horse won't last the distance. I see you have that gray of yours; a fine beast. Give him to me!"

"Gladly," she answered. "Chanlay is not far. You say it's a plot against the king? And we never guessed that! Have you seen Raoul?"

"Good Lord, yes!" groaned Bellegarde.

Swiftly he told her of his escape. He spared himself no whit of blame for his past folly, his lack of realization; except for this, he should have taken the king warning long since. And now Gisy lay bound in his stead, as he rode.

Angele gripped his hand hard.

"Ah, Bellegarde! Things ever fall out for the best, perhaps," she said quietly. "Listen, for I have news. Not half a league away is La Fleche; her coach has broken down. She lied to me, brought me with her—for what reason, Heaven knows! Certainly it was for no good; but she pretended to be a friend."

"Beware of that woman," said Bellegarde in a low voice. "She is charming, beautiful, intelligent—but there is a devil within her."

"Still discerning, in some cases, are you?" and her voice was touched with mockery.

"You'll think I am, my angel, if I ever get free to talk with you! But flee that woman as though she were the plague."

"The plague! Ah, I had forgotten. There is no marriage for

me, Bellegarde; there are no two-score men for Raoul. Aurilly has died of the plague, which is raging at Blois and Paris. That's why the king came to Tours before he was expected. Avoid that woman yourself, for you must pass her on the road, after you are through the forest ahead."

"And you, Angele!" Bellegarde's voice was tortured. "I must leave you here—I must have this horse of yours! I must leave you, leave everything, as I left poor Raoul to his fate; and if I fail—"

"You'll not fail. Do you go to Tours itself?"

"No, to the village of St. Vecin—"

"Ah! That's in the royal, forest, three leagues from Tours! To reach it, leave the highway at the village of Le Loup Sauvage; the one with a stone church directly on the road. You can't miss it, even by night. Take the turning to the right."

"Thanks, Angele, thanks! Dismount, then—"

"No, wait!" The girl fumbled beneath her garments. "Here is a packet; I took it from La Fleche and fled. She was knocked senseless when the coach wheel was smashed. She will miss it; but no matter. It's from Spain, addressed to Duguet—the man you met at Courcelles, remember? It must be about this plot—"

"By the mass!" Bellegarde thrust the packet under his doublet. Then, swiftly, he caught the girl's hand and pressed his lips to her fingers. She laughed and swung out of the saddle.

"Take it, go quickly! You can examine it by daylight. Never mind about me. I'll be all right—I'll go on and see what can be done about Raoul—"

She gave him no chance for further delay, longer talk, but was gone, melting into the darkness like a wraith.

"Farewell!" cried Bellegarde, and, catching the reins of the gray, went ahead on his rushing course, striking into speed almost at once.

Traversing the Parc de Chanlay, he was forced to slow down; the road here was abominable. Presently a light glimmered ahead; the lamps of the coach were lit, vaguely illumining the

horses and men. A sudden thought struck Bellegarde as he
drew rein. Why not, indeed? These animals had come hard and
fast from Tours, were too weary to be sent after him; La Fleche
was helpless to intervene. She would not know what to believe,
what to imagine—

They stared at him as he slowed his pace and rode up to the
side of the coach.

"Where is her highness?" he demanded. For answer, La
Fleche appeared in the open door. He leaned over in the saddle,
and she recognized him.

"You! Bellegarde!"

He laughed lightly. "Aye! With warning, *madame*. Everything
is known; Mendoza told all before he died. You are betrayed.
The king is aware of the whole affair. You have one chance, and
one only; if Gisy dies, none of you will be spared! If he lives, I
answer for your life. See to it, my princess! Adieu!"

He struck in his spurs, his horse leaped forward, the gray
followed. He heard a cry that floated after him—an incoherent,
terrible cry in the voice of La Fleche.

Then the bay stretched out into a long, easy gallop, the big
gray keeping up without effort. Another and fainter cry followed, more frantic and despairing. Bellegarde laughed to
himself and settled down to the long leagues ahead.

For well or ill, he had done all he could. Now his work lay
before him. But, as he patted the neck of the bay, his hand
touched something, warm and sticky. With a shock, he realized
the truth.

The animal's wound had re-opened with its exertions.

CHAPTER XVII

THE KING

I T WAS only an hour later when the poor brute began to fail.

Bellegarde had pressed the pace relentlessly, intent upon getting every possible bit of speed from the bay, but no animal with a heavy rider could keep up such a gait for long. The gray, not ridden all that day or night, was comparatively fresh. At length Bellegarde drew rein, paused to unsaddle and turn the poor bay loose, and mounted the gray.

"Decidedly, Angele proved worthy of her name this night!" he reflected. "And in more than one way."

He rode on steadily, rapidly, but more carefully, now that he had no spare mount.

The packet burned against his skin; he was afire to examine it, but could not. This, like everything else, lessened in importance before the imperative need for speed. The king must be warned ere his hunt began. Afterward would be too late.

Therefore, thought Bellegarde, he had best push on straight for Tours. In this way, too, he would avoid Spanuto's troopers, who would leave the highway for St. Vecin at the village of Le Loup Sauvage. Yes, he had time enough. Even if the king had departed for his hunt, there would be a company or two of the guards at Tours.

So he breathed more easily, as the miles and leagues fell behind.

Midnight was well past when he came into the wider main

highroad, clattered through a dark and sleeping village, and went on. Then he slowed as a bridge loomed darkly ahead of him, and crossing it, indistinct figures blocked the road. A shout rang up.

"Hola! Comrades, here come the fresh horses—"

Bellegarde was among them before he could draw rein. Half a dozen men and beasts, who had fallen out from Spanuto's company and were here awaiting the remounts on the way from Courcelles. They realized their mistake at once. Bellegarde struck them and scattered them, put in his spurs, was through them.

A pistol exploded behind him, then another and another, angry yells pursuing him. A terrific blow struck his steel cap, carried it away; one at least of those vengeful balls had found its mark. The gray leaped wildly, struck into a frantic gallop, while Bellegarde fell forward in the saddle, his head whirling. Everything went black before him. Only by a supreme effort did he keep his seat.

Presently he recovered himself. The gray had taken the bit

Bellegarde lunged and his point went home.

in its teeth and was rushing madly through the night. Bellegarde tried to rein in the animal, but in vain. Neck outstretched, the gray thundered on and on, while Bellegarde reeled again in the saddle, dizzily. He put a hand to his head and found blood.

An instant later something warm flecked his face. The gray was whistling shrilly with every breath, was galloping more furiously but with failing stride. In sharp alarm, Bellegarde realized the horse must have been hit. Again he tried to bring the poor beast under control.

Another bridge, where the flying hoofs rang with hollow thunder. On again—but suddenly the gray stumbled in its stride. Bellegarde desperately freed his feet from the stirrups, and barely in time. Horse and man came down in one tremendous crash.

Bellegarde was pitched clear, and that was all he remembered.

WHEN HE opened his eyes he lay on his back in the ditch beside the road. The stars were out, clear and cold, the haze of cloud had passed from the sky. Scrambling to his feet, he found the packet safe, and stared around. He was unhurt, save for his head; the shock alone had knocked the senses from him.

But, a dozen feet away, the gray lay dead in the road.

For a space he stood in blank consternation. How much time had passed, he could not tell. The extent of this disaster stunned him; then, awakening, he turned and strode out along the road. Sooner or later he must obtain another horse. The gray had been quite cold, so he must have lain here for an hour or more, probably more.

Walking was not easy, however, by reason of the ankle-irons still about his legs, the high boots drawn over them. At every angle he seemed balked and hampered, and he cursed savagely as the irons chafed him. The length of chain still fastened to his right wrist was like a symbol of his own futility. He had failed at every point; every effort, every sacrifice, was vain. After a mile he perceived that walking was useless. He halted, desperate.

At this moment he caught the thud of hoofbeats. A horse was cantering toward him from ahead. Grimly, Bellegarde drew his rapier, stood waiting. In the starlight he presently caught sight of a single rider approaching, unhurried. The rider perceived his figure and drew rein at a little distance.

"Ha! *Cornidious!* Who's there?"

With a thrill, Bellegarde recognized that voice instantly, incredulously.

"Pellancourt! Is that you?" he cried out in savage joy.

"Aye, with orders for the remounts and escorts," assented the Gascon, for it was none other. "Who the devil are you?"

"Messenger for the captain."

Pellancourt urged his horse on again. "Devil take me if I know you!" he rumbled. "On foot, are you?"

Bellegarde came close, seized the horse's reins, threw up his weapon.

"Out of the saddle!" he ordered. "Do you know me now, big ox?"

An oath of astonished recognition burst from the Gascon. Then he struck Bellegarde's rapier aside, drove in his spurs, jerked out his own weapon.

That move spelled his fate. As the horse plunged frantically, the rapier lunged upward, and again, Bellegarde holding to the reins. A cry escaped Pellancourt and he toppled from the saddle, dragging by one stirrup. The horse calmed, Bellegarde disengaged his foot and bent over him, lifting him against a stone beside the road.

"The devil is in you!" murmured the Gascon faintly. A sudden spasm of energy seized upon him; his poniard flew out, all but disemboweled the man above him. Bellegarde leaped back barely in time, lifted his rapier, then lowered it again.

Pellancourt fell over sideways and blood came forth from his lips. He was dead.

Next instant Bellegarde was in the saddle and turning the horse about. The animal was far from fresh, but at least it was a horse; he asked no more. Also, it had pistols at the saddle, with a small horn of powder for priming. At this discovery he was overjoyed. Now, if he met other stragglers, he was ready for them!

The night was farther advanced than he had supposed. Dawn was in the sky when he gained the village of Le Loup Sauvage, recognizing the church which Angele had mentioned. The weary horse was badly fagged, but Bellegarde took the road to the right and spurred him into renewed effort.

The road was a vile one, and almost at once plunged into thick forest. Slower and slower grew the pace of the exhausted animal, who now responded to nothing. Coming to a brook, Bellegarde dismounted and gave the beast a half hour's rest and refreshment; he himself stretched out, but dared not close his eyes lest he oversleep. With the first rays of sunrise he went on.

AN HOUR passed, and another, with interminable forest stretching away on every side. No speed could be made on this road, and Bellegarde had to keep a sharp lookout ahead. The morning was half gone when his alertness was rewarded by discovery of five troopers sprawled in a glade ahead, sound asleep, while another, at some distance, watched over half a dozen horses who were cropping the grass. Evidently they had been resting here for some time.

Dismounting unperceived, Bellegarde removed saddle and bridle from his own jaded beast. Pistol in one hand, bridle in the other, he strode openly toward the group of horses. The astonished sentinel stood staring at him, then uttered an oath of recognition and crossed himself.

"You! The prisoner—"

Bellegarde lifted his pistol.

"Exactly, my friend. With a message for the captain. I'll take one of your horses—and never mind a saddle. This is imperative."

The threat of the pistol sent the man running, calling to his comrades. Bellegarde picked the best of the horses, bridled him, leaped to the smooth back, and sent the others scattering with blows of his sheathed rapier. Then he rode off on his way, and looked back laughing at the discomfited troopers.

Presently smoke curled up ahead of him, and he came warily to the hut of a woodcutter, where a gaunt-eyed woman stood at the door, staring. Bellegarde rode up, dismounted, gave her cheery greeting.

"Fear not, good wife!" he exclaimed. "If you can give me something to eat and drink, do so; I'll remember it and pay you at another time. And put me on the way to St. Vecin."

"Two leagues or a bit more, straight ahead," she said. "We have only some sour wine and cheese—"

This she gave him gladly, and in ten minutes he was on his way again.

It was a little before noon when he came into St. Vecin, which was no more than a large tavern and half a dozen miserable houses clustered behind it. No men or horses were in sight. The tavern was all in a bustle, however, and Bellegarde rode into the courtyard without hesitation, the host coming forth to greet him.

"In the king's name!" he exclaimed, dismounting. "I'm a courier of his majesty, waylaid by robbers. Put a saddle on this horse for me, and tell me if a company of men were here lately."

"They are but ten minutes gone, *monsieur!*" answered the host, calling to his grooms and hostlers. "They went to meet his majesty—"

"In which direction?"

"By that forest lane," and the inn-keeper pointed to a road winding away from the village. "Half a league, in the valley of La Chaudiere; an equerry was here to summon the troop. Faith, this has been a fine morning's business, *monsieur!* Will it please you to break your fast?"

"I've no time," said Bellegarde. "Bring me a stoup of your wine of Arbois, give my horse a handful of oats, and I'll be on after the others."

A saddle was clapped on his horse, and he himself drained an excellent flagon of wine. Five minutes later he mounted, while his host besought payment.

"Later," answered Bellegarde. "The account is good, fear not!"

With imprecations ringing in his ears, he spurred the horse out of the inn yard and along the forest lane, thanking fortune that the animal was fresh and in good wind.

No pause now. No chance to give warning at Tours, as he had known long since. He must find the hunt, break through Spanuto's men, turn back the king—and this was no light affair. Henri of Navarre did not hunt with a majestic retinue of servants, but in headlong pursuit of the stag.

Bellegarde spurred hard, and suddenly thrilled to a clear, far note—the ringing sound of hunting horns. He was closing in, but he was closing in too late, for no men had appeared ahead of him, and he knew that Spanuto must have spurred yet harder than he.

Now the forest opened out, the trees thinned; here was old and ancient growth with velvety sward. A great stag of twelve tines appeared like a shadow, leaped high, twisted in midair at sight of Bellegarde, and went bounding away. Another horn, and another. Then, somewhere just to the left, a shouting of men.

Bellegarde turned from the road, sent the good horse speeding among the trees. And of a sudden he came upon the scene—a dozen troopers closing in, circling. Two figures on the ground, huntsmen, three or four dismounted men above them with stabbing blades, and one proud, bearded man who sat his horse while the troopers circled him. He set a horn to his lips and blew a shrill, prolonged blast. Shouting rippled among the trees. The voice of Spanuto blared forth like a trumpet.

Then, with a rush and a yell, Bellegarde was out of the trees and on them like a whirlwind.

CHAPTER XVIII

A RIDE FOR LIFE

A T THIS moment the net of Spanuto was just closing in—a great, far-flung circle of mounted men suddenly appearing, cutting off any flight of the quarry toward Tours. None of the three leaders were in the little group around the king. Bellegarde, as his horse went rushing at them, bared his rapier and lifted his voice.

"Navarre!" he cried out, ringingly. "Navarre! To me, to me!"

Then he was upon them with a reeling shock, sending two horses sprawling, catching a blade on his own, driving home a deadly lunge beneath it. His staggering animal went on, came to a halt almost beside the king. Bellegarde held out his empty hand, appealingly.

"To me, sire!" he cried. "Spur for it!"

His horse came around. Two of the troopers were upon him, one from either hand. A pistol blazed, but the ball went wild. The rapier licked in and out. One man coughed and fell from the saddle. The other swept in a deadly blow, but Bellegarde's poniard warded it, and then the rapier was through that man's throat. As he plunged down, the king leaned far over in his saddle, came up with the fallen sword and plunged in his spurs.

The two horses leaped away.

In the course of an active and by no means well-spent life, Henri IV had been in many a tight place ere this, and was no man to stop and ask questions when emergency seized him. Although at this period his grizzled beard and pouchy eye showed the advancing age that dissipation was bringing upon him, that eye was none the less steely, the jaw beneath that beard was the pugnacious Bourbon jaw, the man himself was alert, active, ready for anything. In a flash he saw that there was but one avenue of escape, and he took it.

Stirrup to stirrup, the two went straight ahead, riding like madmen.

When they came to the road, the king eyed it, but Bellegarde caught the glance. "No, no, sire! They have men on every road!"

"*Ventre St. Gris!*" exclaimed the king. "This is a plot, then!"

Bellegarde laughed. "It's no love tryst, assuredly! Is your horse fresh?"

"Fresh enough. 'Ware right!"

Three troopers appeared, the end of the far-flung net, on their right. Bellegarde swerved, and the three fell behind, joining in the long rout of horsemen following the pair in the lead.

Bellegarde turned in the saddle, swiftly eying their pursuers. Of Spanuto he saw nothing, for the Italian had been on the far side of that circle, and was now at the end of the line into which the circle had developed. Directly behind, however, and heading a group of half a dozen men, were Theleme and Count Solbeig.

There was a discharge of pistols. The king swore roundly, but galloping horses make a poor stance, and the balls went wide of the mark. Settling to the work, Bellegarde plunged into the thicker forest that now greeted them, letting his horse pick its own way. He was aware of the curious, penetrating glances that the king flung at him, but now was no time for talk.

They rushed among the trees, bending low to escape the branches overhead, following no straight course but driving on madly wherever an opening showed. At least they were keeping ahead of their pursuers, though gaining little.

"What the devil!" exclaimed the king in astonishment. "Were you alone, *monsieur?*"

Bellegarde made no response. Glancing over his shoulder, he perceived that one of the troopers, magnificently mounted, had passed the others and was creeping up on them. The man had recognized him and was grinning at him, blade ready.

"Ride on, sire!" and he checked down the headlong rush of his mount.

FOOT BY foot the trooper gained; but he was overtaking a man fresh from encounters with Turk and Cossack cavalry, the finest horsemen in the world. As they swept on into an open glade, Bellegarde swung his horse suddenly to the left, drew rein for an instant, then struck in his spurs as the trooper rushed past with an awkward and futile cut at him. He came alongside the man, who tried desperately to turn his mount, parried a sweeping blow, and ran the other through the body.

Then, as the trooper pitched from his saddle, Bellegarde caught the reins of the horse and went on after the king. The latter was following a wagon track which had appeared, and flung a word over his shoulder as Bellegarde came thundering up.

"Well played, *monsieur!*" rang out his vibrant tones. "I've never seen a finer bit of work! What are those irons on your wrists?"

"The mark of your enemies, sire," responded Bellegarde. "Never mind all this; here's a remount if your horse fails. Until then, spur on!"

"Follow me, then! *Ventre St. Gris,* we'll ride them to hell!"

So saying, the king quickened his pace, flogging his superb mount with the naked sword in his hand, taking a thousand chances from sweeping limbs, uneven ground, briars. Then he swung abruptly out of the track, across an open glade, and Bellegarde followed him into the pathless forest depths.

They went on and on, but failed to throw off their pursuers. The king's horse, a magnificent animal, showed not the least sign of failing; but that of Bellegarde could not keep up the pace. At the king's insistence, Bellegarde mounted the spare beast. Twice, when they paused, the sounds of pursuit came close, driving them onward again.

"*Diable!* There's the reason for it!" exclaimed Bellegarde, pointing to the ground. "It has rained here within the past few days; the ground is soft, and we leave marks. Also, Spanuto has trackers, men trained in following pursuit."

"Spanuto?" The king gave him a sharp look. "He is among them? That Italian?"

Bellegarde nodded, and gave his horse the rein. "What say you, sire? Shall we separate and so divide them? Not many are following us—"

"No, stick together," came the response. "Ride! Devil take it, they can't follow us forever!"

He dashed away impetuously. Bellegarde sought vainly for any higher and drier ground as he followed on. The pursuers were close enough now to have sighted them, but only for an instant; the forest closed in again, with Henri leading the way and riding like a centaur.

Almost without warning they came to another wagon track; the king turned into it and the trees opened out ahead to show huts of charcoal burners. The two foam-flecked horses went pounding along the track past the huts, and Bellegarde looked back. Into the open came Theleme and Count Solbeig, neck and neck, a trooper behind them. This third man crashed down an instant later as his horse stumbled.

Bellegarde put in his spurs and overtook the king.

"O N L Y   T W O of them close upon us, sire!" he cried out. "Others will be following. Do you ride on, and I'll guarantee to hold them—"

"No, by God'" snapped Henri in his usual forceful manner. "None of that; I can die as well as you. Try them for another league, keep in this wagon track, and if our horses give out, then's time enough to halt. How are you named, *monsieur?* I have certainly seen your face."

"Not for the past three years at least. I'm the Marquis de Brisac."

"Brisac—ha!" With this one short exclamation Henri fell silent and devoted himself to riding. It was a race now, and to

Bellegarde's mind a bootless one, but he judged that the king had some purpose of his own a-brewing, and he was right. Henri never did anything like other kings; nor did any one know his purpose until he was ready to act. If he was no fighter himself, he had seen blood shed in rivers around him, and had emerged unscathed from the perils of field and court by doing the unexpected.

Knowing all this of old, Bellegarde bided his time, held his peace, and was content to keep his seat in the saddle as the horse dashed along under the spreading trees. The king set a cruel and merciless pace which would kill the horses in a few more miles; the more he spurred, the harder spurred those who came after.

Theleme and Solbeig alone were on the trail now. Their men had fallen far back, or had gone astray; but not only did they remain well within sight, they actually gained on their quarry. Once or twice the king glanced back, a gay and reckless light in his eyes, then he beckoned Bellegarde. The road grew more open ahead, and the latter forged up beside Henri.

"Look you, Brisac! When I give the word, turn and face them. Hold them in talk until they realize that they are alone," he exclaimed jerkily. "The stag who runs may lure on the hounds, but when he turns at bay—egad, you hear their bark change to a howl!"

"Then take this," and Bellegarde passed over the packet from Madrid.

The king took it with a nod, eyed it as he rode, glanced back again, and spoke curtly.

"Where the trees close in ahead—turn!"

The two pursuers were within fifty yards when Bellegarde drew rein, turned his heaving animal, and sat waiting. The king, a little behind him, followed suit. At once the two noblemen checked their mad pace, reining in their horses, and a simultaneous cry broke from them as they came face to face with

Bellegarde. Evidently they had not until now recognized him or seen his face clearly.

"It is he—the prisoner!" exclaimed Solbeig, staring.

"Aye," said Theleme, drawing his sword. "*Monsieur,* yield! You are our prisoners, gentlemen. Neither of you shall be harmed—"

Bellegarde broke into a laugh of such genuine and hearty amusement and they fell into sudden and disconcerted silence.

"*Messieurs,* go take the moon captive, and add the stars for good measure!" he responded whimsically. "Faith, if you could do it with words, you're the right men for the job. No, no! His majesty knows everything. Your whole plot has been betrayed; in his hands are the signed agreements from Madrid. The Duchess de Maine—or La Fleche, if you prefer that name—has been taken! She has confessed everything. By this time, the Tour de Gisy has been captured, and Spanuto cut off. Not one of your men will escape. Troops are on every road. Now, if you still desire to use your weapons, we are two to two, and you might better die here than on the scaffold, so fall on!"

Obviously, no other troopers were coming up. It was very silent here in the forest—a deep, dead midsummer stillness, upon which Bellegarde's voice rang out with deliberate force. He had spoken, more to give the king an inkling of what it was all about, than to impress the two noblemen before him; yet he saw how justly Henri had reasoned.

Confusion and doubt settled upon them both. The very fact of Bellegarde's presence here showed them that much must have gone amiss. They glanced at each other irresolutely, and then the king urged his horse forward and broke the silence. The remarkable power of his personality, the authority that clad him like a garment, was felt full force.

"*Messieurs,*" he said gravely, "it is true that I learned of this affair a trifle late, but others knew of it earlier. Your emprise has gone altogether askew. As the Marquis de Brisac has just said, you have only the alternative of dying here, or of being taken by my agents; but I give you another choice. Men enough will die of this matter as it is.

"M. de Theleme, I pardon you what share you have had in this matter; but do not let me see you at court again. I do not know this gentleman who rides—"

"Sire, allow me to present Count Solbeig," broke in Bellegarde ironically, smashing all etiquette in thus interrupting the king. "Late captain of guards of M. de Sedan."

"So?" said the king, as Solbeig bowed in the saddle. "Let me advise you, then, to leave France very quickly, before my pardon is revoked. You may go, gentlemen."

And they went.

BELLEGARDE SAT blinking after them. The quick wit of Henri had turned disaster into an overwhelming victory, as he perceived instantly. These two would bear back word to Spanuto that all was lost, that the king knew of everything, that he had escaped the trap—and the rest would be flight.

"Quick, Brisac!" broke out the voice of the king. "Before they stop to think it over—on! Before they encounter their men—spur, man, spur!"

Bellegarde turned his weary horse. There was little speed left in either animal, but a moment later they were trotting down the forest lanes, while the king broke into a roar of hearty laughter and leaned over to clap Bellegarde on the shoulder.

"How you put the game into my hand for the playing!" he cried joyously. "You're a man after my own heart, Brisac! Devil take me if I understand much of this matter, but time enough for that. What I want now is a bottle of wine—a dozen bottles—and something softer than a saddle to rest my bones."

"Not to mention a company of the guards, sire."

"Bah! Their stroke has failed; they'll scatter like a covey of quail!" said the king, and snapped his fingers. He threw away the sword he had been carrying, twisted his mustache and broke into new laughter. Then he became sober.

"Eh! I forgot those huntsmen they slew!" he said in a different voice. "*Ventre St. Gris!* I'll have that Italian broken on the wheel, and every one of his men I can take! Come, press on faster. We'll surely get out of this accursed forest ere long."

"Have you any idea where we are, sire?"

"Of course not. Have you?"

Bellegarde laughed. "Faith, not I! Nor do I care greatly, so long as you're safe. But there—I smell smoke. This track is taking us somewhere."

A moment later they came into an opening, where men were burning charcoal in pits. Half a dozen blackened peasants, who stared blankly at the two cavaliers. Bellegarde questioned them and found that they lived in the forest, which hereabouts was part of an estate ruined and laid waste during the religious wars.

St. Vecin? They had never heard of it. The highway? They had never seen it. They took all their wares to the Carrefour du Roi. What was that? One said it was a town; another called it a tavern; to a third it was simply a place of wine and girls. They were gawking, incoherent fellows, little removed from animals in point of intelligence.

"Well, at least where lies this Crossroads of the King?" demanded Bellegarde. They pointed along the track. Three hours' ride with a wagon, said one. The king flung them a coin and they fell to fighting for it.

"At the worst, we'll find where we are," observed Henri, who was in high good-humor. "Three hours' ride with a wagon—well, a league at most. And the afternoon's getting on. Death of my life! What a thirst I have! Here, Brisac; these papers. What are they?"

Bellegarde shrugged. "That's for you to see, sire. I suspect, but don't know."

"Then let them wait. Carrefour du Roi, eh? A good omen in that name. Why don't you take those irons from your wrists?"

"For the same reason that your majesty doesn't order up your cooks and vintner and a troop of horse. I can't."

Henri broke into laughter. "Well, I charge you to abandon all titles. I am M. d'Albret, and you'll kindly remember it. Lord! I haven't been so saddle-galled since I was on campaign, and Heaven knows that was years ago! Come on. Let's get this cursed ride over."

The horses were pricked up, and shambled on.

There was nothing to differentiate the king from any ordinary gentleman, except that his dress was shabbier; and as he rightly said, he was now in no danger whatever. As soon as he could reach some château, even some village, he could obtain an escort and send out couriers to Tours. He was extremely cheerful, and when they sighted the Carrefour du Roi he fell into renewed laughter.

For this place, which to the charcoal burners represented everything they knew, was no more than a huddle of huts, an old and tumbledown tavern, and a smithy; however, it had a road, and this promised everything. Also, the inn proved to have several horses in stalls, which hinted at the required messenger.

"I'll take on the horses," said the king, as they came to the smithy, "and make all arrangements yonder. Stop here and get rid of those irons."

"Then give me some money, for I've none to pay the smith," and Bellegarde chuckled. The king searched his pockets, found a few silver coins, and handed them over.

IN FIVE minutes the smith was at work on his somewhat delicate task. In another fifteen Bellegarde drew on his boots again, rid of the irons; and as he strode toward the inn, a mounted man came riding out of the yard and went spurring away. He found the place in a bustle of excitement, the host scurrying about, fowl being killed for the spit, and wine coming into the main room of the place, where the king sat at a table.

Bellegarde half emptied a bottle, then sank down on the long settle before the fire.

"Read the packet I gave you, M. d'Albret," he observed. "As for me, give me twenty minutes to sleep and call me when the meal's ready. On the faith of a gentleman, I'm unable to talk intelligently. Tell you all about it later."

So saying, he turned his back to the fire and was asleep before the king could reply.

It seemed no more than a moment when he found himself being violently shaken, and sat up blinking, to find food on the table and the king excitedly but gravely pocketing the vellum documents, which he had been perusing. He gave Bellegarde a sharp look.

"Can you use tongue and teeth at the same time, comrade?"

"Aye, that I can," said Bellegarde, and pulled up a chair. "Were the papers as I thought?"

"Whatever you thought them, they were more."

"Then take them, with the compliments of Raoul de Gisy."

"Gisy!" The king looked startled. "Eh? Upon my word, I remember something about it—you were mentioned in his conspiracy—"

"Conspiracy be damned!" said Bellegarde. "Pass the wine, and hear a little truth. I'm a soldier, and so are you. Let's forget everything else."

So, while the sun sank in the west and daylight gradually faded, he proved his boast that he could use tongue and teeth at once.

The king said not a word, except now and again to ejaculate one of his favorite oaths, and stare at the speaker. Even when Bellegarde had brought his story to an end, the king made no comment, but opened another bottle of wine and sipped it with long breaths.

"Arbois; the finest wine in the kingdom, to my notion," he said slowly, as though his thoughts were far from what he had heard. "And to find it in this pigsty? We'd best bide here the night, comrade. That fellow who took a message for me won't bring any response before daybreak. The host says we're deep in the forest and the roads are unsafe at night—"

"Yes?" said Bellegarde, as the other paused. "They're still

unsafer for Raoul de Gisy, who lies in the dungeon of his own castle, unless he's dead by now! And if you don't do anything to help him—well, you're not the man I think you."

The king broke out laughing. "You damned irreverent rascal! Have you no respect for me?"

"For a scoundrelly Gascon? My dear M. d'Albret," and Bellegarde's eyes twinkled, "if you had any sort of title, I'd give you due respect; but you haven't. No, no! We're two soldiers with good wine before us—but I'm still thinking of Gisy."

"Well, so am I," answered the king quietly. "And you'll find that my thoughts will get somewhere. What can I do for you, Brisac?"

"More than you will, I fear."

"So? Well, name a request."

"Give me permission to marry any lady in France who will have me."

"What else?" asked the king cautiously.

"Nothing."

"Oh! Then, by St. Denis, I swear it here and now! Who is the lady?"

Bellegarde grinned.

"Oh, that remains to be seen!" He broke off as the host appeared, bearing candles in an iron sconce, and set them on the table. Then his face changed, as he caught a sudden sound from outside. Like a flash he was out of his seat, catching the innkeeper by the arm.

"Quick—take this gentleman away and hide him! Up, Albret—up! Both of you—through the door yonder—devil take you, wake up—"

The king had caught the sound now, and was up and off; a clatter of hoofs from the yard outside, a tumult of voices rising high. He disappeared through a door at one side of the hearth, crowding the host before him.

Bellegarde shoved aside the candles, disarranged the dishes, poured more wine for himself and threw the second pewter cup to the floor. He lifted his own cup and drank from it, deeply, and was aware of some one who had come in at the entrance and stood there staring at him.

When he set down the cup he turned, and met the gaze of Spanuto.

CHAPTER XIX

CAPTIVE

THE ITALIAN had that day lost a great wager, the greatest stake of all his life, by means of this man who sat by the hearth.

Bellegarde was ready for anything except fighting. If he used his sword, however, Spanuto would at once suspect that he was shielding another; this must be avoided at all costs. Still, Bellegarde was not prepared for what actually happened.

Spanuto stood looking at him, then came striding forward very calmly, while his men crowded into the place and stared in utter astonishment at Bellegarde. The Italian showed no emotion whatever, though his face was extremely pale. He came up to the table, pulled up a chair, and with a motion of his arm swept half the dishes to the floor.

"Well, *monsieur,*" he said casually, catching up a bottle, "I see we have wine here."

Underneath that calm of his, as Bellegarde now perceived, there was a frightful tensity. His black eyes were liquid pools of fire. He stooped, picked up the fallen cup, poured wine and drank it off at a gulp.

"Excellent wine," said Bellegarde. "I trust you had a pleasant ride in the forest?"

Spanuto showed his teeth in a grimace, caught up a crust of bread and wolfed it. The inn-keeper and two wenches appeared hastily to serve the soldiers, some of whom were bawling for food and wine, while others came forward and made a half-circle about the table, still staring as though Bellegarde were some apparition.

"Very pleasant," said Spanuto. "I encountered Theleme and Solbeig, by the way. They gave me certain information, and are by this time *en route* to the border of Savoy."

Bellegarde leaned back, and his brows lifted.

"And you, my dear captain? I am astonished that you did not follow their example."

"I am somewhat more practical, *monsieur*, and also a soldier. I think that the story you told them was largely false. The castle has not been taken, for the excellent reason that there was no one to take it. I shall go there, rest and refresh the horses, and ride for safety with my fifty men; we shall not encounter any trouble that cannot be overcome."

"Well, that is true," admitted Bellegarde.

"You spoke to them of La Fleche, I believe. Just where is she now?"

"Probably at the castle," said Bellegarde calmly, and chuckled. "It was really quite remarkable, how those two gentlemen swallowed all we told them. If you had been in their place—"

A spasmodic contortion crossed the pallid features of Spanuto.

"Ah! That would have been different," he murmured. "Where is the king?"

"Probably in Tours by this time. Naturally, his first thought was to reach safety. We separated, I lost my road, and here I am. By the way, I'll thank you to return that rapier of mine, which I see at your side. It's a valuable weapon—"

"You have no further use for it," said Spanuto softly.

"Come, come!" exclaimed Bellegarde. "You're a soldier, my good captain, riding from a stricken field. Not even the Turks slaughter their prisoners."

"No, they use them as slaves," and Spanuto smiled thinly. "There is a good deal that I do not entirely understand; but we shall make everything clear at the castle. At all events, I have

Gisy safe there, and I have you here. Therefore I shall unite you on the gallows before I depart. It will be great satisfaction to leave you both there. Take him, men!"

His order came suddenly, sharply. Before Bellegarde could leave his chair, the circle of men closed in and he was seized in a dozen hands. Then, for an instant, the calm of Spanuto was broken.

The pallid features writhed in a burst of anguished fury, and a terrible light flamed in his black eyes, as he put his contorted face close to that of Bellegarde.

"Accursed one!" he cried out in Italian. "How you came to be here, I don't know; but by the saints, I shall pay you for this day's work! Out with him, men. Tie him into a saddle. Take what wine and food you can find, and be ready to depart in ten minutes."

SO BELLEGARDE was taken out to the inn yard, where certain of the men were baiting the horses, and his feet were lashed to the stirrups of a mount.

He offered no resistance, which would have been futile. His whole attention was centered on the activity going on around, and he was relieved to find that no search was being made. Spanuto, lost in exhaustion and the bitterness of failure, had accepted his story without suspicion.

Ten minutes later, indeed, the men came flooding out. The unlucky host, demanding some payment, was buffeted aside. Spanuto appeared and swung into his saddle, and under the guidance of a trooper who knew this part of the forest, the column set out. A man on either side held the reins of Bellegarde's horse.

From the talk of the men around, most of whom had brought forth loot in the shape of wine or food, Bellegarde gathered that while some of them might suspect what sort of quarry they had been seeking that day, the truth was neither known nor inquired into. They were mercenaries, and Spanuto paid them; they therefore obeyed him and shrugged at all else.

Thus the long night march began, and continued hour after hour, men and horses fagged, jogging along in silence. Bellegarde, like the others, dozed as the horses plodded on. All affairs of his own were relegated to the dim background; nothing mattered now, and after the supreme efforts he had made the reaction was upon him, his vitality was low, and it seemed as though the darkness encompassing them was reflected in himself.

So the night passed.

With a start, Bellegarde wakened, to find the troop halting and the voice of Spanuto giving sharp orders. Dawn was in the air, sharp and chill; the sky was gray, the forest was long since fallen behind.

A dozen troopers swung off behind Spanuto and went riding away on a side road. The others started on again. Bellegarde peered around, but for a space could make out little; there was no sound but the jingle of accoutrements, the slogging thud of hoofs. One of the men spoke,, and another answered with a sleepy laugh, and Bellegarde caught the word "Chanlay." It startled him. He turned to the man on his left with a question as to whither Spanuto had gone, but his only answer was a curse.

Uneasy, refreshed by his sleep in the saddle, Bellegarde found his spirit mounting anew. He even considered an effort at escape, but realized that this would be futile. The sky cleared and brightened, the first streamers of red crept across the eastern heaven. Suddenly he recognized this road, and looking ahead, saw the gallows of Gisy appearing in sight. So they had passed Chanlay—and it was there Spanuto had turned off!

A low moan of consternation escaped his lips. Was the man actually, even at such a moment, thinking of Angele? Then his plan could only be to carry her off in freebooting style, and with her, such loot as he might find at the château. There was no doubt that the Italian meant to ride out of France with his men; perhaps to Savoy, whose duke would certainly welcome him.

A sudden stir of interest among the men, a laugh that rippled through the ranks, caught his attention. He followed their eyes and looked up as they drew under the gallows. A single figure was hanging there, slowly turning in the morning breeze.

It was the figure of Auguste, the old seneschal.

The troop passed on. Presently the castle loomed ahead of them, a horn was sounded, and the gates drew open. More men were here than had remained under Stuart; those who handled the remounts, the spare horses, had already returned from their fruitless task. As the riders halted, Stuart came striding among them and greeted Bellegarde with a grim smile.

"So we meet again, *monsieur!* You are a slippery fellow, you are, but this time you'll stay put. Here, two of you! Bind his arms behind him and take him down where he belongs. Where's the captain?"

"Gone seeking a wench," said some one, amid laughter.

Bellegarde was presently led away, back to the same dungeon which he had so recently left, and saw nothing of La Fleche, though her coach stood in the courtyard.

DOWN INTO the darkness and the cell again. The door clanged shut upon him and the light of the lantern vanished. A voice spoke from the blackness.

"Who's there, eh?"

"A friend," said Bellegarde grimly. "Still alive, Raoul?"

Gisy swore in dismay and excitement. He was across the corridor in the opposite cell.

"You! How the devil do you come here? What's happened?"

"Enough and to spare. They've failed in their stroke—but you don't know of the plot?"

"Aye," came Gisy's voice bitterly. "That she-devil has told me about it; we've had some sweet converse since they caught me, she and I! Plague take it, what's happened? Did they get the king?"

"No; he's safe enough."

"Thank Heaven!"

"But they've got us," added Bellegarde. "And that Italian dog has gone to Chanlay to seek Angele."

"He'll find more than he bargains for, then. La Fleche rode over there yesterday with four men, swearing up and down she'd have Angele's life—about some papers the girl took from her, or so she thinks. She found Angele with a dozen sturdy peasants armed to the teeth, and came back again disgruntled."

"So? Well, Spanuto took a dozen men, and the dawn is always a bad time to be caught napping. But let's hope for the best. I see that somebody hung old Auguste."

Gisy cursed furiously.

"He tried to get me out of here, and they caught him at it. I've a poniard he brought me, but small good it does."

"Eh? A poniard? Aren't you bound?"

"No, thank the saints! But tell me what's happened."

"I bartered you for the king, Raoul," said Bellegarde bluntly, and launched into his story, telling how he had seen Gisy brought in captive.

The other laughed harshly.

"Blame not yourself, old friend! The king comes first. If he's saved, then devil take the rest of us."

"He'll do that, right enough, and before long."

Bellegarde related all that had chanced since his last meeting with Raoul de Gisy, the other listening in silence. When he made an end, Gisy sighed.

"Ah, you have all the luck! Devil take it, I was in my shirt when they caught me—hadn't time for a single stroke! Somebody gave me a crack over the pate, and they had me."

"Where's Breiter, the German?" demanded Bellegarde.

"Badly hurt. When they took us off the horses, he tried to break away, and nigh made it, but that accursed Scot ran him through the body. He wasn't killed, and they carried him off to a room somewhere to mend before hanging him. So our friend

Spanuto gets away after all, does he? That fellow has the devil's own luck?"

"He hasn't got away yet."

"Bah!" said Gisy. "He can well afford to take his time, and is aware of it. You know how these things go. The king gets back safe to Tours and sets about writing letters; no troops there except some of his guards. By the time he can raise men and send them here, Spanuto is gone and we're keeping Auguste company among the ravens."

"Aye, you're right. But what the devil!" and Bellegarde laughed suddenly. "I forgot you had a poniard! With that, you can cut me free when the chance offers."

"What good?"

"Well, I'd sooner die of a sword thrust than of a rope around my gullet."

"Hm! I hadn't thought of that," said Gisy. "But I agree with you. We will do it, then. By the mass, we'll give them something to think about, eh? I want to get my hands on that damned Italian!"

"You'd better not," said Bellegarde dryly. "They say he's ambidextrous and a devil with a sword. No chance to get out of your cell?"

"None. My father had these doors put in during the religious wars. They are stout."

The talk dragged after this. Bellegarde did not ask about Gisy's adventure at Tours, and the other volunteered no information on the subject.

Bellegarde, still in lack of sleep, dozed off.

Gisy's voice wakened him, then he discerned a light. Armed men were at his cell door; two of them seized him and jerked him forth without ceremony.

Gisy was hauled forth in like manner and both were marched up the stairs.

To his astonishment, when he came to the open Bellegarde perceived it was noon or after, for the sun was high overhead.

Stuart met the two, eyed them grimly, and motioned four of his men, who surrounded them.

They were marched straightway to the garden, where Spanuto awaited them; but the Italian was not alone.

CHAPTER XX

TWO AGAINST FIFTY

UNDER THE old gnarled trees, whose sweet shade and fragrant fruit made the garden very pleasant at this season, a table was spread and seats laid out. Spanuto, all in black as usual, sat at the board, with Mme. La Fleche at his side. At first, however, Bellegarde did not recognize her, for she wore a man's costume of blue velvet, a poniard at her hip; besides, his whole attention went to Angele de Chanlay, who sat at one side of the table.

She regarded the two prisoners without recognition. Her face was bruised and her right hand was bandaged; in her eyes lay terror and anger mingled, and a strange desperation had thinned her features, until she looked wan and drawn.

Yet never, thought Bellegarde, had he seen a woman so delicately beautiful and shining with inner strength—aye, though her eyes touched upon him and then lifted again without sign of greeting. Her dress was of silver gray, with a high cape and collar on which were flecks of blood.

Spanuto, who was in talk with La Fleche, looked very pleased with himself. He gestured the Scot to wait and turned to his companion with a scornful laugh.

"What the devil, *madame!* I tell you there is no haste whatever. Not until to-morrow or the day after will any agents of the king arrive here, much less troops! And in two hours more we'll be gone."

"You're a fool," snapped La Fleche roughly. "I tell you, I know

Henri! If you're not ready to leave in an hour, I'll go without you."

"Very well," assented Spanuto, half angrily. "But your coach—"

"Devil take the coach! I'll ride with you, and outride you if need be. What about her?" and she motioned with a certain furious disdain toward Angele.

"Oh, she's well able to ride in man's garments, by all accounts!" and Spanuto chuckled. "What say you, my dear Angele? But wait; I forgot our two gentlemen here. Stuart, are you prepared to hang them?"

"Instantly, my captain," said the Scot.

The Italian surveyed the two with amused interest; behind this expression, however, one might divine a consuming hatred in his eyes.

"Send one of your men and prepare horses."

Stuart gestured one of the four men, who departed. Then Bellegarde laughed slightly, as he met the glare of Spanuto, and broke the silence.

"What, good captain? Are you not anxious to ransom prisoners who can pay well?"

Spanuto smiled thinly, and glanced at Angele. "That has already been discussed," he said. "By the saints, you hang! You may thank this lady that you're not left impaled instead, but I am glad to humor her. You, M. de Brisac, or whatever you call yourself, may depart with my benediction. As for you, M. de Gisy—"

He paused, his gaze roving over Gisy with a sort of relish, as though he found this moment very sweet. Bellegarde glanced again at Angele, but in her frozen manner discerned that she was only too certain of what must come, and had found no help. As for La Fleche, she eyed the two men before her, and a smile came to her lips when their gaze touched upon her.

"As for you, my dear *monsieur*," broke in Bellegarde, before the Italian could continue, "kindly go to the devil, where you belong! We want none of your smooth speeches. You're a base rascal in gentleman's garb—"

Spanuto motioned to the Scot.

"Take them out and hang them."

AS STUART saluted and moved to obey, Angele leaped suddenly to her feet.

"Wait!" she cried, and turned to the Italian, fiercely. "You promised me—oh, you devil! You promised me speech with them—after I had agreed to everything to save them torture—you promised I might have a word in private—"

Spanuto broke into laughter.

"Well, speak!" he returned, and lifted his wine-cup. "Stuart, move your men back a pace or two, that this lady may whisper in the ear of these unhappy gentlemen."

White with anger, Angele faced him. "You can jest, at such a time? God forgive you! Does my agony mean nothing to you? And you, you woman who sit beside him, in woman's form but with the heart of a devil—"

"Oh, have done, wench," exclaimed La Fleche disdainfully. "By the saints, if I have any more of your whining, my lackeys shall trice you up and take a whip to you! Giulio, try it on her. That would break her spirit quickly enough."

"*Per Bacco,* I like her spirit!" said Spanuto admiringly, and stroked his black mustache with a complacent air. "Well, little Angele, do your speaking quickly! We must get them hung and be on our way, since her highness here is impatient."

Angele turned and came to Bellegarde, her eyes on his. As she did so, he backed a step so that he struck against Gisy. If the latter took the hint, well and good.

"I am sorry, Bellegarde," she said quietly, "for I have—"

"Nay, nay," he broke in roughly. "Do your talking to Raoul and not to me! If you have a word to whisper in his ear, whisper it and put your arms about his neck, and have done!"

So saying, he looked over her head at the Italian and laughed coarsely. Spanuto chuckled, and the woman beside him muttered something that brought a hearty grin to his lips.

A shocked, hurt look came into the face of Angele at hearing such speech from him; then she met his eyes as they lowered to her, and heard the word he breathed.

"Quickly!"

Color came in her cheeks and she swiftly went past him to Raoul de Gisy, and put up her arms about his neck, whispering in his ear. Bellegarde shoved back against them. Then he felt cold steel touch his arm.

Under cover of Angele's embrace, Gisy had out his poniard, unseen of any. Bellegarde felt the cords loosen from about his arms. Luckily, they were not so tight that his hands had become numb. He worked his fingers swiftly.

"Time enough!" called out Spanuto. "Take them, Scot!"

The lean Stuart moved forward and laid his hand on the shoulder of Angele. Bellegarde turned a little, facing him, and met the keen hard eyes of the man with a gaze like gray flame. Meeting this look, Stuart paused for an instant, startled by its furious intensity.

"I warned you, rascal!" said Bellegarde quietly.

"Come, enough of this!" snapped Stuart, and roughly jerked Angele aside.

Bellegarde moved like a flash. His right hand went to the Scot's rapier-hilt, his left shoved Stuart violently backward. The rapier—the same that Florio had once owned—slid from the sheath.

As Stuart recovered his balance, Bellegarde ran him neatly through the heart.

He had a swift glimpse of Angele, wide-eyed, of Gisy hurling himself on the three soldiers, his poniard driving home; then he turned and darted forward. Spanuto, in sharp alarm, was on his feet, whipping out his rapier, uttering a call for his men. Then, a laugh on his lips, Bellegarde kicked the table over on

top of La Fleche, and had the Ferrara against his own blade, as
Spanuto met his attack.

"Too good a sword for you, rascal!" he exclaimed. "Ha! You
use it well—"

SPANUTO, HIS face contorted, drove in a deadly riposte.
Bellegarde felt the point go into his shoulder, then engaged
again, as Spanuto attacked like a madman. Try as he would, he
could not hold that furious assault with his own wrist; only luck
saved him, and the crafty notch in Stuart's blade that caught
the Ferrara and wrenched it aside.

From the corner of his eye Bellegarde saw that Gisy had
poniarded one of the soldiers, taken his sword, and was warding
off the attack of the other two. Then he had to give full heed
to himself, for Spanuto was upon him like a whirlwind, with
murder in his blazing eyes and a hoarse snarl on his lips.

This time, however, Bellegarde did not give back under the
attack.

He met it coolly, skillfully; the clink and hiss of steel rang
out as the blades slithered, lunge and riposte, trick and coun-
terplay, arm and sword like one perfect entity, bodies springing
and bending as the steel clung.

In and out, parry and thrust, flaming in the sunlight. Then,
for all Spanuto's amazing skill, Bellegarde knew himself as good
or better, and a laugh came to his lips.

"Ha! You learned that thrust in Milan, my pallid reptile—and
here's the counter for it. A plague on you! Evidently we had
the same teacher—"

A cry broke from Angele as he slipped and came to one knee.

Spanuto drew back and showed his teeth in a grin. "You don't
catch me with that trick, Frenchman! Quick, men—take him
in rear—"

Bellegarde glanced around. Like a flash Spanuto was in for
his throat and only a leap saved him from the thrust. He turned,
engaged, realized that Gisy was still holding off the two soldiers.

As yet, no others were on the scene, though shouts were dinning up from all sides.

Spanuto suddenly shifted the Ferrara to his left hand. And at this Bellegarde unexpectedly took the offensive, attacking for the first time.

Such was the cold fury of this attack that the Italian fell back before it. Bellegarde pressed him mercilessly, saw the pallid cheeks straining anxiously, laughed as he pressed home a yet swifter assault. It was now or never, as he knew well; he hurled himself against the defense of Spanuto, exhausted every trick of play he had learned in Italy and Hungary—and lunged like a flash as the opening came. He drew blood from the shoulder, and Spanuto shifted the rapier to his right hand again.

"Touch for touch!" said Bellegarde gayly. "But now watch your throat, Italian! Your high guard is poor, your fingers are too small for that hilt—ha! At your throat, traitor?"

His body extended as though on coiled springs of steel. He lunged, lunged again, and Spanuto, with sweat starting on his face, protected his throat desperately. Then Bellegarde's point slipped suddenly out and in, disengaged, and stood out between Spanuto's shoulder-blades in a movement swifter than eye could follow.

The Italian was run through the heart, as Stuart had been. He fell forward, wrenching the sword out of Bellegarde's hand.

BELLEGARDE, PANTING, stood for a moment looking at the man, then wakened into life. From the side, a figure in blue velvet was hurtling at him, poniard aflame in the sunlight—La Fleche, wild fury transforming all her loveliness to stark deviltry. Bellegarde let himself fall under that rush of death, came down lightly on his hands, thrust out his foot.

She tripped over it and fell in a headlong plunge, rolling over and over, shrieking out oaths as she crashed into a tree.

Coming lightly to his feet, Bellegarde picked up his own rapier that had fallen from Spanuto's hand. Gisy was backing toward him now, hotly assailed by three men, and others were darting in from the courtyard. Bellegarde sprang to his side just as one of the three went down, coughing blood.

"Back!" he cried, engaging one of the two. "Back, Raoul! Into the corner!"

The long Ferrara warded a savage cut, slipped under the heavier sword, pricked the life out of that man's throat. Gisy's opponent drew back. The two had breathing space, and retreated slowly to where Angele stood watching with wide and horrified eyes.

Here they gained a corner of the garden, under the building, so that they could be assailed only in front. La Fleche had risen. Abandoning further attempts at violence, she was now shouting to the soldiers, her voice rising high and shrill, ordering them on, screaming out offers of pay and reward.

Bellegarde laughed.

"The beldame has spiked my cannon," he observed lightly as they joined Angele. "Faith, with Spanuto down I thought they'd cry quits, but she's too quick for us. Hurt, Raoul?"

"Not a scratch," answered Gisy cheerfully. "Well, it'll be a good ending! You've quick wits, Angele. If it hadn't been for you I'd not have cut him loose in time."

Angele regarded them, terrified. She was all woman now; the high anger that Bellegarde had first seen in her was fled away, for death was all around and she was helpless.

"Is—is there no hope?" she faltered. "Surely—"

"Not with that she-devil loose," and Gisy glared at La Fleche. "Ha! She's yelling at them to bring pistols!"

"She was a bit late thinking of that," and Bellegarde laughed again as a tide of men came pouring among the trees. With the Ferrara in hand, he felt like a new person, himself again. His gray eyes struck at them, calm and keen. "Take the right, Raoul! Angele, get back into the corner. A Brisac! A Brisac!"

"A Brisac!" came a weak voice like an echo from above, and glancing up, Bellegarde saw the face of Herman Breiter at a window there, looking down upon them. He waved gayly to the German, then stepped forward as the foremost of the soldiers came running in.

Now befell sharp work and stern. The troopers rushed up with any weapon that came to hand; with only two men to drag down, they thought to make short work of it, and so fell on with a will. But Gisy, sword and poniard in play, lay on the one hand; and on the other was the Ferrara, flashing like blue fire in the sunlight.

With the first clash of steel, a man screamed out and died, and then another. Two ran together upon Gisy, slashing at him, but he knocked up their swords and the poniard bit into one throat. Bellegarde stood almost motionless, but the Ferrara was like a wall beyond which no man could pass except in death. Those troopers knew nothing of fence. The glittering blades that gave no cut or slash, but glided in like snakes, astonished them, and with wounds and death their rage became redoubled.

Yet the more they pressed in, the more those in the front rank tasted of bitterness, and screamed to get clear. Four men went down, others were hurt and drawing away. Another wild rush, and Gisy staggered as the flat of a blade smote him over the eyes. Bellegarde leaped suddenly at them all, whipped aside their weapons with the long pliant steel, thrust one man and then another through the body, and leaped back again before they could touch him.

NOW THE soldiers drew away, shouting at one another, cursing and bawling for pistols. One man came up with a pike, and headed a fresh attack, striving to hook Gisy with the curved beak of the weapon. He had small luck in this, for Gisy dropped the poniard, caught the shaft in his left hand, and dragged the man close, stabbing him. Bellegarde drove at the others, the Ferrara licked in and out with deadly tongue; but his foot slipped in blood and he pitched forward and was under their weapons for an instant.

He came up again, stabbing as he rose, and with the long pike Gisy transfixed a man in the act of running a sword through his back. The attack drew away, leaving more men groaning and crying out. As he stepped back beside Gisy, however, Bellegarde's face ran with blood from a slash over his cheek, and as he rested his weary sword-arm, blood ran down his wrist and dripped from his fingers over the golden hilt of the rapier.

"Hurt?" cried Gisy, panting. Bellegarde laughed a little.

"Nay; not enough to count."

"They have pistols!" rose the voice of Angele, as the crowd of men split asunder to show two who came with long brass pistols ready, the clumsy weapons lifted in both hands.

Like a flash Bellegarde hurled himself forward. The Ferrara glinted in the sunlight as he leaped in among the foremost men; weapons struck at him, but first struck his own blade, swift and deadly. One of the two with pistols, took the point in his breast, the other was wounded and dropped his weapon.

Bellegarde drew back, but slowly and painfully, for a sword had slashed his hip and another his knee. Then a pistol exploded from the rear of the crowd, and the ball whistled between him and Gisy but did no damage.

"We're at the end, comrade," said Gisy, while Bellegarde leaned on the rapier so that it bent under his weight, and got back breath.

"These dogs will stand off now and finish it."

This was plain enough, none having stomach to test those blood-stained rapiers further. All the men in the place were crowded into the garden or on the walls above, and above the din of their voices rose the shrill tones of La Fleche, promising a hundred crowns to the man who first brought down either of the pair. Pistols were loaded in haste, powder was brought up, and with it all mingled the groans of hurt men and the shriek of one who had been blinded.

Bellegarde stepped back and leaned against the wall, for weakness had come upon him with the loss of blood. Angele came to his side and put out her hand to him.

"There is no pity in them, Bellegarde," she said gently. "Now would you have me say what I meant to say before?"

The old whimsical smile touched his lips.

"Aye, if—"

A pistol roared, then another, but haste spoiled both shots, so that the balls struck the wall and whinnied up through the air. Then, of a sudden, the tumult of voices died, and men stood stock still, staring at one another. A brazen, piercing sound rang up, and again—a trumpet. And on the silence rose a voice, clearly heard.

"In the king's name, open!"

And this sound came from outside the gates.

Before that amazed silence died out, another voice rose in a roaring, vibrant shout that reached every ear.

"Open, you dogs! Open, or *par Dieu*, I'll hang every cursed man I find here!"

A cry broke from La Fleche. Even as men turned, those on the walls lifting shouts of wild startled alarm, yelling that a troop of horse was at the gates, La Fleche uttered a shrill and almost hysterical laugh.

"I told him so! It is the king, the king—"

She shoved the men aside, rushed through them, and was gone into the castle. But they had caught the words, and looked one at another, slack-jawed, while those at the gates made haste to open.

The king had come, indeed.

CHAPTER XXI

KING'S JUSTICE

INTO THE castle filed not one but two troops of horse, being the two companies of the King's Guards that had ridden breakneck from Tours to the Carrefour du Roi, and thence to the Tour de Gisy. And weary men were they from the ride, for the king had spared no time.

Now was wine brought up and what food could be got, while Spanuto's men were lined up in the courtyard. The king embraced Gisy and Bellegarde, and embraced Angele twice, and had her sit and talk with him while their wounds were tended. He was very jovial, somewhat weary, and begged Gisy's hospitality for himself and his men until next morning.

At this, Gisy burst out laughing and pointed to the dead Spanuto.

"Not mine but his, sire! Faith, you've granted him this castle—"

"Devil take your nonsense!" exclaimed Henri, his keen eyes twinkling. "The lands are yours and with them a thousand crowns for the injustice done you, comrade! Sieur de Gisy, eh? *Ventre St. Gris!* Such a goodly castle as this is far above the estate of a simple gentleman. Comte de Gisy—is that better? My word on it!"

Gisy knelt joyfully and kissed his hand, and Henri turned to Bellegarde.

"Well, my friend? I think I am somewhat more in your debt than ever—"

"Your pardon, sire!" and Bellegarde shrugged. "You've more than repaid me already, if you recollect your promise."

"Eh?" The king blinked at him and emptied his wine-cup. "Oh, of course! The woman you desire to marry! Who is she, then?"

Now Bellegarde flushed in confusion. "Plague take it, sire! She's not aware of it as yet, so let that rest, I beg of you."

"As you will." Henri rose and put an arm about his shoulders. "Brisac, I love you, damme if I don't! We're far from quits. Ask of me what you will; take time to think it over. Come, let's have a look at these rascals yonder before I hang them."

They followed him out into the courtyard, where Spanuto's men were drawn up, hands bound, dully awaiting their fate. The king looked them over keenly, French and Italians and master-less veterans from the wars.

"You scoundrels!" he said sharply. "Every last one of you shall hang on that gallows I saw below here! Look you, *messieurs,*" and he beckoned two of the guards. "There is a village near by. Ride to it, and bring peasants. I warrant they'll be glad enough to have the hanging of these foul birds."

"Your pardon, sire," said Bellegarde, coolly. "After all, these fellows are soldiers. And I've found them excellent stout fight-ers, too; no cowards. That Italian was a good picker of men."

"Aye, like enough. I say they shall hang, every one of them."

"I say they shall not," said Bellegarde.

There was a sudden tense silence. The king looked at him, moving his mustaches with quick anger, a sharp flame in his eyes.

"*Monsieur,* I think you forget yourself!" he said. "Have a care!"

Bellegarde bowed. "Sire, I was but reminding you of your promise to me, that whatever I should ask, you would grant. These fellows are rascals, I admit; none the less, they're good soldiers."

"You fool!" snapped the king angrily. "You ask their lives, when you might have asked for money, lands, position?"

Bellegarde shrugged. "Your majesty, I am not a king, thank the saints! I have grown a little weary of killing. Yes, I ask their lives, on your promise."

"Granted, then," and Henri turned his back. "But, *Ventre St. Gris!* Ask me no mercy for any of these conspirators. By the mass, I'll hang each and every one of them that comes into my hands!"

"Alas, sir!" said a soft and gentle voice. "Then send for a priest to shrive me. I pray you, since I have no recourse but your mercy!"

A L L   T U R N E D in astonishment as the throng parted. La Fleche appeared, making a low curtsy to the king. Bellegarde stared at her. Gisy's mouth flew open in blank stupefaction.

For her man's attire was gone, and with it every sign of her recent fury. Her hair was done up neatly, glinting with jewels; she wore a low-cut gown of pale yellow silk, and pearls were draped about her throat. Her loveliness, her allure, were as Bellegarde had glimpsed them at first meeting. She was all woman, and she was bewitching.

"*Madame!*" The king regarded her with sparkling eyes, then bowed very courteously over her hand. When he straightened up, however, his gaze was direct and stern. "I know your part in this affair. Is there any reason why you should expect mercy?"

"None, sire," she replied, and sighed a little as she looked at him. "I have no excuses. I can only throw myself on your clemency."

"What is more to the point," said Henri, "you played me a certain scurvy trick last year, *madame*. You affronted me then; now you dare to plot against me."

"It is true, your majesty," said La Fleche, and she had never looked so helpless, so lovely, as now. Her voice was low and quivering, appealing. "Ah, sire, you have broken my pride and my effrontery! You are a truly great man. I perceive it too late."

For an instant, Bellegarde thought that she had won her bold play, for the eyes of the king kindled. Then they grew cold again. After all, Henri IV was a very wary gentleman.

"There is your coach, *madame*," he said, motioning across the courtyard to the vehicle. "Take it; depart from France forever. To make certain of your departure, six of my *gardes nobles* will attend you to the frontier! Ho, there! Six volunteers to see this lady to the frontier! Step out!"

There was a movement, and the entire front rank of the guards took a step forward and saluted.

The king bit his lip, then motioned to an officer.

"Choose six men and let them depart with this lady." So saying, he turned his back upon La Fleche. "M. de Brisac, take command of these rascals whose lives you asked and gained; they shall enter into a regiment that you will command in my name. M. de Gisy, I expect you to produce a marvelous fine dinner later in the day. Until then, I shall rest in this château of yours."

And disregarding the staring La Fleche, whose bewitching smile had quite fled her lips, the king was gone.

Bellegarde turned, saw the stupefied expression of Gisy and the sly smiles of the guards around, and clapped his comrade on the back.

"Wake up, Raoul! Why so gawking, man?"

"Eh?" Gisy started. "Devil take me! Where am I going to get the dinner he ordered?"

Bellegarde broke into laughter.

"Faith, we may find some help at Chanlay!" And striding across the cobbles, he came to where Angele stood, and laughed again as he met her eyes and bowed. "*Mademoiselle,* here is no lack of true cavaliers to escort you home again. Will you have a dozen gentlemen to ride with you, or would one alone serve the purpose?"

A smile touched her lips.

"I think, *monsieur,* that one would serve—if he were the right one," she said, and held out her hand to him.

THE TRUTH BEHIND
"BELLEGARDE"

IT MIGHT be of interest to *Argosy* readers to know that the plot indicated in the story, "Bellegarde," to found a Calvinist republic within France itself and to partition that country, is no writer's dream. The written proofs of it, the signed agreements, were captured and laid in the hand of Henri IV, much as related in the story of Bellegarde. It was a very complicated affair, however, which I have here tried to make somewhat plainer and simpler in the telling. As Sully says in his memoirs, the folly of the nobles and princes in putting their signatures to such a scheme was almost incredible, but was none the less a fact.

H. BEDFORD-JONES.

H. BEDFORD-JONES

BEDFORD-JONES IS a Canadian by birth, but not by profession, having removed to the United States at the age of one year. For over twenty years he has been more or less profitably engaged in writing and traveling. As he has seldom resided in one place longer than a year or so and is a person of retiring habits, he is somewhat a man of mystery; more than once he has suffered from unscrupulous gentlemen who impersonated him—one of whom murdered a wife and was subsequently shot by the police, luckily after losing his alias.

The real Bedford-Jones is an elderly man, whose gray hair and precise attire give him rather the appearance of a retired foreign diplomat. His hobby is stamp collecting, and his collection of Japan is said to be one of the finest in existence. At present writing he is en route to Morocco, and when this appears in print he will probably be somewhere on the Mojave Desert in company with Erle Stanley Gardner.

Questioned as to the main facts in his life, he declared there was only one main fact, but it was not for publication; that his life had been uneventful except for numerous financial losses, and that his only adventures lay in evading adventurers. In his younger years he was something of an athlete, but the encroachments of age preclude any active pursuits except that of motoring. He is usually to be found poring over his stamps, working at his typewriter, or laboring in his California rose garden, which is one of the sights of Cathedral Cañon, near Palm Springs.

Bedford-Jones has written stories laid in many corners of the earth, but among his most popular tales were the John Solomon stories which started many years ago in the *Argosy*.